Resounding Acclaim for *The Hunt Club*

"A gripping, wrenching, and devastatingly good book."

—Chris Bohjalian, author of *Midwives*

"Bret Lott has written a suspenseful mystery that is also, for its young protagonist, an intense emotional journey into adulthood with all its dangerous secrets, its acts of grace and courage. As always, Lott writes with a fine feel for the landscape of his fiction, and a gifted generous eye for the memorable people who live there."

—Michael Malone, author of *Handling Sin* and *Time's Witness*

"If you've ever found yourself chewing your fingernails while you're reading or skipping ahead almost unconsciously because you've got to know what happens next, you'll love this book."

—*Men's Journal*

"Mystery fans who dote on stylish writing and strong characters will love *The Hunt Club*."

—Tony Hillerman

"An emotionally charged thriller that places the reader in the labyrinth of the human heart, where such qualities as devotion, greed, love and dishonesty stand out with near-terrifying clarity."

—*Chicago Tribune*

"Action, suspense, and a hint of Southern folklore."

—*Library Journal*

"A wonderful read."

—*Charleston Post & Courier*

"The writing is splendid."

"Reads quickly and compellingly. . . . Resembles a John Grisham tale . . . yet Lott's writing is far superior to Grisham's. *The Hunt Club* unfolds like a movie, always in motion, always seeing its world with a camera eye."

"A gifted and expert storyteller."

"A well told novel. . . . Highly believable and very entertaining."

"This nerve-jangling thriller . . . is a tenderly crafted coming-of-age story that is worthy of the author."

"A beautiful romance of *Shane*-like quality."

"Wonderfully well written. . . . This may well give Lott and his layered, hypnotic prose the visibility they so richly deserve."

"Lott has potential to go the way of James Ellroy or Walter Mosley."

"The pace is brisk and the set-piece action sequences vividly imagined. . . . This spirited novel boasts an exotic locale, full of earthy characters and their attendant superstitions; life lessons about bravery and integrity; and an earnest rendering of an adolescent's emerging consciousness about community and identity."

—*Washington Post Book World*

"Lott builds his story with an architect's skill, mixing suspense with emotion into a glue that grasps a reader tightly. Each time you think you know where the tale's going, Lott jerks you in a new, unexpected direction."

—*Indianapolis Star*

"Thrilling, suspenseful. . . . Rich depictions of Southern lore and landscape are combined with a chilling tale of murder, suicide and greed."

—*Daily Citizen Entertainer* (Searcy, AK)

"Lott knows how to paint a scene and animate his characters. The action is crisp and credible."

—*People* magazine

"I stayed up an hour past my bedtime, just to see how things turned out."

—*Milwaukee Journal Sentine*

ALSO BY BRET LOTT

THE HUNT CLUB

BRET LOTT

HarperPerennial
A Division of HarperCollinsPublishers

HarperCollins books may be purchased for educational, business, or sales promotional use. For information, please write: Special Markets Department, HarperCollins Publishers Inc., 10 East 53rd Street, New York, NY 10022-5299.

First HarperPerennial edition published 1999.

Library of Congress Cataloging-in-Publication Data is available from the publisher.

ISBN 0-06-097770-1

99 00 01 02 03 ❖/RRD 10 9 8 7 6 5 4 3 2 1

The sins of some men are obvious,
reaching the place of judgment ahead of them;
the sins of others trail behind them.

—I Timothy, 5:24

THE
HUNT
CLUB

My name is Huger Dillard. You say it YOU-gee, not like it's spelled. It's French, I heard.

I'm fifteen years old, and my mom and dad are divorced, and I have my driver's permit. I am telling you this because driving figures in to what happened, as does my mom. My dad, too, in a way, because it's his brother, my Uncle Leland, this all happened to. Him and me both.

It started with a body, the head of it pretty much gone, the hands skinned.

We found it the Saturday after Thanksgiving, out to Hungry Neck Hunt Club. Uncle Leland owns the hunt club, which might make him sound important, or rich. But he's not. The club is just what the family has had in its hands for the last seventy years or so, and is a tract of 2,200 acres, some of it trash land, good for nothing, some of it pretty, set on the Ashepoo. It's forty miles south of Charleston, just past Jacksonboro. Live oak and pine, dogwood and palmetto and poison ivy and wild grapes and all else. Marsh grass down to the Ashepoo. That's about it.

But it's where Uncle Leland lives, in a single-wide. Unc, I call him. For short.

And it's where we found this body.

The body was between stand 17 and 18, twenty yards back off the road and fifty yards or so up from the Ashepoo. Saturday after Thanksgiving is a big day for deer season, most all the members there. The members: doctors and lawyers and what have you from Charleston, the sorts of people you see on the news for whatever reason each night, or in the paper, all of them getting honored or interviewed for one matter or the other.

The body was there on the ground, not much of a head left on it for what I figured must have been a couple rounds off a shotgun. Its hands were skinned, too, from the wrists on down, the muscle dark red and glistening, the tendons all white. Two hands like skinned squirrels.

I wanted to throw up for looking at it. I've seen deer skinned and gutted before a million times, done it a million times myself. I've seen even the fetus taken out of a doe a time or two. I've seen dead things all my life, seen the blood involved. I've seen it.

But this. This.

Unc stood next to me, behind us and beside us a good dozen or so of these doctors and lawyers, all of them decked out in their clean crisp camo hunter outfits, all of them shaking their heads.

They had heads left.

The body, too, had on its own set of crisp camo hunter fatigues, had on a hunter-orange vest.

And in those hands was a shotgun, over-and-under twelve-gauge. Maybe the same one that did what it did to his head. It lay there in the weeds and grass just before the woods started up, where if he'd been one of the ones we'd dropped off, he would have been down on one knee, or maybe on a camp stool, waiting for Patrick and Reynold to let loose the dogs back on Cemetery Road, just this side of the levee. Then the howling'd start, and a buck might've skipped out from across the road, heading back into those woods and toward the deer trails down by the river.

He'd have watched and waited for that howling, that bust loose in the brush, that deer.

But this was a dead body.

And here's the thing. Here's the thing:

A piece of cardboard lay at its feet, one whole side of a toilet-paper box, like you can pick up out back of the Piggly Wiggly. And on the cardboard was written this:

> Here lies the dead son of a bitch
> Charles Middleton Simons, MD,
> killed and manicured by his loving wife.
> Busy hands can be the devil's workshop as well.
> PS: Leland, can you blame me?

It was all written in a girly curlicue, a black marker. And here was my uncle's name, plain as day.

Nobody'd yet said a thing, none of the dozen or so of us standing at the edge of these woods. It wasn't even sunup yet, the sky still gray and yellow.

"Talk to me, Huger," Unc said, and I felt him put a hand on my shoulder. "What is it?" he said, though I knew he already knew. He'd been the one to tell me to stop the truck.

But he couldn't see it. He'd only smelled it, his head quick turning to my left, my window down. I'd been driving, like always him beside me in the cab, in the bed our load of men. There were three truckloads, us letting off a man at each stand. "Stop," he'd said, too loud. "Stop here," he'd said.

"We aren't even to eighteen yet," I'd said. "Seventeen's not but twenty yards—"

"Stop," he'd said again, his voice no different. Still too loud.

Now here we were. And I could smell it, too. Blood smell, something like the metal smell off the deer when we butcher them back to the clubhouse. But sharper. It smelled dark red, and sharp, like metal in your mouth. That sounds crazy, but that's the words that came to me: dark red, metal.

"Tell me," he said, almost a whisper in my ear now, his hand heavy on me. "What is it?"

He couldn't see it, because he's blind.

I opened my mouth. I wanted to say that the body had no head to speak of. I wanted to say the hands'd been skinned. I wanted to say it had on crisp camo fatigues, and those squirrel hands were holding an over-and-under twelve-gauge. I wanted to say it had on a hunter-orange vest, and that there was a cardboard sign at its feet, right there in the grass just below his newly oiled duck boots.

And I wanted to ask Unc why his name was on that sign.

My uncle is blind, and it's been left to me to be his eyes, my job here at the hunt club. Why I spent every weekend out here with him in his single-wide. Why my learner's permit figures in here.

I'd never seen a dead body before. That's what I wanted to tell him.

I turned to him, the sky above us, it felt, going a brighter yellow even in the second it took to turn.

He was looking at me, him a couple inches taller than me. He had on his sunglasses, that Braves cap he wears. He had on the same khaki shirt and pants as always, the same green suspenders.

And in his free hand was that walking stick he carries everywhere.

I found that stick when I was seven, not but a quarter mile from the trailer. Back when he'd just lost his sight. Back after the fire at his house in Mount Pleasant, in which his wife, my Aunt Sarah, died.

Back when my dad and mom were together, and we three lived here at Hungry Neck in that single-wide, my dad the proprietor of the hunt club.

They brought Unc here from the medical university, where he'd been for two months, his house and wife gone.

He lay in bed for six months in what had been my room, me in a sleeping bag on the couch in the front room. But I didn't mind. I talked to him each day, too. I told him about where I'd been on Hungry Neck, about the turkey I'd seen back past Baldwin Road or about the dove up from the clear-cut on past Lannear Road. I talked to him. And I read to him: the Hardy Boys, *The Chronicles of Narnia, Field & Stream.*

And I brought him things: a jay's nest once; a single antler, three points; an eagle feather. He took each thing in his hands, felt it.

Sometimes he smiled, other times he didn't. His eyes were bandaged, and he said next to nothing.

But he was what I had: someone who'd listen, while my mom and dad howled at each other out to the kitchen.

Then came that stick, a stick so straight and perfect I knew it'd been dropped off that hickory only for him. And for me. I brought it to him, and I remember he'd smiled at it, and'd sat up, turned in my bed, and stood.

"Huger?" Unc said now, his hand still on my shoulder. "You okay?" he whispered.

"Unc," I said. I said, "It's a body."

I turned back to it. I tried again to line up words that would give Unc what he couldn't see.

This was my job. Nothing I could have figured on when I'd handed him that stick when I was seven.

I swallowed, looked away from the body, from those hands, but all I did was look at my own, there at the end of my pale, skinny arms.

I'm only a kid, was what I saw. Fifteen years old. Thin brown hair just like Unc's, ears too big to the point where I can remember my daddy, before he left us, calling me Wingnut for fun. But though I'm too skinny, have these ears, I can knock shit out of most anybody in the sophomore class. There's nothing much I'm scared of.

But now.

I took in a breath. "It's a body," I said again, "and it doesn't have hardly any head to speak of. And the hands've been skinned."

His hand was still on my shoulder, but he turned, faced where that smell he'd found came from. He whispered, "Son of a bitch."

"And your name's involved here, too, Unc," I said.

He was quiet a moment. Still nobody'd said a thing.

His hand went tight on my shoulder a second, then relaxed. He said, "It's Charlie Simons, ain't it." Not a question, but a fact.

I looked at him, saw he had his upper lip between his teeth, biting down hard: what he'll do.

He turned then, started off on his own toward the truck, that stick out in front of him, leading him on.

That was when the dogs started up, way off to the levee, their howling not unlike the sounds of my mom and dad. Just howling in the hopes of turning something up.

2

"I got my bag phone in my daypack," one of the men said from behind me. "I'll call it in."

"Good idea," somebody said.

"Charlie Simons," somebody else said. "God."

"Ol' Charlie Simons," somebody else said. Then, almost too low to hear, "Head and hands. Not the prettiest job of degloving I've seen. The irony here's pretty thick."

Then somebody else whispered loud enough for everybody to hear, "She got that son-of-a-bitch part right."

Some of the men gave out a quiet laugh.

I didn't say anything, only turned from the body, my eyes do~~
and started back through the brush for Unc.

He knew all these men. He knew them because they'~
part of the whole thing out here long as he's been alive:
men from South of Broad entertaining themselves w?
they were hunters. When what they did every Satur
son long was just show up here, have breakfast—
and biscuits all cooked up before dawn by Mis~

black woman who lived five miles out County Road 112, and her deaf-and-dumb daughter, Dorcas, a girl a year older than me—at the clubhouse.

The kitchen where they cook it all up is just a big old iron stove and a sink set up at one end of the long, low white dining cabin we called the clubhouse, the rest of it picnic tables, screened windows, the rafters all open. Miss Dinah and Dorcas show up around 4:00 A.M. to get things started, and Unc is always in there with them, too, laughing and talking, carrying on when I stumble in, me trying to sleep as late as I can before the members arrive. Over the years he's learned some sign language he tries to use on Dorcas, who stops from stirring the grits or working the bacon and goes to him, puts her hands in his and slowly spells out a word or some such, the three of them laughing again for whatever it is they're messing about, me never a part of things, only looking for coffee and heading out to build the campfire.

Then, after breakfast, Miss Dinah and Dorcas washing things up and readying for fried-chicken lunch, the members'd stand at the fire, bellies full of good food they didn't have to make, while Unc parceled them out.

Unc knew all these South-of-Broaders. And knew it was Charles Middleton Simons, M.D.

I knew them, too, but only by the shiny Range Rovers and Suburbans and Grand Cherokees they drove, each one polished, detailed. I could size up the parking area next to the clubhouse while they were all in there eating, and know if the six-and-a-half-foot-tall ear, nose, and throat doctor was here, or the lawyer with the wire-frame aviator glasses and goatee, or the fat radiologist who was always chewing on an unlit black cigar.

But I didn't know their names because I just didn't want to commit to memory the names of adult men who thought piling into the back of a beat-up Luv like mine and then hopping out at a stretch of road was hunting. Why, too, I kept my eyes down. I just didn't look any of them in the eye.

He was already at the truck. The Luv didn't have a tailgate or bumper, and he was leaned against the bed.

I sat next to him. He held the top of the stick in his lap, the tip on the ground a few feet in front of him. He was moving the stick, making small shapes in the dirt, like he was thinking about writing something but wouldn't.

He said, "One of them call sheriff's office yet?"

I put my hands on the tops of my legs, moved them back and forth. I said, "Yep." I waited a second, said, "You smelled it."

"You got that right." He stopped a second with the stick, held it still to the ground.

"And?" I said, though I knew he didn't like that, didn't like anybody making him give up what he didn't want to give up.

"And what, boy?" he said. "How'd I smell it? Because I got no choice." He stood, took a step away toward the woods on the other side of the road.

"Listen," he said, his back to me. "Just listen."

All I could hear was the dogs, coming closer. His back to me, he could have been anybody out here.

"Listen," he said again, and now he turned to me: those sunglasses, the stick. It was my uncle. Nobody else.

"What I hear is all I got," he said. "And what I can touch and what I can taste. And—" He stopped. "And all I got is what I can smell." His shoulders fell, and he took a step toward me. "I can't see."

I said, "Unc, we got to talk." I paused. "The police are on the way. You got to talk to me."

"Listen," he said one more time, as though I hadn't yet said word one to him.

But this time I listened. There were a few squirrels barking. And there were the dogs working their way here. A mourning dove.

And past all this, beneath it and behind me, was the low sound of the men talking amongst themselves.

I turned. There they stood, all of them, back in the brush and looking down, a batch of hunter-orange hats at the edge of woods, between us a dirt road and twenty yards of weeds.

"They're talking," Unc said, "about what a son of a bitch Charlie Simons was, because he was. A son of a bitch if there ever was one." He sat beside me again. He started with the stick in the ground again, too, still like he was almost writing.

I said, "Somebody made a joke. Said something about the irony is heavy-handed."

He let out a breath, and I saw a smile come up on him, though I could tell he didn't want any part of it. But it came.

"Charlie was a plastic surgeon," Unc said. "And shot in the head." He paused. "Hands skinned." He took in a breath. "I imagine it was Cleve Ravenel made the joke. Him, or Buddy Rose." He paused, moved that stick again. "Neither of them cared for that bastard much. But truth is no one give much of a damn for him." He took in a breath. "And they're talking about me," he whispered, his voice gone so low I could hardly hear him for those dogs, still a good couple hundred yards off. "Because there was a time when I would have killed the man, too."

I looked at him. Here was my uncle, somebody I thought I knew. Somebody I knew I loved.

Then I looked back to the men. Now and again one of those hunter-orange caps turned our way. I couldn't see faces for the high weeds, only those hats turning.

"Yep," he said. "They're watching us."

I quick looked at him, amazed for the millionth time at what he could figure out.

He started moving the stick again, and now, finally, I could see some kind of pattern to what he was doing: he was making a row of spiral shapes in the dirt there, like coils, each one about a foot or so across. He'd made five so far.

They were strange there on the ground, these shapes, and I wondered what he'd meant with it. But even stranger was the fact he could do it without looking: the coils were shaky but there; no line touched itself as it grew bigger. He knew what he was doing.

I said, "There was a sign with it. With the body."

He stopped with the stick. "No doubt that's where my name came in."

I said, "Yep. The sign said he was a son of a bitch, too."

The dogs were coming closer, and I wondered if they hadn't picked up it was human blood they were coming up on.

I said, "There was a P.S.," and looked at him. "It said, 'PS: Leland, can you blame me?'"

He shook his head, this time let out a small laugh, short and sharp.

He said, "Constance," and still shook his head.

"You better talk to me, Unc," I said.

But he only took that stick, dragged it back and forth through the row of shapes, wrecked them.

He stood then, faced the hunters. "Boys," he hollered out, and all those orange caps turned this way. "The dogs are coming up," he hollered. "Make sure and keep the damn things off that poor boy."

"Yessir," came a few voices.

"And Cleve Ravenel—" he called out.

"Yeah-man," I heard, and here came one of the orange hats.

"Get your truck and go down to the clubhouse, wait for the sheriff to show up," Unc hollered. "Then usher the brethren on back here."

"Yessir," the man said.

He was the one who drove the third truck out here, the cherry-red Ram 2500 with the black bed liner, the black cargo net. Unc'd picked him out to carry the last load of men, bring up the rear. He was a big man, red-faced and white hair, a beer gut that made his belt buckle disappear. He was a cancer doctor, as best I knew.

He took off his hat, rubbed the back of his head, put the other hand at his hip. He squinted at Unc, looked back to the men, then to Unc again.

"Mighty nasty work," this Cleve Ravenel said, and I recognized his voice: the one who'd agreed with the sign.

Unc was right again.

"Sounds like," Unc said, and nodded.

Cleve Ravenel stood there with us a few seconds, looking at Unc and the men and at Unc one more time. Then he looked at me, smiled. He winked.

"I'll be back with the troops," he finally said. He put the cap back on, headed past the pearl gray GMC that belonged to the short, crew-cut orthopedic surgeon.

"Cleve," Unc called to him.

"Yeah-man?" he said, and turned, maybe too quick. He was a big man, and he looked scared. But I figured even though he was a doctor and'd seen more dead bodies than I ever would, seeing one without a head might could do that to you. Make you scared.

"On your way out stop at each stand, tell every man what's going on over here." He paused. "Won't do no good to tell them to stay put. But tell them to walk on over here in the weeds on the east side of the road. Stay off the road so's they don't muck up any oddball tire tracks or such."

Cleve Ravenel had a hand up at the bill of his cap to block the sun. He said, "Why's that, Leland?"

"Just tell them," Unc said, and turned his back to the man.

Cleve Ravenel stood there a moment longer, looking, then headed for his truck.

And now the dogs were upon us, busting out from the woods and crossing the road, the dozen of them howling and carrying on, tails wagging, most of them soaked and muddy for the low-lying land between here and the levee. It'd only be a couple minutes more before Patrick and Reynold would come through on horseback, following the pack, their purpose to scare up one last time any deer hadn't yet moved.

Unc looked down at me, and I could see me in his glasses, two of me reflected there, me small and far away on the tail end of the Luv. Which is exactly how I felt: small, and far away.

He knew things.

Cleve Ravenel did a three-pointer, then headed away.

Unc said, "Before your Aunt Sarah ever came around, it was Constance. Then came Charlie Simons." He paused. "Then I was out on my ass. Him a resident over to the medical college, me a snot-nosed private with the police department." He stopped, looked to the men again. The dogs' howling had slowed down some, as though finding what they were ape-shit over all this time was some sort of letdown.

"Then Wednesday night she gives me a call," Unc said. He was still looking at me. "I haven't heard from her in twenty-one years, not since the last night I ever saw her. The night I told her she was the one I was going to marry, like it or not." He smiled, slowly shook his head. "Wednesday night she's crying, and she tells me she's going to kill the son of a bitch Charles Middleton Simons, M.D."

He let out a slow whistle. He looked to the ground before him, and I was gone, my reflection. "Twenty-one years," he whispered.

I watched him. His job with the police was something we didn't talk about. He never said word one of it to me, not since before the fire, when he and Aunt Sarah used to come out for Christmas and Easter and he'd talk about things.

But since the fire he hadn't said a word.

He moved his hand again, working the stick, and looked at the ground. He'd already gotten one whole spiral done, this one even clearer than the rest, steadier.

He finished the thing, said, "Better get hold of one of them bag phones. Give your momma a call."

Then he put his boot to the shape, moved his toe back and forth in the dirt, and it was gone.

3

If I called my mom, she'd make me come home. And if I told her I wouldn't—I wouldn't—she'd haul ass down here and drag me back.

Which is why I didn't call her, like Unc told me to. I didn't want her to come screaming in here in that old Stanza she drives, didn't want her making a scene in front of everyone here.

So I left Unc there at the Luv, made like I was going over to use the bag phone off the man who'd called the sheriff. But I only went to the edge of the weeds across the road, and I turned, watched him.

He'd held back a piece of truth from me, this woman Constance calling him this week. I'd hold a piece from him: the fact Mom wasn't on her way here to get me.

A minute later I went back to the Luv, leaned on it.

He said, "What'd she say?"

"She shit bricks."

"Such talk," he said. "Clean up your mouth."

"Yessir," I said. I was quiet, then said, "She told me to come home soon as I can."

"You're lying."

"I am," I said. Mom wouldn't have said that. "She said come home now. But I told her I couldn't, because I might have to talk to the sheriff, seeing as how I'm a witness."

He didn't move. His head was down, the bill of the Braves cap covering his face, the stick still against the ground. The light was coming up around us now. We had the whole day left, a day I was certain wasn't going to be like any other I'd known.

Then he looked up, called out, "Boys, party's over. Come on back to the road now. Single file. Bring them dogs with you, too." He paused, took a breath, as though he were tired already. "Then just take a seat in the weeds or back in the trucks."

"Yessir," came a few voices again.

Here came the orange hats.

He turned to me. "And where in hell do you think Patrick and Reynold are?"

Patrick and Reynold: the horsemen, their job to let out war whoops while they rode through the woods, the dogs in front of them, scaring up deer from where they hid. Both of them carried rifles in their saddles and were given the right to shoot anything they startled up, this their form of payment. Unc could count on the two of them to run the dogs exactly where he wanted, though past that he couldn't count on them for much.

Last I'd seen of them was just after Unc'd parceled out the men at the campfire, then we both walked like every Saturday deer hunt to where they waited at the front of the line of trucks. Patrick and Reynold sat in their black and rusted Dodge pickup, in the bed the dog cages, all of the dogs moving, yelping, behind it all their horse trailer.

"Drunk again," Unc'd whispered as we came up to the driver's-side window, Patrick behind the wheel. Already I could smell the beer off them, that smell mixed with the smell off the dogs.

I'd known these two men my whole life and still didn't know them enough to say word one to them. Or care to. They'd been the ones to run the dogs since their daddy was killed in a bar fight in Beaufort before I was born, and lived in a shanty back toward Jacksonboro. Neither of them had ever married, though there was word every now and again about there being a girl or two living with them in that shack, but never for long. And I'd never seen one of them without the other. They were just the men who ran the dogs, stinking of beer every Saturday-morning deer hunt the whole season long.

We stopped at the window, and Unc said, "Head up Cemetery. Let the dogs out above Baldwin before where it crosses Levee."

Patrick rolled his head over to Unc, smiled. He had a heavy ponytail I don't think he'd ever washed, his forehead working back on him, and from the light off the dash I could see in his smile where teeth ought to have been.

He grunted, then Reynold leaned forward, his bald head soaking up the green of that dash light. "Sir yes sir," he said, and saluted.

Patrick gave it the gas, pulled away. And just like every time, once they were past the clubhouse Reynold gave off the same old high-pitched, hard laugh, a laugh out of control and ugly: his own rebel yell, Patrick and Reynold's way of getting in the last word on the blind man they worked for.

Forty-five minutes after Unc'd sent him, here came Cleve Ravenel's Ram 2500, behind him two cruisers, the first with its blue lights on, siren going, the other only following along. Ravenel blinked his lights on and off a couple times. Leading the parade.

And still Patrick and Reynold hadn't shown up.

Unc was already moving toward them, and I wondered if maybe he didn't need me here after all. If maybe I shouldn't have just called Mom and headed home. I hadn't done squat yet in all this, only followed him, watching.

"It's two of them," I said. "Two cruisers." I caught up with him.

The first cruiser cut the siren and lights. "I'll wager it's Doug Yandle in the lead," he said, and shook his head. "A siren."

Cleve Ravenel pulled to a stop, his truck sliding a couple feet, the wheels locked for how hard he'd hit the brakes.

But Unc kept walking quick, a step ahead of me. When he came even with the truck, he let the stick drag behind him, his hand down, and I watched him pull his index finger along the front quarter panel, leave a stripe of clean red metal in the fresh mud splashed up there.

Ravenel let us pass before he popped open his door, climbed out. "Sorry it took so long," he said. He hitched up his camo pants over that beer gut. "Got lost," he said.

The door of the first cruiser was already open, an officer climbing out, Smokey the Bear hat in hand. He was tan, had a perfect mustache, creases starched into the light brown uniform.

I didn't like him already.

"Mr. Dillard," the officer said, and started to put on the hat.

"Deputy Yandle," Unc said. He was at the front quarter panel of the cruiser, dragged his muddy finger along the white metal casual as you please, leaving behind a thin brown stripe the officer couldn't see for Unc headed toward him.

He was wiping the mud off on the cruiser, and I felt myself smile. Him giving shit to this droid already.

Yandle stopped, hat halfway to his head, surprised Unc knew who it was already.

Unc stopped, pulled the stick up, held it. "Who's your backup?" he said.

"Mr. Dillard," this Yandle said, his voice loud, like Unc's being blind meant he couldn't hear well either. He slammed his door, put his hands on his hips. "We had a call regarding a possible 763—"

"Leland!" I heard, and looked past this Yandle to the second cruiser, saw a man climbing out.

"Tommy Thigpen," Unc said, and started around Yandle, the stick tapping out the ground. "Haven't seen you since back when I could see," he said. "How's your granddaddy doing?"

"Passed on a while back," this Thigpen said, and shrugged.

Unc paused a moment. He held the stick a few inches above the ground, said, "I'm truly sorry to hear that. He was a good man."

Thigpen shrugged again, rubbed at his nose. "You got that right," he said.

Slowly Unc let the stick touch the ground, then turned toward where the body was across the road. "Tommy," he said, "looks like we got a messy one here."

Yandle looked at Unc, then at me. His eyebrows were all knotted, his jaw working.

I only shrugged. I said, "Guess he wants to talk to your backup."

Unc turned back to Thigpen, leaned the stick against the hood of the cruiser, and shook hands with him.

"Leland," Thigpen said, "I just followed this call. I'm backup for Doug, so don't you start with me. You know that."

He was smiling now, a gold cap on one of his two front teeth. He was skinny, pale except for his left arm, the farmer's tan. He had the same creases in the uniform, even had the same mustache, though his was grizzly, gray and brown and a little long on the edges.

"Mr. Dillard," Yandle said. He was still too loud. "We have procedures as set down by the County Sheriff's Department as regards responding units, and those procedures, when violated, place any investigation in serious jeopardy—"

"Back this way," Unc said to Tommy, and turned.

But I was right there, in front of him now he'd turned to usher this Thigpen to the body.

Police work, I thought. Nothing to do with me.

His stick hit my boot, and he stopped, looked up. Here I was again, two of me there in his sunglasses.

"Huger?" he said.

I said, "You're not losing me this easy."

Past him I could see Tommy Thigpen, now with his arms crossed, his head tilted, looking at me, at Unc. And I knew behind me was Yandle, behind him Ravenel, then everybody else, all those orange-capped South-of-Broaders standing now, dusting off their butts from sitting in the weeds all this while, waiting to see, just like me, what was going to happen.

It wasn't going to happen without me.

Unc put his free hand to my shoulder yet again. "You probably think I'm hoping your momma's going to show up here any second, don't you?" He squeezed hard, and I felt again how skinny I was, how nothing I was out here with everyone looking on at the two of us. "But since you haven't called her yet, I don't suppose she'll be coming anytime soon. Now, ain't that right?"

I looked down. "Yessir," I said.

This was how long we'd been with each other: long enough for him to know I wouldn't be calling this in to my mom, who'd throw a fit one way or the other. And long enough for me to know I couldn't lie to him.

"One thing," Unc said, and I looked at him. "One thing. This is a murder. Not a party. Not a field trip."

His mouth was just a thin line, his jaw clenched.

"Yessir," I said.

He nodded.

The smell had gone worse.

It'd been almost an hour since we were first back here to the body, and some flies had started in. Before, that smell'd been dark red and metal. Now it was something like a whiff of pluff mud up off the marsh.

But what hit me most was how still this all was, and I felt myself in some way ugly for being alive, for moving up to it with Unc and these two deputies. Behind us and looking over all our shoulders was a string of lawyers and doctors and such, eager for a look again at a body, all this movement, all of us alive.

Nothing had changed at all from when we'd first been back here. It was a body. It had hardly any head, its hands skinned. It had on fatigues, held a gun, and just lay there, but for the flies picking at the head and hands.

Thigpen stepped up beside the top of the body, squatted, moved his head back and forth, looking at the weeds there.

"Quite a wound," Thigpen said. "Not enough blood behind him and in the weeds here for a wound that big." He paused, leaned in close. "And them hands. Shit." He reached toward the shoulder, and I could see a tattoo coming out from under Thigpen's short sleeve: the word JUNIOR, homemade.

"We'll leave all deductions to the crime-scene task force, Deputy Thigpen," Yandle said. He had a notepad out, a silver pen he'd taken from his front shirt pocket, started writing in it. "We're already in violation of at least two codes discussing details of the case with Mr. Dillard here. Not to mention the boy."

"We would've heard the shot, too, if it'd been back here," Unc said, ignoring Yandle. He tapped the boot of the man with his stick. "He's been dead a good five hours or so. Me and Huger been here all night, and we would've heard it at the trailer if they'd shot him back here."

"How you know how long he's been dead?" Yandle put in.

"The smell, first off," Unc said, his voice quiet. "It's old. Next how stiff this boy is going. Tap his boot. You can feel rigor mortis already settling in. Quite a while ago."

"Maybe you ought simply to be quiet about anything, Mr. Dillard," Yandle said. He slipped the pad and pen into his shirt pocket. "You might ought to remain silent, seeing as how you are implicated here, on a cardboard sign no less." He paused. "Sir."

I wanted to answer him, wanted to turn to this turd and tell him off, sick of Yandle already and what he was saying here: my uncle was involved. Even though I wasn't sure of anything myself.

But there was nothing I knew to say. It was a body here, going ripe, the hands skinned like dead squirrels.

"Let's go," Yandle said, and started for me. "I'm moving you two out of here and putting up a banner on the perimeter." He put a hand to my arm, started to pull me back toward the road.

But I shook him off. "The hell you are," I said finally, and I could hear my voice gone loud, heard it quivering, too. "This is our property," I said. "You're not kicking us out of here."

This time he took hold of my arm tighter, pinched the muscle there. "Let's go," he said.

"Now the two of you," Unc said, his voice low and solid and

sharp enough to make Yandle stop a second. "Just cut this out altogether."

Yandle, teeth clenched, said, "Unless proper order can be maintained at the crime scene, then all offenders will be—"

"Son of a fucking bitch!" Thigpen said, not a whisper, not a shout, but like it'd taken every bit of his air to say it.

I turned, saw him fast crabwalking backward in the weeds, his hands scrambling on the ground behind him, his feet moving fast, too, though it seemed in the second I took it all in that he wasn't getting anywhere, instead was falling and getting up, falling and getting up.

He was looking at the body.

"What?" Unc said. "What?"

That was when I saw it, too: those skinned hands, red muscles, white tendons holding that gun, an over-and-under twelve-gauge, were moving, starting up, slow and stiff.

It was a body.

It was a body without much of a head.

The arms were moving up, slowly, like he was taking aim at some bird might fly off if it saw him move, and now Yandle's hand was off me, and we were moving back too, my feet heavy in the weeds, and now my throat collapsed, and though I tried to answer Unc, tried to tell him *It's a body, and it's lifting up that gun,* I couldn't get anything out.

"Holy shit," Yandle whispered beside me, and still we two stumbled back, the weeds like ropes.

"What?" Unc said again. "What the hell is going on?"

He turned toward us, and I could see the puzzlement on his face, the way he was trying to figure why he got no answer, but still nothing came.

And then I saw what it was there in the weeds, saw it in the way that gun rose, those hands ready to shoot: it wasn't a body, but a *man,* dead.

It was a dead man.

Then the world out here, the trees, this light, the weeds and Thigpen and Yandle and Unc—"Somebody tell me what's going on!" he shouted now, him pitiful and alone not five feet away from me, and not five feet from a dead man lifting his gun to aim—all of it started to swirl in front of me, and I started falling back, the blue morning sky above me filling my eyes now, and in the last instant before everything went white I saw the bird this dead man was aiming at: a buzzard circled way up there, brought here by a smell old and red and metal, and I couldn't blame Charles Middleton Simons, M.D., for trying to take him out with that twelve-gauge, no matter the son of a bitch everybody here said he was.

4

Mom.

She was leaned over me, her face close. The first thing I felt was her smell: the same thick flowery perfume as every day, but on top of that another smell, like the bathroom after I'd cleaned it Monday afternoons at our house in Liberty Hills. Lysol, maybe. But I couldn't make out her face, like I was looking through water at her, so I blinked.

That's when I felt it: the pain in my head.

"Honey," she whispered. "Sugar."

For a second everything seemed like it hadn't happened: no dead man, no police, no hunting.

Then I heard the scrape of a chair on the floor, steps toward me.

"Huger," Unc said, and I knew.

"Stay out of this," Mom said, her voice just like it was when she didn't want to hear my side of whatever. Like Unc was a kid with no sense at all.

Like she talked to him most all the time, really.

And here was my mom: her red hair in soft curls, her white skin, and those thin freckles across her nose, her green eyes. My petite, beautiful mom.

The same one who could rip me in half for coming in past curfew or getting a B on a test, and who seemed an inch from tearing Unc apart, too, if she hadn't already.

She had on her white nurse's outfit, the ID card clipped to the collar. We were in a room, me in bed, and I saw steel rails beside me: in the hospital.

Mom was trying to smile at me, her chin shaking.

"Everything'll be fine," she said. "Just fine." She touched my cheek.

"Unc," I said, and the word was like a brick on my head.

"You fell," he said. He stood back behind Mom, hat off, no stick. "You fainted, and you fell. Hit your head on—"

"Leland," she said, her eyes moving like she might see him beside her. "You keep quiet."

"What happened?" I whispered.

"You got a concussion," she said, smiling again. Just that quick, like Unc never existed. "You been out a couple hours now. Officer Thigpen and Dr. Morrison brought you in with that other officer." She paused. "And your uncle." She shook her head.

I looked past her to Unc. On the wall behind him was a painting in a brass frame: six black Lab puppies chewing on a duck boot. The footboard was shiny oak, against the wall a huge piece of oak furniture, eight foot tall and with a mirror.

Mom said, "This is the Palmetto Pavilion. We're here at the university." She looked around, smiling. "When they saw you being escorted in by Dr. Morrison, they put you up here on the VIP floor. Pretty sharp, huh?"

But I was looking at Unc again.

"You got quite a bump on the back of your head," Mom said. "You'll have to stay overnight. Dr. Morrison is taking good care of you." Mom reached to the little group of buttons on the rail, pressed one of them. "We'll get one of the nurses to tell Dr. Morrison you're awake."

She was in her scared-mother mode: just keep talking and everything will be all right. When all I wanted was to know from Unc what happened: that dead man's arms.

"Yes?" came a voice from a speaker somewhere above and behind me.

"Eugenie Dillard here," Mom said. "He's awake. Can we get Dr. Morrison in here?"

"Okay."

Mom smiled down at me. "Imagine my surprise to get a call down in X Ray that my baby boy is being brought into Emergency by the sheriff's office. And imagine my surprise that he's unconscious." She shook her head, and now the smile was gone. "Imagine I find out there's been a murder out to Hungry Neck, and my son hasn't called or had sense enough to get the hell out of there, and now here he is being wheeled in on a stretcher through Emergency, and a deputy behind him crying and carrying on about his broke shoulder, and it's me and the girls down there in X Ray who get to shoot pictures of you and your head all banged to hell and then get to shoot that crybaby deputy—"

"Yandle broke your fall," Unc said. "To a degree."

"Leland," she said again, but this time she turned to him, started in with her finger, shook it in his face, like he could see it and maybe fear her for it. "You just shut the hell up. You ought to know better than to let a boy out there in amongst all this grisly murder and whatnot, you sorry excuse for an uncle. As if I don't have enough problems with this child and all he's got going against him back home and over to school, plus everything I have to train out of him every Sunday night when he gets back from that godforsaken broken-down hunt club. The smartest thing I ever did was get us the hell out of there and into Charleston—"

"Mom," I whispered. "I told him I called you. I told him—"

"And now you've gone and give him a dead body to look at like it was some sort of manly man thing to do," Mom kept on. "I'm working my damnedest at providing for him a loving and virtuous home to live in, no small feat I figured you'd know by now, a single

mom and the way the world is crouching at my door ready to take
my precious love, my baby boy, any second now. But no. You give
him this. This looking at a dead man."

"Eugenie," he said. "I'm sorry."

"Sorry?" she said. "Sorry? Sorry don't even begin to do it. Sorry
don't even—"

"Mom," I said, and the word hurt.

She turned to me, her eyebrows up, mouth open, like she'd forgotten me altogether with what she was handing out to Unc.

Then she cried, her shoulders falling in on her, her mouth crum-
pling up, eyes squeezing shut. She was holding back, the sound only
hisses, quick breaths.

Unc went to her, turned her to him. "Now, Eugenie," he said.
"Everything's fine. It's fine."

Mom gave up then, leaned into him, cried into his shoulder.

It was something I hadn't seen before, her giving up to him.

But it only lasted a couple seconds. She quick tensed up, took a
step back from him. She put the back of a hand to her eye, looked
at me, tried that smile again. She said, "I'm a mess," and sniffed,
touched at a run of mascara down one cheek.

"Now let's not hear any more talk like that," somebody said at the
door, and I looked past them to a man in a white coat, stethoscope
draped over his shoulders.

Silverado short-bed, teal blue. Adam's apple big as a fist.

Buck, the name on his personalized license plate.

"Dr. Morrison," Mom said, and quick touched at her eye again,
smiled big for him.

Unc turned, and here came Buck, smiling at me. "How you doing?" he said, and pulled a penlight from the jacket pocket.

I said nothing.

"Now, don't you worry none. I washed my hands since holding
back them hounds at the club," he said.

He was a member, a definite South-of-Broader, handing me redneck talk, like what he'd expect I might want to hear out of him.
Like he thought that's what might comfort us hayseeds.

He leaned over me, held the light to one eye, then the other. The room filled up with a white so bright my head hurt for it.

"Tommy Thigpen and Jervey Morrison here brought you in in Tommy's cruiser," Unc said. "And Yandle and me. Lucky we had a neurosurgeon out in the wilds with us."

"Dr. Morrison's on the faculty," Mom said, her voice all candy. "He's dean of Neurosurgery," she said, "so I'd say it's more like divine intervention than luck."

He looked at my eyes a second time: white, pain. Then he was away, still smiling.

"Just out for the hunt," he said. "Glad I could be there to help y'all." He turned to Unc, crossed his arms. "Luck is that deputy being there to break his fall. Otherwise he might have hit that stump full on, cracked his skull open like an old muskmelon."

Unc only nodded.

Buck looked at me. "We'll need for you to stay the night. Just to make sure you're all right. Then you can head on home tomorrow, if you're feeling at all like it. In the meantime, we need for you to stay awake for long as you can. Watch some TV, football games."

He turned to Mom, smiling, then back to me. "Divine intervention is having a momma as pretty as she is," he said, "and working at the hospital we end up bringing you into."

He glanced at Unc. "Leland, we be seeing you." He turned to Mom, nodded at her to follow him.

She smiled at me, then Buck headed out the door, and she was gone.

Unc already had his hands to the railing. He grinned. "You should have heard Yandle pissing and moaning about his arm all the way down here," he said, his voice down low, like we'd get in trouble if somebody heard us talking. "He was crying the whole way. But it's a good thing he was there, breaking your fall, like the good doctor said."

"But Unc," I said, and swallowed, my mouth dry now too. "What—"

"Rigor mortis," he said. "I seen it happen before."

He stopped, slowly looked to the window, like maybe he'd see something out there could help him. "For whatever reason, the muscles just go taut sometimes, start pulling against the bone." He paused. "You'd be amazed, Huger, what I seen. But I'm sorry you had to see that. Just like I said to your momma. I am sorry."

He let go the rail and reached to me, his hand moving along the white of the sheet, looking for me.

I took hold of it, and he squeezed down hard.

It felt good, that pain.

"But your momma is right," he said.

"About what?" I swallowed again.

"What she's saying is you ought not to be out there anymore. You ought to stay home for a while. Till things get settled."

I let go his hand. "No way."

He shook his head. "I told you. This is no field trip. There's no way I want you or your momma involved in any of this."

I tried to sit up then, pushed my elbows down, scooted my butt up. But the pain in my head nearly knocked me down, and I only lay back, closed my eyes.

"What's *this*?" I whispered. "What do you know, Unc?" I opened my eyes to him. "You said she called you."

"Saturday after Thanksgiving, I imagine there's a couple dozen ball games to choose from," he said, his voice whole and solid. "Now, where the heck's the TV in here?" He put his hand to the rail, found the buttons. "Which one for the TV?"

"Unc," I said, "you can't do this." I was quiet a second, not certain if what I wanted to say was right or not. If he'd take it the way I meant it: that he needed me.

And I needed him.

"Unc," I said. "You're a blind man."

"Damn straight," he whispered hard and looked at me, his lips tight. He forgot the buttons on the rail and quick reached up with his hand, pulled off the sunglasses, like he'd been waiting for this all along.

There they were: his marble eyes, white and fake, held in by the gnarled and shiny skin of his eyelids, the skin melted from where his eyebrows might have been down to his cheekbones, where he'd been burned, and where the glass from the bedroom window exploded out at him, hot shards of it shooting into his eyes and into his chest and arms. It was then he'd fallen back, away from the house, and then the eaves above that window had collapsed, him screaming on the ground.

It'd been my Aunt Sarah inside the bedroom, asleep, Unc just home from a shift at the department, him an investigator, home at midnight every night.

But this time his house was on fire, and he'd run around to their bedroom window, and it'd exploded.

I knew all this only from what my mom told me once, years back and just before we moved to North Charleston. It'd never occurred to me to ask before that, to ask what happened, Unc's presence in our trailer only a given, what other uncles did when they were hurt. I'd known it was a fire he'd been in, known Aunt Sarah was dead.

But in the hush of his moving in, and the moving out of my daddy not much later, it'd always seemed something not to ask after, and so I hadn't. Even when I did venture that one time, the trailer choked with boxes, Unc like a stone on the couch in the front room, Mom folding my clothes up and into yet another box, her answer had been short, quick: just the fact of a fire, Unc home after his shift, that explosion, all of it whispered to me so Unc wouldn't hear talk of it, I imagined.

And Unc himself had never ventured a word on it to me, and I knew, always knew, not to ask.

"Damn straight," he said again. "I'm a blind man. And if I can't handle something like this on my own, then I might as well up and die. Because—"

"Because why?" I said, my voice finally gone loud. The pain didn't matter. "You think you can walk into whatever it is you know about and work it out yourself, when it's me to drive you to the Piggly Wiggly, and me to write your bills for you, and me to rewash the dishes in the sink because you're—"

"Enough!" Mom shouted, and here she was, moving fast for Unc and me. She pushed him aside while he quick put his sunglasses back on. She looked at me, her face gone red. "I don't know what the hell's going on between the two of you, but you better both of you shut up. We could hear you all the way out to the hallway, like two kids. It's embarrassing." Now she was straightening out the sheet at my chest, looking at it like it was the only important thing in the world.

I looked at Unc. His back was to us, his head up.

"Unc," I said. "You got to tell me."

"Now you just settle down," Mom said, still picking at the sheet, but I pulled it back, tried again to sit up. "Unc," I said, "listen."

He pulled his Braves cap from his back pocket, slapped it on. "Eugenie," he said, and made his way toward the door, found the knob. He reached behind the door, pulled out the stick. "I'm sorry for what-all happened. Take better care of that boy than I have."

"You sure don't ask for much," she said, and put her hand to my chest, eased me back down.

He was leaving me.

I lay back then, felt like I was out of breath, like I'd run ten miles, my mom's hand on me some kind of comfort in it all. But not the sort I wanted.

He stood in the doorway, out there in the hall bright white light. He looked one way, then the other, and put out his stick.

"Unc!" I shouted, and felt like I'd split my head clean open with the word, with how it echoed in this VIP room with brass and oak, when all I wanted was to be curling up to sleep on the couch in the front room of the single-wide, in me the good knowledge Unc was there, back in his room, my old bedroom, snoring quiet like he does.

"Now you shush," Mom said.

I heard that stick in the hallway out there, tapping, Unc walking away.

5

I tried to stay awake.

Mom talked beside me, now and again stood from the chair she'd pulled up beside the bed, put her hand to my face in a kind of gentle slap, and I'd open my eyes, say, "I heard you."

She'd gone to that big piece of furniture down past the footboard, opened up the mirrored doors to reveal a TV, then came back to the rails, pushed a button.

The TV came on, a football game.

I closed my eyes to that, too. I hated football.

But the speaker was up by my ear and turned way low, me too tired even to tell Mom to turn the thing off, so that while I was sleeping and staying awake there were two stories going on: announcers and players and coaches all after something, and Mom talking.

Mom and I live in North Charleston, which might as well be another planet from Charleston. North Charleston is like a joke to people who live downtown, because that's where all the Navy people live, and all the fired shipyard workers are, and where people get shot in the BP minimarts or where some kid will bring a gun to school and start shooting, like what happened at my school last year.

There was a body after that, too. One of the football team, a black kid who everybody said was going to Clemson or USC to play on a scholarship, maybe. They said these things, of course, only after the kid was dead. And he wasn't even a part of the fight that happened, was just like everybody else who ever gets killed in school: one of those Innocent Bystanders.

But I didn't see that body, that black kid. And I remember school after that happened, the counselors they had lined up in the office wanting to talk to anybody who was cracked about that kid getting killed. Like we don't need anybody to talk to until one of us gets killed?

I didn't see that body, but I do remember feeling like death was there with us, like it'd been walking the halls, and maybe I just missed it, just walked into my first-period class a second or so before he turned the corner, headed along the lockers toward me. I just hadn't seen him.

But I saw him today.

And Mom thinks my staying with Unc is a necessary evil: she makes me stay down there, and Unc cuts her a check each month off his insurance from the fire.

She thinks I don't know about the money, but I do. And she thinks she's making me go there. Truth is, I'd pay her, if it came to that.

It takes close to an hour to get to Hungry Neck from where we live in North Charleston, a neighborhood called Liberty Hills. There's no hills there, of course. Just houses, square ones like ours.

I lay there in the hospital bed, listening to my mom talk and the TV playing on and on, and thought of the drive there, that hour, saw myself climb in the Luv parked in our driveway of a Friday afternoon, school over, then heading out to Hungry Neck Hunt Club: the clubhouse, next to it the butcher shed, where we haul the deer in and dress them, past the clubhouse and shed the single-wide, beige with a brown racing stripe all the way around, cinder blocks leading up to the front door.

Hungry Neck Hunt Club. Where my mom lived with my dad for eight years, me there for seven of them. And with Unc for one more year after that, Mom nursing him and taking care of me. That whole year, I saw my dad talk to Unc maybe twice, their words never much more than sharp knives meant to cut out the heart of one or the other of them. Nothing like when Unc and Aunt Sarah used to come out for Easter and Christmas, when there'd be laughter and stories, usually about Hungry Neck and wild pigs they'd snared, or the secret deer stands they used to put up just for watching the woods, the river. Back when I used to envy them being brothers, me having none, not even a sister.

Not a week after Unc took that stick from me, sat up in bed for the first time, my daddy was gone.

Which is why sometimes I blame myself for the whole thing. If I hadn't found that stick.

I've driven this route so many times I don't even have to think about it, a drive I've been doing one way or the other every Friday night since I was eight and we moved to that square house in Liberty Hills, when we'd come back to take care of Unc over the weekend, heading home late Sunday night.

Then, when I turned ten, she took to just dropping me off Friday nights, and going home, me here to tend to him.

But in April, when I got my learner's permit, Unc bought me the Luv from Miss Dinah Gaillard. Now I drive out there myself.

The Friday he gave it to me, Mom just dropped me off, Unc sitting like always on the cinder-block steps up. He waved at her like always, then she was gone.

He'd said, "Let's go," and stood, started around the back end of the trailer.

I followed him around back, saw him standing next to the Luv, navy blue and rust, his hand on the hood like one of those bubba car salesmen we make jokes about when we stay up late Friday and Saturday night in front of the television. He was smiling.

"It's yours," he said. He pulled a key chain from his front shirt pocket, tossed it to me. The keys hit my chest, and I hadn't said a word, not yet able to figure this out.

"This was Benjamin Gaillard's. Miss Dinah's son," he said, and opened the driver's-side door. "Been sitting out to her place since he died. She told me she knew she could trust it to you, knows you're a responsible young man." He paused, grinned. "Not like me on deer-hunt Saturdays, sitting in the kitchen and shooting the breeze with her and Dorcas. She says she's seen you making certain to get that fire going, and saying thank you for the coffee. Guess good manners and following orders sometimes pays off." He nodded. "So take good care of it."

"Yessir," I said. He didn't have to say anything after that. I knew who Benjamin was. Everyone did. He died in Desert Storm, one of those people in the cafeteria when the SCUD missile hit. The Luv had 218,143 miles on it when I climbed in, and I remember pulling closed the door, the hard screech of metal on metal in the door hinges.

Sounded good to me.

I leaned out the window, said, "Unc, let's go."

He stepped back from the truck, started swinging his arm like a traffic cop for me to get going. "She's yours," he said. "You go try her out. Report back to me."

I sat there a second or so, not certain what to do. It was a small truck, the cab tiny compared to the old fenderless GMC pickup he'd let me drive all over the place since I was twelve. The truck my dad'd left here.

But the Luv was mine. And it'd been Benjamin Gaillard's.

"Go," he said, and I gave it the gas, let out the clutch.

I drove out Baldwin, then on to Social Hall Cut, then to Cemetery, where the road goes close to the Ashepoo. That's where I stopped, a place I'd gone to since I could remember, just to look out at the marsh.

Which is what I did: looked out over the marsh to Bear Island and Settlement Island and White House Woods, past them all those little squat islands didn't even have names scattered around, four or five miles away the tree line of Edisto.

All these miles on the truck, I was thinking. Eight and a half times around the world, the ghost of Benjamin Gaillard thrown in for free. And out there looking at the marsh, I thought of Miss Dinah, how she'd always just been a part of the way things worked here at Hungry Neck, cooking for the members for as long as I'd ever known, and I thought, too, of her daughter, Dorcas, the deaf-and-dumb girl, and how she and Unc seemed somehow to share something, the two of them working their hands to talk to each other, and the laughter with it.

Unc had a life, it came to me. He knew people, laughed, talked, lived. All of it out here to Hungry Neck.

And then the sun going down, back behind me and just touching the tops of the trees, hit that point where everything changes. The marsh went a green you couldn't name, mixed in and down inside it browns and reds and a color like bone, miles of colors you can't see except for that time of day.

And past it all, above and behind it, the blue sky, going a darker blue every second.

I sat there, watched it all, until the marsh grass went dark and the colors started to bleed out. Until those islands parked out in the marsh became these dark humps, islands of no color. Just there, never even named. I sat there on into dark, past that time when, back when I was a kid, the stories of the ghosts that haunted these woods and islands and everywhere down here used to start creeping in on me, stories I'd hear from Miss Dinah herself while she cooked up the breakfasts, me watching her in the kitchen of the clubhouse, Dorcas on a stool, reading her mother's lips to hear of the Gray Man up to Pawley's Island, and of the *Silver Trade,* a ghost ship that appeared out in St. Helena Sound only at new moon, shipwrecked two hundred years ago in a storm.

Or she would tell us the best story of all, the one every kid knew but wanted to hear as many times as he could: the Mothers and Fathers, those first slaves to work this land, the holy kings and queens and princes and princesses all buried together on a plot guarded by their green-eyed ghosts, ghosts who would come up on children lost in the woods at night, ghosts that swarmed and swooped and swirled around you, their green eyes a kind of fire that struck anyone who saw them with a kind of fear that would turn their hearts inside out, make their hair fall out, make their minds turn into grits.

And once the stories were over, Dorcas would turn to me, look at me, and sometimes we'd shiver at the same time at the scare of it, and then we'd grin, locked for a second inside the story, though everyone knew these stories for the myths they were, especially the one about the Mothers and Fathers, the way those ghosts would follow you through woods if you were out too late.

But the myth of it didn't matter. It all seemed the truth in the moment of that shiver, me and a black girl I didn't really know sharing for that instant fear and delight at the same moment.

These were the ghosts that were with me that evening—my childhood, that shared look with Dorcas, all the stories I'd ever heard about this place—me now in my own truck and no longer fearful of the dark out here on Hungry Neck for the presence, it seemed, of Benjamin's ghost himself.

But then I shivered in that dark, and headed on home, back to Unc.

That's what I saw, there in my hospital bed: those nameless islands, the long stretches of marsh, the tree line, the herons and egrets, the red-tail hawk and the marsh hens, the green-eyed ghosts of the Mothers and Fathers.

I saw above me this sky, the river right up against these woods, saw these ghosts.

I saw all of this, everything I love, exactly where I want to grow old and die.

Huger, I heard whispered.

My eyes opened, and I was in the bed in the dark. I lifted my head off the pillow, felt the pain in my head. The only light was that from the TV, still on, down past the footboard.

"Huger," someone whispered next to me, and I quick turned, saw a woman.

She had on a white shirt, the sleeves rolled up, and a dark skirt. Color from off the TV caught in her gray hair like a halo.

On the TV was what looked like the end of a football game, the locker-room stuff, and I glanced off to my right, saw a cot set up under the window, my mom lying there, a blanket half covering her, still in her nurse's outfit.

I lay back, ready for whatever this nurse was going to check on me about.

"Huger," she whispered again.

I swallowed, my mouth thick and dry. "Ma'am?" I whispered.

She said nothing for a long few seconds, then whispered, "Tell Leland I didn't do it."

I felt my blood go fast, felt my face go hot. I blinked, swallowed again.

I looked at her.

"Constance?" I whispered, the word barely loud enough even for me to hear.

She looked toward my mom. I could see her profile now by the light off the TV: a small nose, sharp chin. She was smiling.

"You have a caring momma," she whispered. "Cherish that."

"Yes ma'am," I whispered. It was all I could think to say.

Here she was: the woman who'd written that sign. The one who'd called Unc and told him what she was going to do. The woman who'd killed the son of a bitch Charlie Simons.

Then she turned to the TV.

The late news was coming on now, a bunch of quick shots of the Lowcountry: the bridges into Mount Pleasant, the mayor saying something, a couple ballet dancers, the beach.

And the lead story: the murder of Charles Middleton Simons, M.D., his body discovered at a hunt club near Jacksonboro.

The anchorman, his big forehead and tiny eyes all wrinkled with concern, gave out the words, quiet and right there in my ear, and now here was the video, all the orange caps and eight or ten uniformed deputies walking slow through the weeds, heads down, looking for whatever. Another shot showed the crime banner up, more men, these in black windbreakers, SLED in big yellow letters across the back. Then came the shot of a stretcher with a blanket over a body, the ambulance with its lights on and back doors open, the paramedics sliding it inside. Nobody in any big hurry.

I looked at her. She was watching it, no reaction. Just watching.

Then came a shot of a man at a podium, at the bottom of the screen the words FILE FOOTAGE. The man had on a gray suit and red tie, was reading something, though it was the anchorman's voice I heard: "Dr. Simons was on the faculty at South Carolina Medical University, where only last June he was awarded the Distinguished Service Award by the president of the university for having founded the Christian Children's Reconstructive Surgery Foundation, a charitable organization providing Third World children with needed reconstructive surgery."

The man in the film footage finished what he was reading, smiled big, and waved to the crowd before him. The camera pulled away to show the whole head table at this party.

Cleve Ravenel was up there. And Dr. Buck. And two or three others from the club, all of them clapping and smiling.

And there was the woman next to me, looking up at him, her clapping, smiling.

Then it was over, the anchor's big forehead here again. "State Law Enforcement Division officers as well as Charleston City Police and the County Sheriff's Department are still searching for Mrs. Constance Dupree Simons, wife of Dr. Simons, in connection with the murder. Mrs. Simons, a trustee and former director of Acquisitions for the Carolina Museum of History, has as yet to be located."

The anchor disappeared again, and here came more file footage, this time of the woman beside me. She was surrounded by children somewhere in the woods, before them a staked-off pit a couple feet deep, strings up around it. Inside the pit was a man stooped to the ground, who then pulled from the ground a piece of pottery, held it out to the kids. Constance smiled, nodded at them, touched the heads of the kids as they looked at the piece.

Then it was over, the anchorman back. "Anyone with information as to the whereabouts of Mrs. Constance Dupree Simons is urged to contact authorities immediately."

He gave a small nod, turned to another camera, on the screen behind him now a lighthouse. "Sullivans Island authorities predict the new leash law—"

I turned to her. She was looking at me, smiling.

"No one more invisible than a doctor's wife," she whispered.

She brought her other hand from where it'd been in the pocket of her skirt. "You need to give this to him," she whispered, and held that hand over mine on the bed, my fingers curled and holding on to the sheet.

I couldn't move. This was her. Constance Dupree Simons.

She reached with her other hand to mine, gently folded open my fingers. Her hand was soft, just like her movements, and like her face, her hair. All soft, and suddenly, with the way she touched my hand, I believed her: she didn't do it. Even if she *was* smiling after seeing her dead husband fed into the back of an ambulance.

She lifted my hand up, put something in it.

It was warm and hard, a little heavy, the size of the bottom end of a quart beer bottle: a warm, flat piece of round glass. I didn't look at it, let her ease my hand back to the bed, my eyes on her.

She nodded at my mom again. "You cherish her," she said, then, quieter, "I have no children of my own, and had always hoped to be cherished."

I nodded.

"And tell Leland," she said, "that I did not do it." She paused, touched at my hand, in it that piece of glass. "And tell him I loved him."

I tried hard to believe what was going on here, that she knew where I was, how to get to me to tell me what she needed Unc to know.

Finally, I whispered, "Yes ma'am."

She turned, slow, like she might be sleepwalking, and started for the door, opened it. Light crashed in on her, made her a silhouette to me. She stood there in the doorway, staring straight ahead, then looked back to me one last time.

Still smiling, she nodded, and stepped out into the light.

I brought my hand up, wanted to see what it was she'd given me, so important she'd walk into a hospital, the sheriff and police both after her for murder.

I held it close to my eyes, tried to see it with the light from the doorway but only caught the reflection of that light. A piece of glass was all it was, a little rough on the edges.

I looked over at my mom, wondered if she'd wake up if I turned the lights on, then sat up, slow, so my head wouldn't fall off, and scooted to where the rail stopped down near the foot. I turned, stepped to the cold floor. All I had on was the thin dresslike thing they gave you, and my underwear, and now my back went cold for the sweat, and I shivered.

I looked to Mom again, then started across the room, my head heavy and big, and I was at the oak door into the bathroom, and I opened it, pulled it to behind me before I turned on the light.

I forgot to close my eyes, and the room exploded white, shot through me for a second, and I squinted hard, opened my hand.

It was brown and shiny, just like glass.

But sealed inside the glass, or whatever it was, was a little pinwheel of pine straw or sweetgrass, every half inch or so a wrap around the straw with a strip of wider straw, like the very center of a sweetgrass basket. It was just three circles, a tiny spiral of a basket, there inside the glass.

A spiral.

Those shapes Unc'd made on the ground, then wrecked. He'd been drawing sweetgrass baskets.

I looked in the mirror, saw a kid with his mouth open, his hair all plastered to his head for sweating in his sleep.

Sweetgrass baskets?

Tell Leland I didn't do it, she'd said.

But sweetgrass baskets?

Sweetgrass baskets, those baskets made of coiled sweetgrass and bulrushes and palmetto leaves, a craft brought here by the original slaves from West Africa, we all learned in school, the tradition passed down one generation to the next to the next, the only ones still to practice it the black women set up at the Market downtown, and on Broad and Meeting streets downtown, too, and at the tiny roadside stands along 17 on the way out of Charleston.

Then came three tiny knocks at the door, my mom's voice: "Honey? You okay in there?" She paused. "Honey, the nurse is here to check up on you."

I looked at the piece of brown glass again. Constance Dupree Simons had come all the way here, the world looking for her, to hand me this, what looked like a paperweight you might buy at the Market downtown, except for the rough edges of the thing.

No one more invisible than a doctor's wife, she'd said.

And tell him I loved him, she'd said, too.

"Honey, everything all right?" Mom said. "Huger?"

I looked in the mirror again. No bandages, my head no bigger than ever. But I knew something. In that head—my head—was something important enough to make her come to me.

The only problem was I had no idea what it could be.

"I'm okay," I said. Then I leaned over to the toilet, flushed it. "Just using the toilet," I said, and held the paperweight in my palm so no one would see it when I came out.

6

Next morning Dr. Buck came in early, woke me up. I lay on my stomach, my hand inside the pillowcase under the pillow, in it this glass thing. I squinted at him for the light above the bed again. I let go the paperweight, rolled over, sat up.

The blinds were open, the sky through them gray, though I could tell it wasn't cloudy. Just early.

Mom's cot was empty, the blanket and sheet they'd given her folded at the foot, the pillow set on top of them.

"Where's Mom?" I said.

Dr. Buck put the clipboard on the bed, flashed that penlight in my eyes a couple times more, the pain almost gone. He put a hand to the back of my head, felt the bump back there.

"Can't say as I know, bo," he said, and gave a quick smile. He picked up the clipboard. "We'll keep you here maybe another hour or so, then you're good to go. Okay?"

I looked back to the window. Through the blinds I could see pieces of the tops of other buildings, pieces of palmettos and live oak and the red metal and gray slate roofs of old houses way off and down.

Charleston.

I closed my eyes. I wanted home: Hungry Neck.

"I'll be ready," I said.

He turned, went for the door, but stopped, and I opened my eyes. He looked at his clipboard, at me again. "That was something, yesterday." He paused. "What happened. What you saw." He put his hand up to the doorjamb, tapped his fingers.

"Yep," I said.

"Hope your uncle's okay." He gave that quick smile. "Hope he's all right out there without you."

"He's been alone before," I said. "He's a big boy."

He tapped the doorjamb one last time. "You got that right, bo," he said. Still his redneck talk didn't sound right, or real. He cleared his throat. "You take it easy, hear? And give my best to your uncle, when you see him next."

"Okay," I said.

Mom showed up around eight, all her makeup on, hair done. She had a nice blouse and pants on and had a little carry bag with her, one of those flowery free things you get when you buy a few dollars of soap at the Belk. She was laughing when she came in, behind her a nurse, a big black woman with her hair pulled tight into a ponytail. She was pushing a wheelchair.

Mom got this big smile on her face, said, "My baby is awake!" and set the bag on the bed. "Dorinda here says Dr. Morrison's signed you out already. I myself went home to get you some clean clothes, not to mention taking care of myself. Nothing like sleeping on a cot to give your hair a royal mess." She sat at the foot of the bed. "But of course the doctor's already here and gone."

"The governor's signed your reprieve," the nurse said, smiling.

Mom was pulling stuff out of the carry bag now: a pair of jeans, socks, a green-and-white plaid shirt. "Dorinda's going to wheel you out, once you get your clothes on."

They looked at me, the two of them smiling.

But all I was thinking on was the paperweight in my right hand, under the sheet, my mind set on how I was going to get my clothes and go to the bathroom and change without either of them seeing it.

"If you'd get out of here," I said, "we can head home all the quicker."

Mom stood, gave me this look, rolled her eyes: *Who do you think you are?*

But I covered it, gave her my shit-eating grin, the one any kid with half a brain has figured out by the time he's three.

"Well," she said, and smiled. "A young man's got to have his privacy, I guess," she said.

"Damn straight," I said, and gave it another good smile, her skinny and pitiful and only child here in a hospital bed.

It was in my pocket. I knew that. But I felt like everybody in the hospital knew it too, though we'd only wheeled out of the room, were only a few doors down the hallway. I glanced into each room as we passed, expecting to see a nurse who'd call out to me, ask who that lady was who came into my room late last night. I saw nobody, just the same oak and brass and wooden blinds as back in my room.

We made it to the elevator, to my left an oak desk on an oriental rug. A woman in a gold suit coat and white blouse sat behind it, hands together on the desktop, smiling like a real estate agent in a TV commercial. She said, "I hope you enjoyed your stay with us."

I just looked at her. She tilted her head one way, still smiling at me.

I felt Mom's hand at my shoulder, squeezing. I smiled at the woman, said, "Thank you," then looked forward, my eyes to the lighted numbers above the elevator doors. We were almost out of here.

Then the doors opened up.

Two men stood inside, both with buzz cuts, both with black windbreakers on. They didn't even have to turn around, show me SLED in big yellow letters across their backs, for me to figure out who they were. Or why they were here.

It was in my pocket. I knew that. But they didn't.

They stepped out, smiled at us as fake as Dr. Buck's redneck words.

"Mrs. Dillard?" one of them said to Mom. He was blond, thick-necked, and had on a red polo shirt, the sleeves of his windbreaker pushed up to his elbows.

"Yes?" Mom said. She turned, nodded at the nurse. "I'll take it from here, Dorinda. I'm a hospital employee, so if something happens while I'm pushing him out, I can sue me, and win." She smiled, shrugged.

"Sound like a plan," Dorinda said, and let go.

Mom pushed me between them and inside the elevator, then wheeled me around, so that now we were inside, looking out at them. She knew something was up.

The second one, black hair and with just as thick a neck, only with a white dress shirt and tie on, put his hand to the elevator door, held it so it wouldn't close.

"We need to talk to Huger Dillard," he said, and looked at me, smiling.

Mom touched the button for the ground floor.

"We're going home," she said.

"Ma'am, this is official business," the blond said, and took out a billfold from his back pocket, flashed a badge and ID card. "I'm Agent Hampton, this is Agent Elliot, State Law Enforcement Division." The other man, still with one hand holding the door open, took out his billfold, too, showed his badge.

"You don't think I know who you are?" she said, and I could hear in her voice where she was headed.

"Ma'am," the black-haired one said, "all we need is a few minutes to go through some questions. You can make it easy on yourself and your son, and just give us that time, or we can waste all our time, and make this harder than it has to be." He smiled at her.

She took in a deep breath, let it out. "We're going home," she said, "and if you'd take your hand off that door, we'd all be spending our time a little more wisely."

They looked at each other, then stepped in.

The door closed.

The black-haired one smiled down at me. He said, "Just a routine interview. He was there at the discovery of the body, and it's SLED policy to interview everyone present at the crime scene." He looked at Mom. "He's the next-to-last one we have to interview. We got everybody else already. Just routine, ma'am."

Mom let out a heavy breath. I couldn't see her behind me, only imagined her eyes on the lighted numbers above the doors, her mouth shut tight.

"Did you hear anything at the club night before last?" the blond one said. "Anything out of the ordinary?"

I was looking at the numbers now, too. "No," I said. "Nothing."

"Your uncle is blind, is that correct?"

"You boys must work nights for the Psychic Network," I said, and Mom let out a small laugh.

They didn't look at her, didn't blink. "How is it you discovered the body?" the blond said.

I slowly shook my head, saw Unc only yesterday morning, telling me to stop.

"I didn't find it," I said. "Unc did."

"And how did that happen?" He crossed his arms.

I said, "He smelled it."

"He *what*?"

I looked at him. "He's blind, and he smelled it. That's why he told me to stop."

The black-haired one cleared his throat. "We'd like to know what you saw once you discovered the body. If there was anything out of the ordinary."

"What's ordinary about a dead body is all I want to know," Mom said. They looked at her behind me. "It's out of the ordinary just to see something like that. So you're asking him what *else* there was about it? Isn't it enough my boy saw it in the first place?"

"Now, ma'am," the black-haired one said, "we're just trying to find out as much as we can about what happened. That's all we're here for."

"You got three more floors to go before we're out of here, and you're out of our lives, so hop to it."

"Ma'am," the blond said, "we'll ask as many—"

"Lee," the black-haired one said, quiet, and this Lee stopped.

The black-haired one knelt, put his hand on the wheel of my chair. I could smell his aftershave, heavy and dull. "What did you see?" he said.

"His hands," I said. "That's pretty out of the ordinary. And that cardboard sign. That's it." I looked at my hands in my lap, and the skin on them, and waited for what was coming next: Have you seen the good doctor's wife?

"And you heard nothing," he said.

"Nothing."

"Did your uncle act strange in any way earlier this week? Or at any time in recent weeks?"

"One more floor," Mom said.

Unc hadn't acted strange. Not until yesterday morning, when he told me he'd wanted to kill the man himself a long time ago. And last night, when he'd told me he didn't want us in on any of *this*, whatever the hell that meant.

"No," I said. "Same old Unc."

"Did you talk about anything at all either before or after the body was discovered?"

I looked him in the eye, almost dared him to try and find what I was leaving out of what I was about to tell him.

I said, "We talked about the stands the night before, took a drive over to them Friday night, looked around. Saturday morning, after we found the body, we talked about the dogs and keeping them off it, off the body. And we talked about police stuff, like making everybody sit in the weeds on the opposite side of the road, walking single file, that stuff, so the scene wouldn't be wrecked." I stopped, took a breath at that place where I could have told him the fact he'd talked to Constance Dupree Simons only Wednesday. "And he told me the person's name, Constance, who was married to that doctor. The one who wrote the cardboard sign, near as anybody could tell. He told me they were going to get married, Unc and that woman, a long time ago." I paused, shrugged. "That's it. Then we went back to the body, and that's when it—"

For a second I saw only that dead man, those skinned hands lifting his gun up, aiming for that buzzard.

The doors opened. "End of interrogation," Mom said, and wheeled me right out. The black-haired one didn't have time even to stand up.

Then we were in a long white hallway, headed for glass double doors down at the end.

"One more question, ma'am," the blond said. "Just one more," and I heard him moving quick up beside us. He took hold of the rail on the chair, pulled us to a stop. The chair wheeled around to him for his grabbing on, and here we were, this big officer looking down at me.

"Now, you look here," Mom said. Then the man moved his eyes to her.

She looked at him a long few seconds. There was no way out. The officer would ask his question, no matter what, no matter where.

The black-haired one was there now, and squatted again, looked at me. "All we need to know is when you saw your uncle last. That's all."

I said, "But he didn't do it."

"We just want to know where he is," he said. "Nobody's convicting anybody here."

"You haven't talked to him yet?" Mom asked, her voice quiet, like she couldn't believe it. "You don't know where he is, do you?"

"That's what we're trying to ascertain, ma'am," the blond said.

I twisted in my chair, looked up at Mom behind me.

Her mouth was open, her eyebrows up: she was thinking maybe Unc really *was* in on this.

I looked at the black-haired officer. I said, "So I'm next to last. That means Unc is all you have left."

He looked down. He was sitting on his heels, his shoes spit-polished. He put his hands together, like a prayer. "He rode in with Deputy Thigpen and Yandle and Dr. Morrison and you," he said. "Nobody had time to interview him. He's the only one left, and we can't seem to locate him."

"He was here yesterday afternoon," Mom said, quick and loud. "He left around two o'clock. I figured he'd just find a way home."

The only one left. A blind man, and they couldn't find him.

The blond pulled his billfold out again, brought out a business card, handed it to Mom. "This here's the number you can reach us at, if you hear anything."

And now they were done.

They weren't here after Constance Dupree Simons at all.

Tell Leland I didn't do it, she'd told me.

It was Unc they were after. Not Constance.

"So what about this Constance?" I said. "The one who killed that boy, the doctor?" I knew the words might draw attention, me changing the subject from Unc and all to her. But I wanted to know, because if they had her already, then maybe she'd told them she'd visited me last night, and these two already knew everything about her showing up. Maybe all they were doing was just waiting for me to cough up what was in my pocket.

The black-haired one stood, and the two looked at each other. The blond made a face, shrugged: *I don't care.* "It'll be on the news tonight," he said. "The TV crews were over there practically before we were. It's no secret."

The black-haired one took in a breath, looked down at me.

"What?" I said.

"She's dead," he said. "Suicide. She hung herself over to the Rantowles Motel, in one of the rooms." He paused. "Somebody called it in at six this morning. A man, wouldn't give his name."

Here came that feel again, the same pinch at my throat as yesterday, the same collapse inside me.

She was dead.

I'd talked to her only last night. I had something of hers in my pocket right now.

Mom turned the wheelchair, aimed us for the door, her silence signal enough to me something inside her was collapsing too.

"You call us, you hear anything," the blond said from behind us. "You have my card."

The automatic doors opened up, and we were out on the street between the hospital and parking garage, out in sharp, white daylight. Mom turned the chair to the left, said, "Now let's stand up," and put a hand to my arm.

I stood, but felt my knees about to fall under me, about to snap.

"Oh, baby," she said, "are you okay?"

I swallowed. "No," I whispered, "but just let's go on home."

We started across the street, Mom's arm looped in mine, leading me, just like I did Unc.

That's when I saw the black Crown Victoria parked about twenty yards down to my right and across the street. Standard-issue SLED.

But behind it was a cruiser, leaning on the hood of it a man with his arm in a sling.

Yandle.

He was smiling, watching us. He had a Styrofoam cup, took a sip, winced for it. He put the cup in the other hand, the one in the sling.

He pointed at me. It was a small move, nothing big or showy. Mom didn't even see him for helping me along the crosswalk.

Then he made his hand like a gun, pulled the trigger. He smiled, slowly shook his head.

It was a small move. Meant only for me.

"Mom, let's go," I said, and tried to walk faster.

7

I didn't look at Mom the whole way home, didn't say a word.

Instead I looked at the same old buildings along I-26: the red-brick high-rise, everyone in there government-assisted; the dead mall and its empty parking lot off Montague; at the concrete barrier between us and southbound traffic, a barrier it wouldn't be all that hard for a car to flip over, kill us right here.

There was a blue sky, too, what pieces of the Ashley River I could see off to my left a dull green, rimmed on either edge in brown salt-marsh hay and spartina and yellow grass.

A sweetgrass paperweight.

Suicide. She'd hanged herself.

The Rantowles Motel was a nothing place on 17 South, where couples from my classes at North Charleston went for a few hours on Friday nights, when they'd told Mama and Papa they'd be at the football game.

She hanged herself.

This made two of them. Husband and wife, and I'd seen both of them.

And if I told Mom anything, she'd become a part of it all, the *this* Unc wanted us out of. What I was already a partner in, though I couldn't say why or how. Only that I had a piece of what was going on.

If I opened my mouth to Mom, even let her see my face, I'd have to tell her about Yandle, too. What was he out here for, him just an idiot droid deputy? If things worked like I thought they did, SLED was in charge of the whole thing, wouldn't have him tagging along. Unless him being there fell under all that first-officer-at-the-scene shit he'd tried to hand Unc when he first pulled up.

I'd keep this all to myself, just go home, sit in the front room with the TV going, watch with her whatever it was she watched here, alone, on Sunday mornings.

Sunday morning. I hadn't been here on a Sunday morning in years.

I'd just sit with her and watch. And wait.

But for what?

We headed down Remount and through that hellhole of an intersection at Rivers, eight or nine lanes plus the freeway off-ramp converging on one set of lights; next we passed the Aquarius Social Club, a cinder-block building with no windows, painted a dull turquoise, next the New Life Congregational Church. Then we turned right onto Attaway, went down the rows of houses just like ours: a short concrete driveway that led to a separate garage at the rear of the lot, concrete steps up to the front door, metal awnings over the porch and the two windows out front. They were all painted pale colors, all of them different shades of green and yellow and blue. Some of the yards were overgrown, some too neat. All of them just there, along with a couple of bushes, oil stains on the driveway, room air conditioners plugged into the windows.

Where we lived.

The first night we moved out here to Liberty Hills, Mom and I set up in that square house, the few things we had still in the boxes, she came into my bedroom and woke me up in the middle of the night, wanting to know if I'd messed in my pants. Me, eight years old. But she was right: the place smelled like maybe something had shit somewhere.

We looked all over the house, all the lights on, searched for where maybe some animal'd snuck in, laid a pile maybe in the corner of a closet or in the cabinets. But I remember thinking it didn't smell exactly like shit. Something else, but close enough.

Finally she opened the back door, and the smell jumped at us. I remember standing next to her, Mom in a thin white nightgown, the same one she'd worn my whole life so far, and looking out to the fence, and seeing above it and above the rooftops of all these houses the dull gray glow of lights way off, like a gray cloud sitting way off in the black. And poked up into the middle of it a smoke-stack with blinking white lights on it, a cloud of white coming up off it.

"It's the paper mill," Mom whispered.

I looked up at her. She was still a moment, then her shoulders started moving up and down, quick and hard. The kitchen light was on behind her, and I couldn't see her face, but I could tell she was crying. She breathed in quick breaths all in a row, let out these hisses, afraid to cry in front of her kid.

I was only eight, and I remember I grabbed hold of her night-gown, bunched a fistful up, and said, "Don't cry about it."

But she went right on.

That was our first night away from Hungry Neck Hunt Club. Our first night living in North Charleston. Only a year after Unc'd moved into the trailer, nine months after Dad'd left us.

Our new life.

Now I had friends inside some of these houses, people a lot like me, which meant they didn't really give a shit about everything you were supposed to give a shit about in high school. We weren't in band or on any of the teams. We didn't belong to any clubs, didn't all sit together at lunch and smoke or toke out to the back fence.

Truth was we didn't even like each other. More like a group that didn't belong to any group, even its own group. And if I wasn't with them or out to Hungry Neck, I was in my room, reading.

Because I had a plan. I wanted to go to college. Duke, maybe. And I read. I read my way through the Harvard Classics, for one thing, Mom subscribing to that book club from about the time we got out here, though some of that stuff was so dull and dry getting through it was like trying to breathe sand. That's what I thought of Milton, for one, Spenser for another. Shakespeare was fine, as was Chaucer. I'd read everything C. S. Lewis put out, everything by this guy Mircea Eliade, too. And there was *Moby-Dick,* which every clod in my English class threw up over but me, and which I even laughed at in places, it was so funny, like when Ahab is going over to the other ship for a little meeting, and he's standing up in the rowboat, and everybody rowing is wishing the hell he'd just sit down so that they didn't have to worry so much about timing their strokes with the waves so he wouldn't fall down and embarrass himself.

At least *I* thought that was funny.

Sometimes we all hung out together out where the railroad tracks turned toward the paper mill on the other side of Storie Street, there under the Mark Clark Expressway. Just us: Matt, Jason, Rafael, Tyrone, Jessup. And the girls: Trina, Roberta, Polly, LaKeisha, Deevonne. We'd sit and pass around five or six bottles of Colt 45 somebody'd gotten, and talk about what shits everybody was. Even ourselves.

Blacks and whites. Good grades and bad grades. Stupid and smart. None of us had nipple rings or tattooed chains on our ankles. None of us was failing.

Just us. Just nothing. All the more reason to see Hungry Neck as my home, and not here. North Charleston was only where I slept, kept most of my clothes.

But as we turned left on Sumner and passed the C&S Grocerette and McTV Repair, then turned right onto our street, Marie, I was hoping I'd see somebody. Anybody.

There was nobody, everyone still in bed and asleep this Sunday morning, all of them oblivious to what I knew.

We moved along Marie, and I could see the Mark Clark Expressway down where the street dead-ended, high up on huge concrete pilings. Then we were home: pale yellow, brown trim, the awning brown too. The yard neat and trimmed—I mowed it every Wednesday—the oil stains the Luv left on the driveway.

We pulled in, the chain-link fence gate open, ready for us, and back to the garage. Mom put the car in park, and I started to open my door, go pull up the garage door.

But she put a hand to my arm, like she used to do when I was little and she slammed on the brakes for traffic or whatever. Protecting me.

"No," she said, and I looked at her. "You have to take it easy."

Her lips were together, her eyebrows knotted in the smallest way. She had on the makeup, the nice clothes, her hair done. Nothing any different from when she'd walked into the hospital room this morning.

But everything different.

We sat that way a few seconds, her hand on my arm, us looking at each other.

Then I climbed out, opened the door.

The kitchen table was set for one: an empty plate and juice glass, a knife and fork and spoon. On the stove was a half-empty bag of grits, a pan, and the skillet.

I sat down, watched Mom move around without looking at me. She hooked her purse over the back of her chair at the table, pushed the sleeves up on her blouse, pulled from inside the pantry door her yellow plaid apron. Then she went to the fridge, pulled out bacon and two eggs.

"How do you want your eggs?" she said. She didn't look at me, only set the eggs and bacon on the counter, took the pan to the sink and filled it.

She finished with the water, headed for the stove.

"Well?" she said, started peeling off bacon into the skillet.

"Stop it," I said.

She paused a second, held a strip over the others. Then she went right on, dropped a last piece in, tore a paper towel from the roll underneath the cupboard, wiped her hands.

"I said stop it." I took a step toward her, put my hand to her shoulder like Unc did to me all the time.

But this was my mom. I'd never touched her that way before, in comfort.

She gave way, her shoulders heaving, and I turned her to me, put my arms around my mom, felt her face on my own shoulder. Slowly she put her arms around me, too, and for a second that first night here came back to me, us finally finding the source of that smell we've grown used to over all these years: the paper mill.

Don't cry about it, I'd said then. But I'd been wrong. Crying, I saw only now, was about the best thing anybody could have done.

"You cry," I whispered. "You go ahead and cry."

Slowly she nodded, her face still on my shoulder, and she cried, hard and long, the two of us alone in the kitchen.

8

I lay there in bed, thought I heard the tapping in a dream, but then heard it for real, right there at the window: *tap tap tap. Tap tap tap*.

I sat up, felt the cool of the room through my T-shirt; Mom turned the heat down at night to save money, and for a second there was in my head the idea of Mrs. Constance Dupree Simons floating into this room here, tonight, and I thought again of the paperweight, remembered it was in the pocket of my jeans, on the floor in front of my dresser.

Then, *tap tap tap*.

Matt or Tyrone or Jessup, I thought. Somebody'd seen something on the news, figured out maybe it was my uncle's place all this was going on at and was over here to bug me about it. And my bed was next to the window, after all, for exactly this reason: easy out and easy back in whenever we felt like going over to the tracks.

I pulled back the curtains, gray in the dark.

It was a black person, just the head and shoulders at the sill, and for a second I thought, Tyrone. Then I saw the long hair down to the shoulders, a white hairband holding it all back, and I thought, LaKeisha, or Deevonne.

The only light out there was the same old dull gray cloud up above the blinking smokestack of the paper mill, and I saw it wasn't LaKeisha or Deevonne.

It was Dorcas. Miss Dinah Gaillard's daughter, Benjamin's sister, looking in at me.

I'd seen her last just yesterday morning, when she and her momma'd cooked up breakfast at the hunt club. I'd known her all my life, this black girl who couldn't talk or hear, but I'd only known her out to Hungry Neck.

Now here she was in North Charleston and looking in my window, and it made me inch back and away.

She looked behind her, like maybe there was somebody watching her, then lifted a hand up, and I could see something in it, white and square.

She pressed it to the glass: a piece of paper, writing on it, but it was too dark to read.

She moved the paper up and down, quick: *Read this.*

I finally stood from the bed, held the quilt around me like a cape for the cold and the fact, too, I was just in my underwear, and I went to the dresser, pulled on my jeans, and found in the top drawer the pocket flashlight I kept in there. I looked at the alarm clock on the dresser, saw by the pale hands it was a little after one.

I went to the window, cupped my hand over the flashlight, held it just below the piece of paper against the glass, and clicked it on.

Leland is with us, it read. *He isn't aware of my being here to get you, but I can tell he needs your help, whether he likes it or not. But we need to go, now.*

It was printed, the letters perfect, and I clicked off the light, let my eyes adjust for a few seconds. The paper was gone now, only Dorcas there, looking at me.

I nodded, the decision made just like that.

She took a step away from the window, then crouched, made her way across the backyard to the trees at the fence.

This was what I'd been waiting for.

But Mom was in the next room, asleep.

What would happen when she got up tomorrow morning, found my bed empty? She'd know I was out looking for Unc, and she'd kill me whether I found him or not, but first she'd break down worse than this morning. She'd break, then get royally pissed at me, maybe burn my clothes out in the yard for all I knew, and then there'd be even more hell whenever I came back.

But it was Unc I was after.

I went to the closet, dug in my bookbag for some notebook paper, tore out a sheet quiet as I could, then found a pencil at the bottom of the bag.

School tomorrow. Monday, the day after Thanksgiving vacation. The least of my worries.

I went to the dresser, wrote as best I could in the dark, *I love you, Mom. But I'm going to Unc and help him out. Don't worry.* I stopped, wondered what else I could put. That I knew where he was? What?

But I only wrote, *I love you, Mom* again.

I threw the quilt back on the bed, tried to straighten it out, and set the paper on the pillow. I pulled out a flannel shirt from the closet, and my Levi's jacket, slipped on a pair of wool socks and my duck boots, then I was out the window. I dropped to the ground and pulled the window closed.

It was colder than I'd thought it would be, my breath an empty pale cloud, and I squatted, afraid even that cloud of breath might give me away.

And I smelled it: the paper mill. A smell, it only occurred to me then, a lot like the smell of that body once we'd come back to it, flies on it, the sun starting to work it over.

I heard a finger snap at the back fence, and I ran.

She was crouched behind the row of redtips back there, and had on a jacket, white tennis shoes, and jeans. She lifted a finger to her lips, made the *shh* sign.

My hands were already freezing, and I rubbed them together, made to blow in them, but then she was up and over the five-foot chain-link fence that separated our yard from the house behind us. She hadn't made a sound.

I was just to follow her. Just shut up and follow.

So I climbed the fence and fell flat on my ass on the other side, gave out a grunt I thought you could hear for a mile around, and then I was up and running through the Pinckneys' backyard, headed for the sidewalk at the foot of their drive where Dorcas now stood, a hand on her hip and waiting.

I made it to the sidewalk, and Dorcas turned, started away, me expected just to keep up.

We were headed now down Pennsylvania Drive, toward where it dead-ended at Storie, past that the tracks beneath the Mark Clark. These were houses just like ours, the street just the same.

We walked, walked like it was all we'd ever done: taken a stroll at one in the morning, and then all the questions started coming to me: How did she know where I lived, if Unc didn't send her? How could she know which window was mine? How did she get here, and where were we going?

Then, up at the corner, I saw light on the pavement and against the green weeds across Storie: a car coming.

Dorcas looped her arm in mine, pulled me close to her. She was a little shorter than me, leaned her head against my shoulder, kept walking.

The car started around the corner toward us, and Dorcas quick turned me so my back was to the headlights, put her arms around me, brought her face right up next to mine.

Then she kissed me, full on.

The car went by us before I could even get my arms around her for my part of this disguise. They didn't even slow down.

Her lips were warm, her arms tight around me warm, too, though I knew I couldn't really feel anything through my jacket.

Dorcas, kissing me.

Soon as the car passed, her arms were down, and now she was running up the street.

We crossed Storie into the weeds, then came the crunch of our feet on the gravel beds that lined the track, the only other sound the whine of tires from the Mark Clark forty feet above us. I had a hard time keeping up with her, now already into the trees on the other side of the overpass, headed off toward the neighborhood over there, Lancaster Park.

All this was going on in the dark, and I was still feeling that kiss, and feeling the pinch of this cold air in my lungs, me running in the middle of the night through woods, hoping this would all end up with Unc.

I saw her jump a few yards ahead of me, and I wondered what that was all about in the same second I fell into the ditch, maybe three feet deep.

I landed on my knees, felt cold and wet weeds right in my face and beneath my hands. I struggled up, climbed out of the ditch, the front of my pants soaked through.

I ran, crashed through and crashed through weeds, until I was out in Lancaster Park, standing on a street no different from Storie, no different from any of the houses that trailed along the freeway in this part of North Charleston.

Dorcas stood on the sidewalk, a few houses past her a streetlight, so that she was lit from behind. She was bent over, hands on her knees. I could see her shoulders shake, like she was crying.

Then she stood up. She put a hand to her mouth, her shoulders still shaking, the other arm pointed at me.

She was laughing at me. No sound at all.

I looked down, saw in the weird purple light from the streetlight my pants wet from my crotch down to my shins.

I looked up at her. Now she was pointing down the street from us, her eyes on me.

There, just past the streetlight, was the Luv.

We climbed in, me on the driver's side, like we'd planned it all a year before. She gave the door over there a hard pop with her fist, too, the way you had to to get the thing open, her move so quick and perfect I realized right then she'd ridden through more miles on this thing than I ever would, and for a second I pictured Benjamin Gail-lard driving all around the Lowcountry with his deaf-and-dumb lit-tle sister, running for groceries, say, to Hollywood, or to the Solid Rock I Stand AME Church out past Gardens Corner, or just out to one of the roads that ran along the Ashepoo.

She reached into her jacket pocket, pulled out my keys. I nodded, put out my hand, and she dropped them. Our fingers never touched, and we looked at each other a long couple of seconds. Then she looked away, sort of pushed herself into her seat a little deeper. She put her hands together and between her knees, her shoulders up: she was cold, all movement and silence.

The engine turned over the first time, like every time. I patted the dash, and she smiled. Then I turned on the headlights, and she nearly jumped, quick opened the glove box. Before I could even put the truck into gear, she'd pulled out a small tablet of paper, peeled off the top sheet, held it out to me.

I looked at it in the pale light from the streetlight, made out the words *Leave off the lights until we're at least two blocks from here. Take surface streets as far as you can.* She'd written this out in the same perfect printing before she'd come for me.

I turned off the headlights, nodded at her. But she'd already pulled off the next sheet, held it out to me.

Don't drive as though we're in a hurry to get anywhere. We don't want to be stopped by anyone. Once we get to the railroad tracks at Hungry Neck, I'll tell you which turns to make.

She was faced forward again, hands between her knees again.

I knew where she lived. I knew: the haint purple half trailer, half shanty up on Hutcheson Road. I knew that.

I motioned to her for something to write with.

She stared at me a second, then let out a hard breath, reached into the glove box, and pulled out a pen. But instead of handing it over to me, she started writing on it, hard and fast. She tore off the sheet, pushed it at me.

You turn where I say, she'd written. *And we go NOW.*

She was leaning into the corner of the cab, her mouth in what looked like a snarl, the way you look when you can't believe how stupid someone could be.

Me.

I crumpled up the paper, let it drop to the floorboard. She was right, and this was new, all of this as new to me as the look of a headless man raising a gun to the sky, and I only nodded, put the stick into first, and eased out the clutch, somebody else's world out there moving into motion, and we were gone.

She wrote more notes, handed them to me once I'd turned the headlights back on and while I drove all the surface streets I could in order to avoid the Mark Clark, hanging up above us and to my right, then to my left like some huge and well-lit concrete snake just above ground. Stoplights and stop signs, and neighborhoods and grocery stores and frontage roads and minimarts, all just to keep off the freeway.

And these notes. She peeled one off, expected me to read it while I drove, peeled off another, and another. I took each one, held it up to whatever light there was: intersection street lamps, gas-station lights, whatever.

If I were you, the first one read, *I'd ease off the clutch going into second a little more slowly.*

The next read, *Thirty-five miles per hour means you cannot exceed 35 miles per hour.*

And *Keep an eye on the rearview mirror for anyone who might be following us.*

Then, *When you hit Dorchester Road, you'll have to turn left at the Piggly Wiggly where—*

I wadded every one up, dropped them to the floorboard, didn't even bother to finish this last one. If she wanted to tell me where to go once we were to Hungry Neck, that was one thing. And I knew to work the clutch easy into second. But telling me where to turn here, where I lived. No.

I pulled up to a red light. My eyes on the empty intersection before us, I whispered, "For somebody who can't talk, Dorcas, you sure talk a lot."

The light went green, and I pulled through. Across from us, on the left, sat a Pantry market, a single car out at the gas pump. Its lights came on just as we passed, and I watched it for a second out my window. I eased into second, still watching the car, a big old green Plymouth, the white landau top of it peeled and ripped, like huge scabs on white skin.

I faced forward. Here was another of her notes, her holding it not an inch from my face so I couldn't even see the road. I pushed her hand away, looked in the rearview a second. No headlights. I shoved it into third.

She went off on another fit with the pen and paper, and I held up the piece she'd given me, read it.

If you have something to say to me, you redneck peasant, say it to my face. I can read lips, even if they're as white-boy thin as yours.

I looked from the paper to her. She had yet another one torn off, and pushed it to me again.

Call me Dorcas again, and I'll knock you on your skinny white butt so hard you'll be spitting up shit.

Acts 9:36: Now there was at Joppa a certain disciple named Tabitha, *which by interpretation is called Dorcas: this woman was full of good works and almsdeeds which she did.*

I wadded this one up, too, dropped it. "Okay, *Tabitha*," I said, my eyes hard on her, hands tight on the wheel, "I said I think you're a wonderful person, and a gifted Bible scholar."

She leaned back into the corner of the cab again, the pen and pad still in her hands. She was facing me, and now I could see her a little more, one side of her face growing slowly into light: here was her cheek, her eyebrow, her nose. She was smiling, her face lit with light through the rear window.

Light.

I looked in the rearview again. Headlights, the scab car right up on us.

I hit the gas, took off and away, watching him the whole time. A second later his blinker came on. He pulled down one of the streets we'd passed.

Dorcas—Tabitha—tapped my shoulder, and I turned to her.

She was sitting up, and made a sharp move with her hand toward her chest. She held out her hand to me, and I could see her first two fingers were crossed. Then she made the move again, her fingers crossed brought quick to her chest.

She pointed at me, did it again, nodded: she wanted me to do it. So I crossed my fingers, made the move, smiled at her because she was smiling at me and nodding away, and I did it again.

She wrote, tore off the sheet, handed it to me.

That means "I am a liar." You are. You said something about me talking a lot, not about my biblical acumen. That makes you a liar.

I shrugged.

And a truck shot out from a side street, stopped dead in front of us. I hit the brakes hard, sent Tabitha forward, her shoulder rolling into the dashboard, the big yellow Ford pickup not two feet from the hood.

Two men sat in the cab, the one closest to me, on the passenger side, with a hand up to block the shine from my headlights. He had a beer in the other, and waved it in a sort of salute. He had his baseball cap on backward, a face that needed a shave a few days ago. The driver had his cap on straight, faced forward. He was grinning and chewing on something at the same time, his mouth working away.

"Sorry, y'all!" the one with the beer hollered out, then, "Happy Thanksgiving!" and the truck slowly moved on across the street, back into the neighborhood.

We sat there a few seconds, Tabitha with a hand to the dash and breathing hard, her mouth open wide. She looked at me, then at the taillights of the truck.

We were only one more block from Dorchester, where we'd turn left. Then we'd finally be on the Mark Clark, headed over the Ashley River, then on to 17 South, the Savannah Highway. And maybe, if we were lucky, Hungry Neck, sometime tonight.

I pulled up to the intersection with Dorchester, the street we were on dead-ending into it. Across from us was the Piggly Wiggly, and a Phar-Mor Drugs, and a Piece Goods store, a video store, a dry cleaner's. Everything was dark but for the Piggly Wiggly. It was a twenty-four-hour job, the inside still lit up and sparkling, a couple cars in the parking lot.

And there at the curb right in front of the automatic doors, its lights off, was the Plymouth with the scab roof.

I took in a breath. Maybe he knew a shortcut to the Pig. Or maybe it just *looked* like the same car from here. Maybe it meant nothing at all.

Tabitha tapped me hard on the leg, and I turned to her and in the same second felt the hard crack and lurch of the truck, us bumped from behind.

She was turned in her seat, looking out the back, and I turned, too, saw the yellow Ford, the headlights right up against the bed of the Luv, above and behind the lights those two shits.

They backed up a few inches, hit the bed again, that same crack and lurch.

She looked at me, her breath going faster. They hit us again, only this time kept going, pushed us three or four feet into the crosswalk.

They were pushing us out into the intersection, wanted us broadsided all on our own.

They pushed, and I jammed on the brake hard as I could, put it in neutral so I could let off the clutch, then mashed down on the emergency brake. If they were going to push on us, I'd make them work for it.

I heard their engine going harder behind us, and now my tires were sliding, and that was it: the light, still red, didn't matter, nor the few cars out on Dorchester, headed toward us from both directions. None of it mattered. I sat with my foot on the brake one last second, watched for these cars coming, watched, watched—there were three of them, two on the right, one on the left—and then, when it seemed all things might work together for us in the next second, I reached down and released the emergency brake, popped it into first, and stomped on the gas.

We shot out between the oncoming cars, and I turned left hard. The Luv went sideways, hit the curb across the street, and the cars coming at us all screeched at once, all three squirming to stay straight and stop, even though we were already through.

And of course the pickup behind us shot out, too, his gas gunned for trying to push us.

The two cars on our side of the intersection hit him, one at the rear panel, the other at the front fender, and the truck jumped up off the pavement a good foot or so, landed hard on its left two wheels, sort of hung there a second, balanced like it had an idea to just go right on over. But it didn't, and with a slow pitch fell back onto all four tires.

It was a good sound, loud and stiff, metal bitten and chewed and spit out all in a half second, and there was the sound, too, of scattered glass from one of the truck's front headlights and all the headlights on those two cars. It was a good sound.

Then people jumped from the driver's side of both cars, already shouting, waving fists. Next somebody climbed out of the car that'd been headed the other way, and now that guy was running toward us, and I realized only then we hadn't gone anywhere, just sat here against the curb, watching it all.

I pulled away, headed for the Mark Clark on-ramp only a quarter mile or so ahead, hoped whoever it was running along behind us and yelling wouldn't be able to see my tags.

I watched in the rearview, saw the man finally give up, stop right there in the middle of Dorchester Road.

And then saw the pickup swerve out of the whole thing, one headlight busted out, his tires squealing. The back end wagged one way and the other, the driver trying to get hold of a straight line, one that would deliver him right to us, headed up the ramp and onto a freeway that wouldn't let us off until we were over the Ashley River, a good couple of miles from here.

Here came Tabitha's hard breaths, a high-pitched shard of sound, and I looked at her. She had both hands to the dash, looked forward and behind us and forward again, and I could only push harder on the gas, push harder and harder, and forget easing anything into any gear.

9

The freeway was a freeway: big and wide and empty this time of night. The first thing I did was cut across for the fast lane, the little yellow reflectors set down in the concrete skipping past beneath us, and I looked down, saw we were doing seventy, just like that. I'd never gotten it going this fast, only drove the speed limit. I still had only my learner's permit, and then I felt something small in my throat, thought it might be a laugh too scared to get out: here I was, with only my learner's permit, doing seventy in the middle of the night and being chased by who knew who, me not even old enough to be at the wheel after sunset by South Carolina law.

I looked to Tabitha, tried hard to get a smile out, and said, "Did your brother juice this baby up? Because neither me nor Unc has."

She stared at me a second, then quick moved her hands on the seat, the dash, the floorboard, and came up with the pen and paper.

I held the note to the window, caught the words in the light from a passing freeway lamp: *He worked on it, we went places. That's all I know.* The letters were shaky now, like they were under water.

"Let's hope he did," I said, and looked in the rearview, saw a single headlight back there, rolling up the on-ramp.

The pedal was flat on the floor now, and I glanced down again, saw we were up to seventy-nine, and still the needle moved up, the sound of the engine big and loud and ready to burst, the steering wheel trembling in my hands. We were on the way up the bridge over the Ashley now, to our left the marina and boat ramp, rows of lit-up boats anchored out there and going by too fast. Then I looked back to the freeway, gray concrete and tall lamps lining it, ahead of me the lit-up green highway sign: HWY 61 1¼. I looked in the rearview, the pickup gaining on us now. We were up to eighty-five, still on the rise up the bridge.

I edged to the middle lane so I could take the off-ramp. I didn't know this area over here, West Ashley, like I did North Charleston; knew only that 61 North headed to Summerville, a good twenty or so miles away, the road a two-lane hung over with live oak. And if I went south, there was a street off 61 that went over to the back end of Citadel Mall, the big place with Sears and Dillards and Belk and the movieplex.

I glanced in the rearview. They were still gaining, and now we were doing eighty-nine, that wheel trembling even harder in my hands. But it felt, too, like we were above the ground, the tires trying hard to hold us down on the concrete, like we were just gliding along here, and I knew this feeling was a dangerous one and a good one at once: we were doing near ninety, gliding along, but if I turned the wheel we'd flip, lose it all.

We crested the bridge, the road making a smooth twist down and to the left, beneath us now that marsh. Tabitha's fingers tapped hard on the dash, her mouth open, teeth clenched. Still she took in quick breaths I could hear even over the engine screaming.

We hit ninety-one on the downhill, then fell back to eighty-nine. Then the engine shuddered, a kind of quiver that made the wheel jump. Tabitha turned to me: she'd felt it, too.

I looked down at the speedometer. There, next to it and to the left, was the gas gauge.

Empty, the little white needle down past the E, not even touching it.

I looked at her. She did nothing, only stared at me.

The engine flinched again, and now we were doing seventy-eight, up ahead another green highway sign: HWY 61 NORTH with an arrow to the right.

I moved to the right lane, saw them coming up behind us, that single headlight growing in the thin strip of sight the rearview gave me. We were doing sixty-four now, the off-ramp just ahead, right there the yellow speed-limit sign, 35 MPH, and the big curved arrow showing where to go.

And now they were behind us, right on our ass, like they'd been at that intersection, and they bumped us, the steering wheel wild in my hands, and I pulled hard on it to keep it straight. We were only fifty yards or so from the ramp now, doing fifty, and I tried for the exit, leaned the wheel to the right.

Then the headlight in the rearview disappeared, and here they were on the right shoulder, the big yellow hood pulling up beside us.

The truck slammed us to the left, the steering wheel flying of its own, and Tabitha's window exploded into a shower of glass pieces all over us, cold air flying in after it. She jumped over to me, pushed herself into my shoulder, her hands to her face, that sound she kept coughing out the back of her throat lost to the roar of the truck pushing us to the left, and to the cold air shouting in on us, and now we were past the exit, in the middle lane again, and we had only the chance of the next one, 61 South, not two hundred yards ahead.

Here was that yellow hood still riding right up against us, edging up, both of us slowing down and slowing down, and now here was the cab, higher than ours, so that the first thing I saw as they pulled up even with us was the pistol, thick and shiny, in the driver's hand, his arm just hanging down out his window like he had hold of a beer bottle, then the driver himself with his baseball cap on straight, still grinning, his mouth moving fast, chewing away. He wasn't looking at me but at the road, his other hand at the top of the wheel, holding on. The one with the cap on backward was leaned over and look-ing at us. He held that beer up, made that salute again, but he wasn't smiling anymore, their faces all moving shadows and angled light for the freeway lamp passing above us.

The driver gave out a little laugh, then lifted the gun, held it right there inside the Luv's cab, pointed at us.

I tried to think what Unc would do.

I looked down: forty, thirty-eight.

"Best just to stop altogether," the driver shouted, his voice loud and low. "You need to talk to us. About your uncle." He glanced over at us, lost the grin. Still he chewed.

There went the exit for 61 South, the off-ramp on the other side of the pickup. Gone. Next stop, the end of the freeway, where it hit Savannah Highway. Only a mile ahead, but what might as well have been twelve light-years away.

I thought of Yandle, his finger pointed at me, shooting it at me, and of a hanged woman, and of a dead man at Hungry Neck, and of Unc hidden away somewhere.

And I thought of the paperweight.

The driver held the gun at us, his hand still to the wheel, thirty-five now, thirty.

Maybe it wasn't what Unc would do at all. Maybe it was a cow-ard's way out. But it was a way.

I shouldered Tabitha away so I could get at my pocket, pulled out the paperweight.

"Is this what you want?" I yelled at him, and held it up. "Is this what you want?" I paused. "I don't even know where Unc is!"

Tabitha pushed herself into me again, hands to her face.

The driver looked at the paperweight. He quit chewing, his eye-brows up, then turned to the other guy.

I thought the gun went off then, that he'd fired at us without even looking, and I shouted for the sound, jumped, felt Tabitha do the same.

But it wasn't a gunshot at all, only the sound of his truck hit from behind, and in that moment his arm, there inside my cab, jolted forward, caught against the blown-out window frame, twisted back and upside down, and I heard a hard pop: his shoulder torn from the socket, just like that.

The gun flipped up, fell to the seat.

The scabby green Plymouth cruised past us fast, pushing the truck along from behind, behind the wheel somebody with his sleeves rolled up, a cowboy hat and a pair of heavy sunglasses on.

They were out in front of us now, the truck and Plymouth in my headlights and flying away. The Ford driver's arm just hung there out his window, flapping and turning, and then the Plymouth cut sharp to the left, pulled up alongside the truck, and turned into it, just like the truck had done to us, slammed it hard to the right.

The truck held its own for a second, then slipped to the right, slipped again, and all I could think of was that dead arm, pinned between the truck and the Plymouth, and then the Plymouth finished the job, edged the truck over onto the shoulder, where it disappeared down the embankment.

The Plymouth stopped, maybe a hundred yards ahead of us, his brake lights flaring up, him there on the shoulder.

Then the Luv shuddered all over, and I knew we only had a few yards left before we'd be stopped dead, and I turned to the right, edged over to the shoulder.

Tabitha held my arm, held it hard, her fingernails biting into my skin through the jacket. Her eyes were on the Plymouth, just sitting there, us moving closer to it and closer, until, finally, the engine died, and we stopped, my right wheels just off the pavement.

I could see the Ford from here, down at the bottom of the embankment. That single headlight was still on, and the taillights. But it was on its back. That's all I could tell for the dark: it'd rolled, and it still had lights on. Nothing else, no movement.

Then the Plymouth's reverse lights came on, and he started backing up, fast. My headlights were on still, and I tried to read his plate, but he'd caked mud over it. All I could see was the driver with his arm up over the seat, head turned back and looking at us, big dark sunglasses.

Here came the sound from Tabitha again, and I looked at her, felt my own breath going fast now. My heart'd slowed for a few seconds inside all this, the Plymouth taking care of the truck and that gun and all, but here was that adrenaline again, my arms heavy and light at once for it, my face hot and wet. Who was this guy, and what did he want with us? And the fact I couldn't even come close to answering any of it made that sound she gave out seem about the best thing anybody could do. Here we were, shit out of gas.

I turned to Tabitha. There, on the seat beside her, lay the gun. Thick and shiny.

He came straight at us. I jammed the paperweight in my jacket pocket, quick reached across Tabitha for the gun, put it inside my jacket. She hadn't even let go my arm.

Then he swerved, passed me on my side, just driving along backward, his arm still up, his head still turned, and he was gone, behind us now.

I looked in the rearview. He pulled right in behind us, edged up to my tail, just like the truck had done, and I turned to Tabitha, shook her with my arm. She looked at me, blinked.

I said, "He pushes us off the embankment, we jump out and roll." I pulled out the gun, patted it. It was a .45 Smith & Wesson, I only now saw. I'd never fired one. But I figured I was ready as I'd ever be. I said, "Get ready."

She nodded, and then he hit us.

Only a tap, contact.

I looked in the rearview. He rolled down his window, then leaned his head out, hollered, "Put it in neutral." He paused, put his bare arm out the window, made the helicopter sign with his finger and hand: *Let's go.* "I'll push you on in," he hollered.

I looked at Tabitha. She hadn't heard a thing, only stared straight ahead.

I found the trigger, knew enough not to let my finger hang around there but still let it settle there a second.

He started pushing. I was still in gear, felt the car give, but only a little.

What would Unc do?

He'd get his finger the hell off a trigger, was the first thing came to mind.

"You need gas," the man hollered. "Checked the gauge myself once the little girl left for you."

And, too, Unc would tell me don't look a gift horse in the mouth.

I looked in the rearview one more time. He made the helicopter sign again, nodded.

I let go the gun, shifted to neutral. I tried to make my hands stop shaking but gave it up, just let myself tremble, and then we were rolling down the Mark Clark, big and wide and empty save for a scab-roofed Plymouth and a '73 Luv.

We made it to the Amoco on Savannah Highway, light from the canopy above the row of pumps too bright down on us. He gave me one last shove with the Plymouth, and I rolled to a stop beside the pump, him right behind me. He cut off his lights, and I did the same.

I could see the worker inside the booth, a black woman in a red smock, orange hair greased into a single big cowlick just above her forehead. She was reading a magazine, the booth only big enough for cigarettes and a register.

His car door slammed, and I put my hand to the gun, looked in my side-view mirror, saw him stretch. He was skinny, not too tall, and had on jeans and boots and a blue shirt, those sleeves still rolled up. The hat was a straw one, the sides folded up, the front end bent down. And those sunglasses.

He looked familiar.

He came toward us, and I found the trigger again, just touched it.

Then he was at my window. I didn't look at him, only saw out the corner of my eye his belt buckle and belt, the blue shirt, his jeans. My window was still up, and he made the motion with his hand for me to roll it down.

I let go the wheel, hoped he wouldn't see my hand shake as I rolled down the window.

"First thing is," he said, his voice light and sunny, like we were talking fish and how many crappie we'd caught today. He leaned against the truck, his forearms against the roof just above the window.

I knew this man. I'd heard this voice before. I knew him.

"Yessir?" I said, my hand back to the wheel, the other still inside the jacket.

"First thing is, I figure that badass pistolero either ended up in your cab or onto the road somewheres." He paused. "If you got it, keep it. You might could use it."

He tapped the roof twice, let out a breath.

"Yessir," I said, and glanced at the woman in the booth. She turned a page in the magazine.

"Second thing is," he said, and I made my eyes go straight ahead, "calm that girl down. Sounds like a stuck pig."

Tabitha'd been scratching out that sound all this while, though I hadn't heard it since we'd started past that rolled Ford. I just hadn't listened.

"Yessir," I said, and finally let go the gun. He'd told me to keep it, he'd pushed us here, he'd taken out the Ford.

A gift horse.

I put my hand out in front of Tabitha, sort of pushed down on the air a few times. She looked at me, and I mouthed the words *Calm down.*

Her eyes moved from me to the man at the window. Then she looked at me a long moment, gave a short, sharp nod, and the sound stopped.

"Next on our agenda," he said, "is the fact Leland's sinking in seven kinds of shit, and he thinks he knows how to swim." He paused. "Problem is, he don't. Thinks he can figure it all out, come up smelling like a rose. But he can't."

He took his hands from the roof, pushed them deep into his pockets.

"You tell Leland," he said, all that air and light in his voice gone, in its place a black gravel whisper. "You tell your uncle we don't care where he's hid. It don't matter. Those two fuckhead shits back there don't matter, neither." He paused. "You tell him the people who count don't give a good flying fuck where he's hid out. The only way through this all is for him to do what he's been asked to do. You tell him things'll be fixed. We're on his side. All's he got to do is what's been asked." He stopped. "You tell him he's got forty-eight hours, and it's over and done with."

"Yessir," I whispered.

He took a hand from a pocket, slapped hard the roof of the Luv, a sound so loud even Tabitha jumped. Then he turned, faced the Plymouth. Still I hadn't seen his face. But I *knew* him.

"Now," he said, and in just that one word here was all sun and blue skies. "Y'all got money for gas?"

I breathed out, looked to Tabitha. She hadn't seen anything, so hadn't heard anything, either. I said, "You have any money for gas?"

She tilted her head, her forehead wrinkled, mouth squinted up: *What kind of question is that?* She shook her head no.

"No sir," I said, and turned back to him.

There on his arm, sneaking out from beneath the rolled-up sleeve, was the bottom edge of a homemade tattoo: JUNIOR.

Officer Tommy Thigpen, the second cruiser at the scene. Backup for Sergeant Doug Yandle.

The only one Unc would talk to.

They'd shaken hands. And he'd just run a truck off the road, pinned a man's arm between a car and a truck. An officer of the sheriff's department.

I faced forward, afraid he'd seen me see it, and the thought occurred to me, what if he wanted me to see it?

But he just pulled a roll of bills from his jeans pocket, peeled at it, dropped some in on me.

I looked down: five twenties.

He stuffed the roll back into his jeans, then turned one last time to me, knocked twice on the roof.

"Drive careful," he said.

10

We reached the railroad tracks. There'd been next to nobody from the Amoco on out, though I'd breathed shallow the whole way here, afraid somebody'd pull out of the woods and ram into us or take a shot at us: anything seemed possible.

And as we'd gotten closer to the Rantowles Motel, just past Hollywood, I'd wondered for a few seconds if there'd still be cruisers parked out front, lights going, crime-scene banners up everywhere, everything still going on though it'd been six this morning Mrs. Constance Dupree Simons's suicide was called in, and I thought of those two buzz-cut officers at the hospital just this morning, thought of them being the ones to tell me of her dying, and I wondered for a second whether SLED were in with Thigpen on this.

And Yandle? Was he with them too, every cop in the Lowcountry party to a murder and suicide, all of them part of the people who counted who could fix things, if only Unc would do what'd been asked?

Then here came the hotel: only a brick box of a building, six parking slots in front of six doors, six windows each with a room air con-

ditioner plugged into it. One lamppost sat to the far end of the little parking lot, everything gray in the wash of light it gave up.

There, making an *X* across the third door to the right, was the
crime-scene banner.

Nothing else. There'd been no lights on anywhere, not even a single car.

The tracks banged beneath us, no closing gate this far from
Charleston, as though people down here weren't worth that kind of
safeguard. Now we were on Hungry Neck, Tabitha's time to take
over. Though I'd been back here a million times, maybe more, the
dark of it all seemed too dark now, too heavy, all of it full of something could happen: the moss off the live oak above us looked too
much like that man's arm out the window of the yellow pickup, or
like a woman who'd hanged herself might look: gray and twisting in
the low wind out there, the half-moon I could piece through the
branches more dead and bright than any moon I'd ever seen before.
Anything could happen now.

I slowed down, and I looked at her, shrugged: *What next?*

She'd written me no notes the hour it'd taken to get here, only'd
latched back on to my arm when I came back from paying for the gas.
The black woman with the orange cowlick at the Amoco had only
yawned as she slipped nine beat-up dollar bills into the metal drawer.

Now Tabitha let go, looked around for the pad and paper, reached
down. I heard her paw through the broken glass on the floorboard.
She came back up with the pen and pad again, wrote, and handed it
to me.

2.2 miles to SR321, right. 3.5 miles to clear-cut on left.

In the light from the dash I could see the printing was still shaky,
watery. She was still scared.

I looked up at her. "You told me Unc was with you. You don't go
State Road 321 to get to your house." I said it big, my mouth exaggerated for the dark.

She wrote.

That's not where we're going.

"But you *told* me Unc was with you." I felt my jaw go tight. "Just what the hell are you pulling on me?"

She held her hand out in front of her. She crossed her fingers, quick brought them to her chest: that same move. She tried a smile, but it came out as shaky as her printing.

"You got that right," I said. "You're a liar."

I looked out the windshield, my jaw still clenched tight. Moss still hung like dead arms from the trees out there, the road still shrouded as heavy as it would ever be.

As dark and heavy as it'd always *been*, too.

This was Hungry Neck. My place as well as hers. That tract of land, the Hunt Club, and all those acres belonged to my family, all the way back to my great-grampa, who bought it off the lumber company back in the twenties for next to nothing, the land shaved clean. It wasn't worth much now, either, but it was our family's land, all we had.

Hungry Neck. Where I wanted to be, even if my mom loved me and might've been crying over me gone this very minute. Even if my uncle was tied up into the ugly something I didn't know just as tight as anybody else. This was where I wanted to be.

I turned to Tabitha. "You just get me there, now. Do it. And don't lead me on." I paused. "Just tell me the truth."

She let her shoulders fall some, slowly nodded, and wrote again.

Just don't treat me like I'm some idiot. You haven't yet, but people act like I'm retarded. I know a thing or two.

Then she reached to the floorboard and pulled something flat from beneath her seat, big as a shoe-box lid.

KKF 428, between the F and 4 what was supposed to be a Carolina wren parked on a jessamine branch, though it wasn't a wren at all, just somebody's idea of a bird: my license plate, off the back of the Luv. She'd taken it off before all this.

Nobody at the wreck back on Dorchester would be able to name us now.

I held the plate in both hands, looked up at her.

She put her index and middle fingers together, brought them to her chest, then pointed them at me. She did it again, just as when she'd taught me how to call myself a liar.

But now the fingers were together, not crossed.

"I trust you," I said.

She nodded hard, smiled, did the move again.

I put my fingers together, touched my chest, pointed at her.

She wrote: *He's in Benjamin's old shotgun shack. Nobody knows about that place except us. At the end of the clear-cut, pull off left. Park in the weeds. We walk.*

I drove off the road, the weeds white in my headlights, the truck bucking with the uneven ground as we plowed through. Then I cut off the lights and the engine, and the cab filled with a silence that rang in my ears.

I pushed open my door, stepped into the weeds, Tabitha doing the same. Here was that moon, banging down on the field and trees, on us and the whole world. I had the pocket flashlight I'd gotten from my dresser, felt it in my left pocket once we were out of the truck. But we didn't need it. The moon was enough.

And I felt, too, the deadweight of the gun in my Levi's jacket, just loose where I'd buttoned the jacket up.

I pulled it out, held it there in the moonlight.

Thick and shiny. Heavy, still warm from where it'd been inside my jacket.

Tabitha looked at me from across the hood. Past her was the end of the clear-cut, where the woods picked back up, a thick black wall, the wind moving the tops of pine and oak and birch.

She couldn't hear the sound of that wind, a sound I'd fallen asleep to most every night I'd been at Hungry Neck, and I swallowed at how strange all of this was, unfolding in front of my eyes and in my ears: a deaf-and-dumb black girl I'd kissed full on the lips, a car chase, a pistol in my hand bright with the moon. I couldn't help but think none of it all was happening, that just like in some bad TV show this was all a dream meant for me to wake from.

I looked at the gun, held it there in front of me like it would say something. Suddenly it was cold, the dark and dead cold a gun takes on with being outdoors. I held it with both hands, my hands gray and small and just a kid's, the cold off the gun feeling like it'd burn through my fingers any second now.

This was real. This was happening.

I heard the thin crack of weeds being walked through, saw Tabitha already on her way toward the trees.

I put the safety on, slipped it in the back of my pants, like an undercover cop on the same bad TV show.

We walked maybe a mile through the woods, Tabitha leading. There were times, too, when I thought maybe I'd gone deaf myself: she didn't make a sound as we climbed over trunks, moved through dead leaves down from the hickory above us, wove between low spots where wetlands lay in black pools littered with more leaves.

The moonlight gave piecemeal shadows to everything, the palmetto and pine and dogwood moving, a thousand gray and black shapes changing shape, the only sure thing Tabitha ahead of me, and those white sneakers, her pale gray jacket. She didn't look back, only moved, held back a wax-myrtle branch for a second before letting it go; it was up to me to make it to that branch before it slapped back, hit me in the face. And still she moved, around us all these shadows, above us the treetops moving, this big empty sound falling down on us, though Tabitha couldn't know.

Then she stopped. I came around her, looked at her, into the woods.

Something sat not twenty yards ahead of us, no moonlight through it, no shadows inside it, no movement. Only a black shape, square, no bigger than the butcher shed over to the hunt club.

Benjamin's shack.

We were here, Unc just that far away. But I didn't move, couldn't.

It had to do with what I'd know next about him, about my uncle, the one a fire had blinded, made him move from Mount Pleasant back here through no choice of his own nor mine neither.

I'd been the one to nurse him back as much as my mom'd been.

And I'd been here with him every second I could, sat with him through breakfast, lunch, and dinner, helped wash his dishes, burn his trash, fold his clothes.

I'd walked the woods of Hungry Neck with him for more hours than I could count.

And I'd been the one, finally, who'd stood with him beside a dead body at Hungry Neck, and to talk to the next one to end up dead. I was the one carrying a message to him from her: *Tell Leland I didn't do it.*

And tell him I loved him, she'd said.

I thought I knew him. But I didn't.

Now I figured I'd know something about him I didn't want to know.

Tabitha turned to me, nodded hard toward the shack. She wanted me to call for Unc.

I looked to the shed, tried hard to open my mouth. But nothing happened.

Then lights came on, flooded over us, the world lit with white so white I flinched, ducked to the ground, eyes squinted tight for it all.

"Huger?" Unc called, his voice flat, the word barely a question.

I was crouched on the ground, like I could hide from this light. Or my name.

Slowly I stood.

There on the shack porch—a door lying flat on cinder blocks— stood Unc, in his hand the walking stick, Braves cap and sun-glasses on.

And next to him Miss Dinah Gaillard, Tabitha's mom, a double-barrel shotgun pointed at us.

I said, "Sir?"

"You better be alone."

Tabitha slowly stood, blinking and blinking.

"Just Tabitha with me, sir," I said.

"You don't be calling her by that demon name," Miss Dinah said, and lowered the gun, let back both hammers. "It's Dorcas. Dorcas only."

She had on a powder-blue parka over a flowery purple dress down past her knees, duck boots on her feet. "That name you call her a demon name for that program *Bewitched* come on while back." I glanced at Tabitha, her head down and shaking slow, eyes closed: she'd seen all these words before. "Them TV people take a godly girl's name and give it to a witch. No Tabitha round here. None I know."

Unc didn't move.

She stepped down from the porch. The shack was only gray boards, one window, a rusted tin roof. A stovepipe came out at the peak, smoke snaking up out of it, white in the light everywhere.

The light. I turned, looked around, still squinting: floodlights twenty feet up in a couple trees behind us, in a few trees on either side of us, and at the top of two poles, one at each end of the shack. It might as well have been noon.

Here came Miss Dinah, shotgun crooked in her arm as natural as a shopping bag, heading for Tabitha.

"Certainly weren't any surprise, you two loud as elephants coming in," she said. "No surprise, too, when I find Missy Dorcas bed empty as the tomb Easter morning. Truck gone, too. No surprise whatsoever."

She was to us now and took hold of Tabitha's arm.

Tabitha jerked her arm up and around at her mother's touch. Her eyes shot open, her chin up. She looked out into the woods past the shed, mouth shut tight.

It was the first I'd seen her in light this whole time: that white hairband holding back a big, full turn of straight black hair, her skin smooth and brown, that jaw set hard as concrete.

She was beautiful. It was something I'd never seen before, this beauty. Tabitha. Before this, she'd only been the girl I'd looked at after being told stories about the Mothers and Fathers, the Gray Ghost, the girl I'd shivered with.

But now.

"We got a mile and a half walk now, Missy Dorcas, breakfast to make up for these two not three hours from now, too," Miss Dinah said, making certain to be in Tabitha's line of sight so she could see her mouth the words. "I be surprised if the Mothers and Fathers don't haint us on home," she went on, "chase us through the woods, they green eyes a-glittering, a moon like this and that far to go."

I cut my eyes to Tabitha one last time, saw her roll her eyes at her mother's words: as though the old ghost story were all we had to worry over.

They started away then, to the left and toward the black out past the ring of daylight the floods gave, Tabitha out in front, Miss Dinah talking to the back of her deaf daughter: "You be safe out to here," Miss Dinah called from nowhere. "You got nothing to worry over out to here."

I knew these words were meant for me and Unc, not Tabitha.

"Six-thirty, Miss Dinah," Unc said, his voice still flat. "We'll be there."

They passed the post at the left end of the shed, and the dark swallowed them up.

He let the stick hang off the edge of the porch, touch the ground. He leaned on it and stepped off.

He said, "Come here, boy."

Between us lay thirty feet or so of dry leaves. I thought of Tabitha with her eyes closed, her mom headed straight for her. But Unc was going nowhere, was waiting for me to head to him, so he could give me whatever hell he thought I was owed.

Thirty feet of ground. I swallowed, started for him.

He held the stick above the ground now, his hand holding on tight, knuckles white, the other at his side, in a fist.

Then I was in front of him, all this light around us, light so clear and sharp I could see myself in his sunglasses, just like I'd been able to see myself in them Saturday morning, two of me reflected there, still just as small and far away as I'd felt there on the tail end of the Luv.

Then he slapped me, the hand up from his side so quick I couldn't have flinched if I'd wanted to, the pain of it white and sharp, a blast of cutting light through my jaw and teeth and tongue.

But I didn't move.

The stick fell to the ground, lost for the force of his other hand across my cheek.

He said, "You don't have a clue, do you?"

It wasn't a question at all, I knew, and now I could taste blood in my mouth, the inside of my cheek cut.

"Miss Dinah comes out here about two o'clock," Unc said, his mouth barely moving. "Walked a mile and a half through the woods to tell me she just got a call from somebody won't give his name but who tells her he knows where I am. Tells her, too, her daughter and you are on your way here." He paused. His voice hadn't changed at all from when he'd called out my name: just there, and knowing everything. "Says you about got killed out on the Mark Clark, and that he gave you money for gas, and to be expecting you."

He stopped. "Now," he said, his voice gone to a whisper meant not for a secret, but for the anger in him. "Now you're in it, and you don't even know. You. And your momma. You don't even know it, but you are, and so is Dorcas, and Miss Dinah, who's probably going to spend the rest of this night playing watchdog with that shotgun, waiting for somebody to show and look to drag me away."

"He ain't coming for you," I said quick, and Unc flinched at the words, like they'd scared and surprised him both. Like he'd figured I had nothing to say.

But I had words, words hidden inside the blood and metal and dark red of my mouth, inside that blast of pain he'd given to me, a piece of the hell he thought I was owed. I'd had no idea they were there, lined up and ready to go, but here they were, and the next ones, too: "And I know who it is."

I leaned over, spit red on the leaves between us, my tongue thick in my mouth.

Unc was wrong. I had plenty of clues.

Thigpen's words, to begin with: *Leland's sinking in seven kinds of shit, and he thinks he knows how to swim.*

I leaned over, picked up the stick. For a moment I thought to throw it far and deep into the black past all this false light, throw it somewhere he'd never find. Then maybe he'd see how he had no choice in this matter whatsoever: that I was here, and that it'd be my arm he'd have to hang on to, and that whatever end this all came to I was part and parcel to it. For better and worse.

He was what I had. And I was what he had.

I leaned the stick against his chest.

He stood there, mouth open, like every word he'd had ready for me had suddenly dried up, turned to dead leaves underfoot, my blood and spit on them all some kind of pact sealed between us.

I moved around him and onto the porch, for the door standing open, inside it more black.

But mounted on the gray board beside the door was a switch, one of those industrial kind, a red plastic handle on it you pulled down and clapped into place to turn it on or off. The switch for all these lights, and I wondered for a second how Benjamin Gaillard had gotten electric all the way out here.

I reached to the switch, pulled hard on it, clapped it back.

Here was the night again, only now it was pitch black for the way my eyes'd adjusted to the floods. I stood there, waited, waited, and then the shadows surfaced again and I could see.

"Unc," I said. "Let's go."

He didn't move, a gray man in gray light, piecemeal shadows moving above and beside him.

Then he turned, and I could see the stick in his hand. He leaned over, laid it against the porch floor, stood.

We were silent a long while, and I heard again the empty song of wind down on us from above.

Then he held up his hand to me.

I took it, our hands the same color gray in this moonlight, and helped him up.

11

I talked.

I just sat in the dark in a big chair, the armrests under my hands, the material pulled and torn, the stuffing and wood right there at my fingertips. Some old hunk of furniture from the Gaillards' shanty, parked here by Benjamin for drinking and hunting and sometimes, I figured, even nights like this, when talk was all that mattered.

Unc'd led me in, had gone to the far end of the room, where a cot was laid out. I couldn't see this at first, saw only black, my eyes needing time to adjust even more to this newer, deeper dark. The window across from me was papered over, I finally could make out, the moonlight through it just the barest hint of gray.

The woodstove sat against the wall on my left, the iron door of it dull red for the fire must've been burning in there since sometime early in the evening. Now and again Unc'd tell me to chunk up the stove, him able to tell precisely when the cold'd start seeping in, and I'd go to the stack of wood next to the stove, pick up a piece, then with my other hand pick up the small hooked stick that lay on the floor before the stove, with it lift the latch on the door. Here came firelight, strong and harsh, and I'd settle in that piece of wood, quick close the door, head back to my chair.

I told him of Tommy Thigpen, to start off, and how it'd been him to call Miss Dinah, or must have been, because he was the only one saw us. Except, of course, for the two bubbas in the pickup who'd been rolled, and I told him of the way the driver's arm'd hung in the window with that gun, and I told him of the gun, too, and stood, pulled it from my pants, handed it to him. In that dark I could see him, the barest figure of a ghost holding the gun, thinking on it. Then he held it out to me, and without a word I took it.

It was mine now.

I told him of how it hadn't been me to strike out for this place on my own, told him of how Tabitha—"Dorcas," he interrupted me, "is what her momma named her, so you make sure and observe that fact"—had tapped on my window, and I told him of the walk in the woods here, the quiet of it all, and how much the floodlights'd hurt my eyes.

But I didn't tell him about kissing her.

Now and again I stopped, waited for him to say something. At times I thought maybe he'd gone on to sleep, and I listened for his deep, steady breaths in and out. But each time I stopped there'd be only a few moments before he'd let out, "Go on, Huger."

I told him of the two SLED clods when we were on our way out of the hospital, and how they believed it was him to call in Constance Dupree's suicide, and I told him of what I'd seen on the eleven o'clock news. I waited for something from him. But still nothing came, only "Go on, Huger."

So I waited for last to tell him what seemed the biggest items to me. This would get him, I hoped, these words next:

I said, "Doug Yandle was outside the hospital when we left. He was looking at us, Mom and me, and he had his arm in a sling, and with his free hand he made like he was pointing a gun at me, and pulled the trigger."

"He's a pussy, plain and simple," Unc said. He was quiet, then said, "Next?"

"Next what?"

"Next thing you want to tell me."

I looked up, said, "Tommy Thigpen said to tell you the people who count don't give a good flying fuck where you're hiding." I paused. I'd never talked like this in front of him. But I'd never carried news like this before, either. "He said the only way through this is for you to do what you've been asked to do. He said to tell you things'll be fixed. All you have to do is what they've asked you to do." I stopped. "He said you have forty-eight hours."

I let that hang in the dark, waited, waited, then said, "What did they ask you to do?"

He said nothing.

I was quiet a little while longer, then said the one last piece I had, something I hoped might flush him out: "Constance Dupree Middleton came to my room last night. At the hospital. And she said to tell you she loved you."

He moved. It was just the squeak of the wooden cot, but I heard him move.

I said, "And she told me to give this to you." I stood again, crossed the shack to him, pulled out the paperweight.

In the dark it was nothing I could see, only the same warm glass thing Constance'd handed me last night, and for a moment I thought I might know a piece of what it was like to be Unc, and be blind. Here was the thing in my hand that all of this had come to, and I couldn't see it.

I said, "It's like a paperweight. It's made of something like brown glass, but I'm not sure. But inside it is the center of a sweetgrass basket, a little coil of a sweetgrass basket."

His fingers stopped dead. "Inside it? A sweetgrass coil?"

"Yes," I said, then put to him what I was sure was a connection now. "A sweetgrass coil, just like the ones you were drawing in the dirt with your stick." I paused. "After we found Simons."

He moved his hand up and down, like he was weighing it. "I don't know what this means," he said. "When she called Wednesday night, she was crazy, crying and all. Threatening to kill him." He gave it a small toss, caught it. "She said something about sweetgrass baskets. Something about graves and sweetgrass baskets. I took it to be crazy talk, her raving on about what a bastard her husband was." He paused. "And she told you to give it to me?"

"Yessir."

"Well," he said. He brought it to his nose, sniffed it, turned it. "It's resin. Pine. Hard as a rock." He made a fist again, with his thumbnail tried to pick at it. "And she didn't say anything else. About this thing, this paperweight."

"No sir." I paused. "Just the part about telling you she loved you."

He was silent.

"And she told me to cherish my momma," I said, not certain why I ought to tell him that, except that now it seemed all the more important, and all the more impossible. "She said she could tell Mom cared for me. Mom was sleeping in a cot under the window. She spent the night there for me."

Now I couldn't even hear him breathing. He was holding on to something had hold of *him* in a way must have been bigger than anything yet to hold him.

He said, "They want me to sell the land. Hungry Neck."

"Who?" I said, my voice whole and loud, and I quick sat down beside him on the cot, leaned forward, said, "No!"

"Settle down," Unc said, and now here was his breath, let out low and long, a hollow whisper of air in the dark. "Settle down. And no, it wasn't me to call it in. About Constance." He paused, took in another breath, but let this one right back out. "I only heard of it on the radio," he whispered. "Over to Miss Dinah's."

I leaned back, the shack wall hard and cold through my jacket.

"Unc," I said, "Unc, I don't know what's happening."

"Join the big ugly club," he said, and reached in the dark for my hand. I held it up for him, and he put in it the paperweight, still warm. "You hold on to this," he whispered.

I woke up, didn't remember falling asleep. I was on Unc's cot, and there was light in through the papered window, and in through cracks here and there in the walls, and I sat up, called out, "Unc!" to the empty room.

The chair, the stove. This cot. That was all.

It was an old sleeping bag I was wrapped up in, and I'd slept in my clothes. I sat up, saw on the floor my duck boots, taken off by Unc, set next to each other and waiting, neat as could be.

And there, rolled up and slipped into the top of the right one, was a piece of paper. I picked it up, saw it was a note, handwriting on it: Unc's scrawl, big and wide. He could write still, left me notes now and again if he was out somewheres when I came in on Friday afternoons.

I'm at Miss Dinah's. Follow the electric wire. Hot food waiting.

Then, beneath it in letters too small for the hand I'd come to know so well, was the single word *love,* and *Unc.*

I slipped on the boots, went to the stove, took what little heat was left from what had become a dead black stove, that warm red long gone. I put on my jacket and started out, stepped off the porch and looked up to the trees for those floods from last night. A wire came down from one to the right, took off back and away, the same direction Tabitha and Miss Dinah'd taken last night, and I was off.

It was the same old woods as everywhere down here, same low water spots and water oak and whatnot as always, only colder than the day before. But it seemed different in a big way now, and for a second I couldn't get it, couldn't feel what it was.

And then last night started in on me, and I knew what it was: somebody was trying to get the land away from us, trying to get Unc to sell it. Hungry Neck, a place for some reason people were being killed over—a plastic surgeon, his wife—and trying to take it out of my family's hands, who the hunt club belonged to.

Me, I knew. Hungry Neck belonged to *me,* and I didn't feel a second of remorse for that feeling, this big selfishness I had in me for wanting our land, all 2,200 acres of it, no matter some of it was trash land, some of it good for nothing.

It was what we had.

But to kill over it? To kill a man, a son-of-a-bitch doctor, and then to tack on a suicide too, when the place didn't belong to any of them?

I walked through the woods, an eye up now and again to catch that wire. Wild grapevine had grown over it this spring and summer, now only the gray dead fingers of vines here and there, the wire tacked to a tree every few yards, the trunks nearly grown over the wire, swallowing it, telling me how long it'd been that Benjamin Gaillard had had this shack to himself. Most likely since he was a kid, I imagined, maybe since he was my age, and I wondered what it would have been like to be him, a kid living out here with these woods seven days a week, every day of the year.

Which is what I had before my father left us, and Mom decided to move us out. Back then it was Hungry Neck, every moment I breathed.

Mom.

I stopped. She'd have found the note hours ago, when she went into my room and tried to wake me up for the first day back to school after Thanksgiving. And now the woods went cold on me, the wind up in the treetops sharp and loud, the dead leaves everywhere making more noise than I could take in. Mom would most likely have called the police on me by now and would be crying there at our kitchen table over where I was.

That, or she'd be at the trailer this very second, the Stanza pulled up out front, waiting for us. Like that was where we'd be.

I looked up to the treetops, saw them sway in the wind, saw the bitter blue sky up there above it all, a midday sky in November. Somewhere deer were feeding, chomping on acorns, living like they had nothing to fear, because, it seemed to me, they didn't. Sure, they heard something, they got spooked, took off. But what did they know of what they heard? It was only sound, and if it was a hunter, and if that hunter got what he'd come looking for, then one of those deer was just gone, and the next morning these same deer would be out there in that same field, chomping on the same acorns, walking the same trails, settling down in the high grass for night, and that life gone, the one taken by that hunter, whether he was a South-of-Broad surgeon or me, a fifteen-year-old kid who didn't know shit about how the world worked, those same deer would just take a look around, maybe, and see one of them was gone, and everything would just start over again, like that deer'd never existed, like he'd just been some dumb dream all those deer'd been having together.

And I wanted, I guess, to be one of those deer right then. Then nothing would worry me, a sound out in the woods only something to duck away from and run for cover. And then next day I could just pick up again.

Because now I knew there were things out there, things that weren't going to be reconciled and tossed away with just going to sleep at night. Somebody was out there, waiting for something to happen from Unc. For him to sell off the land in order just to let Unc live.

Tell him the people who count don't give a good flying fuck where he's hid out. The only way through this all is for him to do what he's been asked to do.

Sell Hungry Neck.

I jammed my hands into my pockets deep as they could go, shoulders up, that bitter blue sky too big, too wide, me too small against this all.

I felt stuff in my pockets: in the right, the money, that wad of bills Tommy Thigpen'd given me.

And in the other, the paperweight, there at the bottom of my pocket.

You tell him he's got forty-eight hours, and it's over and done with.

I ran.

There stood Miss Dinah Gaillard's place, half trailer, half shanty, the whole of it painted haint purple.

I'd been here a few times before, driving Unc over to deliver a ham at Christmas and Easter, flowers on Miss Dinah's and Tabitha's birthdays, and every time we pulled up in the Luv I sort of shook my head at the place, at the way these people thought painting a house a hideous color might actually scare off ghosts and demons and all.

I was in the backyard, if you could call it that, and like in the front yard there were those tires painted white and split up to make planters, pansies in them. There was a clothesline strung up out here, an old dead refrigerator, next to it a dead washing machine, the two of them side by side beneath a live oak.

Same as always.

But as I went up the cinder blocks and onto the back porch, reached for the screen door, pulled it open to knock, I thought for a second this color wasn't such a bad thing, saw for an instant Unc's place painted this same shade, and I wondered if, had our trailer been painted this color years ago, all the bad that had happened since might not have been averted somehow: Unc's accident, my daddy taking off, a murder.

Haint purple. It was a thought.

The door opened before I could knock.

There stood Tabitha, a smirk on her face: *What took you so long?* She nodded, pulled the door open, and Miss Dinah hollered from inside, "She can feel in the floor somebody coming up the porch. No surprises round here."

The first thing I took in, even before I got through the door, was the smell: biscuits, bacon. Hot food waiting, no matter I'd been expected at six o'clock this morning.

I stepped in, and stopped.

I didn't know what I'd expected of the place; though I'd been here so many times before, I'd never actually been inside. I'd never given it a thought, really, only assumed it'd be like every other black's house I'd been in: a TV, a sofa, a table and chairs, and somewhere a picture of Jesus on the wall. Deevonne's house, and Jessup's, LaKeisha's and Tyrone's houses. The only blacks' houses I'd ever been in.

Not any different from my own, to tell the truth.

But here.

Here there were books. Everywhere.

Bookshelves lined the walls, from floor to ceiling. Books were piled in stacks on the floor, too, and lay on a coffee table to my right.

A sofa sat just past the coffee table, behind it bookshelves, floor to ceiling, and at either end of the sofa were more books piled up.

The only clear wall space in the whole room was across from the sofa, where a set of shelves stopped three feet from the ceiling. There, centered on the wood paneling, was a framed photograph of Benjamin Gaillard in full Marine dress uniform. The American flag was behind him, and he seemed maybe about to smile, his eyes right on me, like he was ready to tell me something I could use.

The kitchen was to my left, a little counter right there where, if it'd been any other place, there might have been a couple of stools so you could sit, eat, talk to whoever was at work in the kitchen. But beneath the counter were bookshelves, all full. A hallway led off the kitchen, back into the house, and from where I stood I could see bookshelves down that way as well.

Unc sat at the table in the kitchen, sunglasses on but with the baseball cap off. He was smiling at me, one leg crossed over the other, stick behind him and leaned against the bookshelves, floor to ceiling, behind him.

Bookshelves in the kitchen.

Miss Dinah, dressed in one of the same old flowery print dresses she always wore, was bent over in front of the oven, then stood, in her hand a plate heaped with biscuits and bacon, a puddle of grits.

"Breakfast at noon," she said, and gave me something of the same smirk Tabitha had: *What took you so long?*

"Thank you, ma'am," I said, and turned, looked for Tabitha. She was gone.

"Hurry 'fore it goes cold," Miss Dinah said, and I went around the counter, stood at the table, next to Unc. A place had already been set: napkin, fork, knife.

"Quite a luxury," he said. "Sleeping till noon. Like you're the Prince of Wales or whatnot."

Miss Dinah put a hand at her hip, the plate still in her other hand.

Unc said, "Take a load off, son." He'd lost the smile now.

I said, "Why'd you let me sleep for so long? Unc, we got to get going," and soon as I said it, I wondered, Get going for what? To where? Forty-eight hours to get what done?

"You don't have a good breakfast, you not going to have a good *day*," Miss Dinah said, and set the plate on the table.

I'd kissed this woman's daughter.

I sat down, looked from her to Unc to her again. I said, "Where's Tab—" and stopped. Miss Dinah's jaw got a little bit tighter, her eyes narrowing the smallest bit.

I scooted my chair in, without looking at her said, "Where's Dorcas?"

"She's got a little homework assignment," Unc said.

He had his Braves cap in his hand, was turning it with his fingers, a habit I'd seen him do a million times when he was worried over something: somebody at the club saying something nasty to someone else, the two of them threatening to quit their membership; Patrick or Reynold beating holy shit out of one of their dogs for no reason whatsoever; those few times a doe'd be brought up for butchering and we'd find a fetus.

I said, "What's the plan?"

He was looking down, chin almost to his chest, thinking. Miss Dinah put a plastic tub of butter down on the table, and a cup of coffee, heavy on the milk. Just like I liked it. She'd seen me fix it this way for years at the club.

She leaned against the kitchen counter, arms crossed. Books were stacked on the kitchen counter, too.

Unc fingered his hat; Miss Dinah stared at me. Something was going on here already.

I tried a smile, said, "What's with all these books?"

"As a rule," she said, and turned her head, gave me the other side of her jaw, "we read them."

"Ease off on the boy," Unc said. "He's scared as the rest of us, Dinah. So please." Still he worked the hat.

I turned back to Miss Dinah. "I guess I meant how is it you got so many of them. Books, I mean." I shrugged. "I mean, what did—"

"You mean how come a shanty like this one have a better library than any high school in the county. That's because I know what to spend my money on. My baby." She seemed to soften then, talk turned to her daughter. She smiled, looked out to the front room, all those shelves, all those books. She nodded at them. "We go to the library sale every year, stock up and stock up. Proud to say, too, Dorcas read every one of them." She gave a sharp nod. "I home-school that girl since day one. She never seen the inside of a public school, and already she got the universities of Duke, Princeton, Harvard, Yale, and Stanford banging down the door to get ahold of her. Not to mention ten dozen other schools we don't even wink at." She nodded hard again. "She going be somebody of noteworthy mention. I tell you."

Duke, I thought. Harvard and Yale. Stanford.

Shit.

I read. I've read all my life, and right then, right there, something started to twist in me, something had nothing to do with the matter at hand, namely what the hell was going to happen next. And I thought maybe that something had to do somehow with the word *jealousy.*

Here was Tabitha with offers already from places I'd only dreamed of.

"She got fifteen-twenty combined on her SAT, and she only a junior," Miss Dinah said.

Shit.

Then here came Tabitha, walking fast from the hallway that led out of the kitchen. She had some paper in her hand, her forehead all worried up, and I thought she was even more beautiful than last night.

Fifteen-twenty SAT. Shit.

I looked down at my plate and didn't feel like eating anymore.

"What you find, Missy Dorcas?" Unc said.

She sat beside him, spread the papers out on the table. She hadn't yet looked at me, and it seemed she had no plans of it, either. She started in with her hands, motioning and motioning, her eyes right on Unc, as though he knew exactly what she was saying.

"She get in, start to download the information," Miss Dinah said. Her eyes were on Tabitha, focused, translating. "Had seven baffles between the password and the line in." She paused, watched Tabitha.

Unc nodded.

"Once she make it in, she find the file you looking for." She paused, watched.

"Hello?" I said.

Still Tabitha motioned, eyes right on Unc: she made a fist, slapped it twice into the palm of her other hand. She crossed her arms, sat back.

"She say somebody find her." She paused. "Somebody know she in there monkeying round." Miss Dinah paused again, and now she looked down, shook her head. "Whoever it be cut her off. Just now."

Unc stopped with the hat.

I said, "Why is it everybody knows more about what's going on than me?"

Unc looked at me, then Tabitha. He said, "Do they know who you are?"

She moved her hands, all the while shaking her head. Miss Dinah said, "She had to break down seven baffles to get in, but she loaded in ten of her own on the way."

Unc gave a small smile at this. "You get anything?"

She quick moved the papers on the table, shuffled them, lay them back down again.

Unc set the hat on the table, touched the papers. "Just like I figured. Like every overeducated clod I ever run into, he's kept records of everything. Like someday somebody'd make a book out of it."

He looked at me. He said, "Here's your chance. Read these to me." He pushed the papers toward me until they touched the plate. He picked up his hat, started with it again.

Tabitha finally looked at me. She leaned back again, crossed her arms again.

I glanced at Miss Dinah, saw her arms crossed, too, waiting, like everybody else, for me.

I pushed the plate away, picked up the papers. They were printouts, at the top and bottom all kinds of garbage codes and whatnot. Stuff Tabitha'd done to get in wherever she'd gotten in.

She had a modem, of course, not to mention a computer, a laser printer.

I had an alarm clock at home whose hands glowed in the dark: about the extent of the technology I had going for me. But I'd worked with computers at school, had read enough magazines, and a couple books, to know it wasn't easy to steal mail. Or lawful.

"Read," Unc said.

"This is somebody's e-mail?" I said. "You stole this?"

Tabitha let out a hard sigh: *Get on with it!*

I took a breath, said, "There's the stuff at the top. All this first page says is, 'Meet with Pigboy Wednesday. Got the goods, good to go.' " I stopped, the rest of this page blank.

"Next," Unc said.

I turned the page, more codes at the top. This one was a little longer. " 'Turn left at CR221, follow to Pigboy roost, thirteen miles, for pickup. Maersk Line at Chucktown Terminal, container 1118, will wait for you. Crate up goods, lots of popcorn. Next parcel to the boss man. We be seeing you.' "

Tabitha was watching me. Both she and her momma had their arms crossed, heads tilted the exact same way.

"This making any sense to anybody here?" I said, and both of them quick cut their eyes to Unc.

"Next," Unc said.

I looked at the next page, read, " 'CMS fucking pain—' " and stopped, looked up.

Miss Dinah slowly shook her head, eyes narrowed down to nothing. "They be evil people," she whispered. " 'The tongue also is a fire, a world of evil among the parts of the body. It corrupts the whole person, sets the course of his life on fire, and is itself set on fire by hell.' James three: sixteen, King James Bible." She paused. "You read they words. You go ahead, and let evil reveal itself."

I looked at Tabitha. She hadn't moved.

" 'Pain in the ass,' " I went on. " 'Gone maverick on us. All measures must be taken. Pigboy and Fatback notified, sent packing. Must be voided by 11/24. And? LD put away, of course, if he gets in the way.' "

"LD," Unc said. "One guess who that is."

Miss Dinah said, "Leland Dillard."

He whispered, "None other."

"CMS?" I said, though I thought I already knew.

"You saw the man day before yesterday," Unc said. "There between stand seventeen and eighteen." He paused. "Dr. Charles Middleton Simons."

We sat there, no sound at all, for a long time, that hat twirling slow as ever.

Finally, I said, "Whose files are these? Whose mail?"

Unc stood, took his stick from the bookshelves behind him. He said, "Your friend and mine, Dr. Cleve Ravenel."

Cleve Ravenel, I thought. Cleve Ravenel. The cherry-red Ram 2500 with the black bed liner. The red-faced and white-haired club member with a beer gut that made his belt buckle disappear.

The one who'd turned too quick, scared when Unc called out his name, asked him to meet with whoever was responding to our call about a body with not much of a head left.

And look who'd responded: Yandle, Thigpen.

Pigboy and Fatback?

Unc started for the door. We were on. Going.

I said, "And who sent this stuff? Who did these come from?"

"That's a fine question," he said, and pulled the door open. "You just fold these up and keep them in your back pocket." He stopped, turned from the door to us. "If I know anything at all about the way these things work, it's easier to find out what the message is than who's the messenger." He looked past me, smiled. "Ain't that right, Missy Dorcas?"

I heard her chair scrape against the kitchen floor, turned, saw her standing, smiling at him. Then her eyes were on me, and she handed me the papers, already folded square, and it seemed for a second she was looking me over.

Cold air fell in from the open door, and I think I shivered.

Tabitha made a quick move with her hands.

"You watch your mouth, child," Miss Dinah said. "Who taught you to talk like that?"

Tabitha grinned, pointed to Unc, nodded hard.

"What'd she say?" I asked Miss Dinah, but it was Unc to answer.

"I'll wager her turn of phrase was a short and simple 'Damn straight,' " Unc said. He was grinning now, too.

I looked back at Tabitha. She had a hand over her mouth, shoulders moving up and down, the same laugh she'd given me when I'd fallen in the ditch last night. Only now it was at her momma, scowling down at her from there at the kitchen counter. "I appreciate you don't corrupt my only child any more than she already is," she said.

"Yes, ma'am," Unc said, and nodded. "Missy Dorcas's next assignment is, if you can make sure you ain't going to get yourself identified, to try and poke around, get hold somehow of who the bad boy sent these might be."

She motioned, shrugged. Miss Dinah said, "She say she try but can't promise nothing."

"All I can ask for," Unc said, and Tabitha turned, headed back down that hallway crammed with bookshelves.

But at the last second, just before she disappeared, she looked back over her shoulder. She gave me the smallest wave, just her fingertips.

I smiled, nodded.

"Lose whatever idea you got in your head right now, you hear?" Miss Dinah said. She missed even less than Tabitha. "You hear?"

"What do you mean, Miss Dinah?" I said. "I was just saying good-bye."

"Lose it," she said, and crossed her arms.

"Yes, ma'am," I said.

Unc looked from me to where Miss Dinah stood to me, puzzled. But it wasn't enough to make him stop what he was working on in his head. He said, "I believe these boys we're dealing with will play by their own rules. They told Huger last night we have forty-eight hours before they're going to do whatever it is they're going to do. I believe you have nothing to worry about." He paused. "For another thirty-six hours or so, I guess."

"You guess," she said. "What happens then?"

Unc took in a breath, said, "We'll burn that bridge when we get to it."

He turned, went out onto the porch, and started down the cinder blocks, while I stood there in a shanty flooded with books, just watching him. Then he was off into the woods behind the house, on the trail back to the shed.

"You be careful, child," Miss Dinah said from behind me, right there at my back. "That man dangerous if he want to be. But you the one he really counting on. You the only one can feel what he feel about what you both stand to lose in all this." She patted me on the back. "You the one he counting on, but he be the last one to let you know."

Then for some reason I looked up, above the door, and saw up there about the only other bit of wall not covered over with book-shelves.

Here was their picture of Jesus, but it was a picture like none I'd ever seen before. It wasn't one of those prefab things, Him here with his robe open and heart bleeding, all wild and sharp colors made to make you wince. This one was just a penciled Jesus, pretty poorly drawn, looking down on us. No smile, no sorrow. Just a man in a robe looking down, watching, like all he had to do was wait and see what each of us chose to do with our lives. Like it was up to us what was going to happen, one way or the other.

It seemed about the truest painting of the man I'd ever seen.

"Benjamin drew that for us," Miss Dinah said. "Bless his heart."

"It's beautiful, ma'am," was all I could think to say, and I looked at it a moment longer before I stepped outside, started after Unc, already disappeared back inside the woods.

12

We made it to the Luv, buried there in the high weeds off the road, and once I was actually onto the blacktop, out here in the world again and in my own truck, it seemed that world was watching one more time, could see exactly what we were up to.

Even if I had no idea what we were up to.

"Is this a good idea?" I said. "Just hauling around in the truck so's anybody could spot us?"

Unc looked straight ahead. "You told me Thigpen said nobody cares where we're hiding. So we're going to take him at his word. Testing the waters." He nodded at the road. "So you just drive on over to the trailer. We need to shower, get some clean clothes on."

"Unc," I nearly shouted now, "we need to shower? Unc, there's no time for this. We got to do something. We got to—"

"Drive," he snapped. "Now. To the trailer."

I looked at him a second longer, then jammed it into gear, hit the gas.

"You settle down now, boy, or you and I both will be dead," he said. He turned to me, put his hand on my arm, gripped it until the pain started in on me too much, and I let my foot off the gas a bit.

"You got to know," he said, "that unless we keep our heads on straight, we'll both be dead. Do you understand this?" Still he hadn't let go my arm, and finally I jerked it free of him.

"Do you understand?" he said again.

I could feel my eyes going hot, the back of my neck.

"Huger?" he said, calm now.

"Yes," I said.

"We keep our heads on straight longer than they can, and we'll win this thing." He looked out his window, then back to me. "You blink, you lose. They already made one mistake. Cleve Ravenel did."

I was quiet, knew he was waiting for me to ask after what that mistake might be. And of course I bit, but only once I'd let a full minute or so of silence go by.

I said, "What mistake was that?"

He held up his hand, the index finger. "Cleve Ravenel took too long coming back with Yandle and Thigpen Saturday. He comes back, says he got lost. But he's been a member of the club over thirty years now. Since before I made sergeant on the force. He shoots turkey out here, knows every parcel near well as I do. I know this, so when he says he got lost, just for fun I let this finger drag along his front quarter panel."

"And you come up with mud."

He turned to me. He smiled. "You were paying attention. A boy after my own heart. Now if you were really paying attention, Huger, you'll tell me the rest of what happened."

I thought about what I saw, then gave the steering wheel a slap. "Then you dragged it on the front quarter panel of Yandle's cruiser. You wiped it off."

"And?" he said.

"And he didn't have any mud. So Cleve Ravenel went somewheres Yandle and Thigpen didn't."

"Who gives a damn about fifteen-twenty on the SAT when you

figure out something like that?" he said, and put his hand down on his leg.

I didn't say anything. It wasn't that funny.

"So Cleve Ravenel slipped somehow," he went on. "For some reason. He went somewhere he ought not to have gone, because if he hadn't, he wouldn't have been late. Mistake one. And hence why I figured to get Missy Dorcas to scour his garbage can. I never met a pompous ass who didn't keep all proof of his pomposity. And now we know something about CMS and about Charleston Terminal and about goods."

"And about LD," I said.

"None other."

I looked at him, his mouth straight, a thin line.

I said, "You think Pigboy and Fatback are Yandle and Thigpen?"

"Possibility," he said. "We'll find out once we hit mile thirteen on County Road 221. A detail out of the electronic trash heap: CR221, thirteen miles to Pigboy roost. Our first stop after we hit the showers. I don't know where either of them live, Yandle or Thigpen. But we'll find out."

"Are goods drugs, you think?"

"Possibility, too. Whatever it is, it's crated up in popcorn and sent out by container ship. Maersk Line." He paused. "But why pack it in popcorn? Why crate it up? You want drugs out of here, you do like everybody else: hire a Puerto Rican out of Miami and load up his Pinto, send him on his way up I-95. Charleston Terminal." He shrugged, slowly turned to me. "So what was this between you and Miss Dinah? What's this about you losing an idea?"

I looked at him. "I thought nothing got past you."

"What gave you that idea?"

"Past experience. But apparently a few things do get past you."

"On occasion." He shrugged again.

I looked back at the road. Here was coming the intersection with Ferry Road, Hungry Neck and the trailer only a couple minutes from here.

I said, "Then I'm keeping hold of this one. See how long it takes for you to figure this one out."

There was Mom's Stanza, parked out front of the trailer.

Shit. *Mom*.

I let off the gas a second too soon for seeing her car, and Unc said, "What's wrong?"

"Mom's here."

"Dammit to hell," he whispered, and I pulled up, parked beside the car.

We climbed out, the two of us too slow for the knowledge of what was about to come: Mom flying out the door and right at our throats.

And what were we going to tell her? To let us alone, to trust Unc to whatever plan he had of dealing with people named Pigboy and Fatback who, as far as we could tell, had voided Charles Middleton Simons? Was I supposed to tell her about Thigpen and being chased on the Mark Clark, about two assholes in a pickup truck rolled off the freeway? About a gun pointed inside the cab?

A gun.

I looked over the roof of the Luv at Unc, who was looking at the trailer. Then he leaned back into the cab, pulled his stick from beneath the bench seat, and stood straight again.

"Unc," I said.

"We got to face her at one point or another," he said. "You just let me talk."

"Unc," I said, and he turned to me. "I left the gun in the shed." I paused. "I forgot it."

Then he leaned the stick against the hood, undid the middle button on his shirt. He pulled open the shirt for me, and I could see the white of his T-shirt, and the gun, tucked into his pants.

"Only a few things get past me." He pulled it out, moved around the hood. He handed the gun to me, even thicker, shinier than last night.

I tucked it in the front of my pants, inside the shirt. Just like Unc had, and buttoned up.

"But not much. Brought it with me when I left you in the shed this morning." He nodded, moved back to the stick. "Now let's go face the music."

I pushed open the door, hollered, "Mom?"

I figured she'd meet us on the porch, but she hadn't, and now here we were in the front room of the trailer.

No different from any other time I'd ever entered: the place spotless, the shag carpet vacuumed fresh so you could count the number of strokes it took, only a few footprints in it from us walking through it Saturday morning.

Fifteen strokes is how many it took, to be exact. I'd vacuumed enough times.

To the right was the orange-and-brown plaid foldout sofa I slept on under the bay window at the end of the trailer, and the TV on its stand, and Unc's brown La-Z-Boy, the coffee table with a stack of *Field & Stream*s.

To the left was the kitchen counter. Ours had stools on this side of it, and for a second I thought of all those books, and wondered if Tabitha might loan me some of hers sometime. Past the counter was the kitchen, clean as ever, not even a coffee ring from when I'd poured our two cups Saturday morning.

Everything perfect, like nobody'd been here.

Unc stepped in behind me, called, "Eugenie?"

Nothing.

I started for the kitchen, wanted to head back to the bedrooms, see if maybe she'd fallen asleep or something.

But Unc took hold of my arm, stopped me.

"No," he whispered. He was moving his head slowly, back and forth, chin up.

He was smelling the air.

I whispered, "What is it?"

He moved past me, let his hand touch the counter between the front room and the kitchen.

"Unc?"

He started for the back of the trailer, to the bedrooms.

"Unc, maybe I ought to go first," I said, and now I could feel myself starting to sweat, my chest pinching down on me, and I felt too the sudden heft of the gun, and I thought of drawing it, and now I started to smell the air myself.

I was looking for dark red, for metal. But I got nothing.

We were in the hall now, dark for the cheap wood paneling all the walls in here had. He moved slowly, the stick in hand, the other hand to the wall, feeling it, feeling it, and then we were at my mom and dad's old room, which I'd never slept in, even though there was a bed in there, waiting. It was the foldout bed I slept in. Not there.

We passed it, headed down the hall, maybe for Unc's room, the one I'd had as a kid. He kept it as clean as the rest of the house, his bed always perfectly made, the clothes in his drawers neatly stacked. On his dresser sat photos of Aunt Sarah and him, and of me, and of Mom, and one of Dad, too. He had that antler I found for him on it, and that jay's nest, the eagle feather.

But we passed that room as well, the only room left the bathroom at the end of the hall, the door partway open, the light on.

"Mom?" I called out, hoped one last time she might simply be in there, or maybe, I thought, outside, and I stopped, said, "I'm checking outside."

Unc kept walking, his hand out in front of him, and then he pushed open the door. He paused in the doorway, stepped in.

I held my breath. I bit down on that tear in my cheek, just for the pain of it.

"Huger," Unc said, my name low and solid. "Come in here."

I didn't move, pressed my back against the cheap wood paneling, closed my eyes, and felt that gun I had on me, bigger now.

"Huger," he said. "I need you."

I moved in, saw Unc at the sink, his hand up to the mirror on the medicine cabinet above it.

"What does it say?" he said, fingers to the glass.

There, in the mirror, was written in red lipstick:

BE HERE
AT 9:00
OR YOUR
FUCKED

Beneath it was taped a photograph. It was a Polaroid, and it was of my mother, just her face, behind her cheap wood paneling, the makeup from her eyes running in streaks down her cheeks, her mouth covered in silver duct tape.

I only looked at it, then reached past him, took the photo off.

Unc moved his fingers, smearing the message a little, the letters bleeding now.

"What does it say?" he said, and turned to me.

I sat on the toilet, the photo in both hands, looking at it. My mother. And I could see she was looking at me, that it was *me* she was thinking on when they'd taken it, whoever'd taken it.

Here were the tears, the hot feel of blood to my face, and I looked up, saw Unc, the stick leaned against the wall behind him, and he touched my shoulder.

He whispered, "What does it say?"

" 'Be here at nine o'clock or you're fucked,' " I whispered back, the words choked down, tough in my throat, sharp as knives. I whispered, "They took a picture of her."

He stood up straight, took his hand from my shoulder. He said, "Is she all right?" His lips barely moved, his teeth tight together.

I looked back at the picture. "She's alive."

He exploded then, screamed out louder than I'd ever heard before, just shouted, his head back, mouth open wide, and he turned, took the stick in his hands, held it like a club, and smashed the mirror with it.

I sat there, watched, the photo in my hands.

Then he headed into the hallway, ducked into his room, where he started banging away at everything, and in the sounds of glass—he'd hit the windows in there, busted them out—I heard mixed in the sounds of everything on his dresser cleared off, the stick smashing everything. Then he was in the hallway, and I heard him slam along the walls and on into the kitchen, screaming the whole way.

There were no words, only his screams, up from his gut and heart, while I only sat there, in my hands some ugly proof: my mom gone, kidnapped.

He smashed at the cabinets in there, the sound of the stick a hollow thud against the wood, and then I heard plates, heard glasses breaking and things falling. Then came more glass, the heavy shatter of the window above the sink in there, and I stood from the toilet, looked out into the hallway, saw him stagger into the front room, saw him swing at the TV, saw the thing explode with a clap of sound something like thunder.

And then he started in on the bay window, swung and swung and swung, glass exploding out, and now I ran for him down that hall and into the front room, him still swinging, breaking, screaming, and I tackled him into the sofa.

I knocked the wind from him, Unc down, the stick still tight in his hands, the two of us there on the sofa, above us cold air coming in, cold November air at Hungry Neck, while somewhere my mom was being held, her mouth taped over.

Unc's mouth moved, gasping for air, but I didn't move off him, only held him, pinned to the sofa. I'd knocked his sunglasses and hat off, saw his marble eyes, the lids, gnarled and flat, moving open and closed, open and closed, like some near-dead deer gutshot, unable to move.

That was when I sat up off him, and finally, finally, he took in a breath, took it in big, those gnarled lids closing while Unc breathed again.

He let go the stick, and it fell to the carpet, then put his hands to his face, covered his eyes, and cried.

It was a strange sound, as strange as the screams he'd made, and came from the same heart and gut. It was a broken sound, too, an

old man's sob, cluttered up with more pain than I'd known this far
in my life, and I wondered for a second if he wasn't crying somehow
for Aunt Sarah.

And I heard then my own crying, crying for Mom, and I took in
a breath, another one, and another, as though it'd been me tackled,
the wind knocked out of, and I looked at the picture of Mom in my
hand, crumpled now for the fists I'd made running down the hall
toward Unc, and I saw in those same eyes, the ones looking at *me,*
that in fact we were all she had. Unc and me.

She needed us.

I said, "You told me this was no field trip. This is the real thing."
I stopped, breathed in and out, looked again at the picture. "You
make a mistake, you die. You blink, you lose." I felt the air down on
my shoulders, felt myself shiver. The room was a wreck, the kitchen
cupboards emptied, everything on the floor. Smoke rose from the
broken TV.

I said, "Don't blink." I took in a breath. "We have to hold on."

He took in quick breaths, tried to catch up with his own breathing. Slowly he sat up, his hands still to his eyes. He whispered, "I
didn't want Eugenie in on this. Nor you. I didn't want any of this
to happen." He took more quick breaths, wheezed with them in.
"None of it," he whispered.

I turned to him. There was more, I knew, to all this than just a call
from Constance Dupree Simons on Wednesday night. There was
more. I said, "How long has this been coming?"

He said, "They been on me for almost two years now."

"Who?"

He took his hand down, those lids still closed. This was my uncle,
a blind man, face deformed for a fire he'd been in.

"Delbert Yandle," he said. "Doug's daddy. Over to Walterboro.
Yandle Development. He's two-bit, a shitass to boot. But somehow
he's come up with a wad of money." Unc just sat there, hand in his
lap, shirt all pulled out, his right suspender off his shoulder. "Two
years," he said. "Almost."

"But what does Cleve Ravenel have to do with any of this?" I said. "And Simons? And Miss Constance? And why do they want Mom?"

He turned to me. He opened his eyes: those white marbles. And it seemed he saw me, seemed to me those marbles were the real thing. He took in another breath, this one a big one.

"That's what we got to figure out." He paused. "That, and why these boys aren't playing by their own rules."

"What do you mean?"

"You said Thigpen give us forty-eight hours. Now they shaved it down to nine o'clock tonight." He stopped, swallowed, took in a breath. "That gives us eight hours."

I looked at him, looked at him, tried as hard as I could to remember back before the fire, to what he'd looked like then, to what his eyes were like, his face. I tried to remember him before.

But all I could see was Mom, her face, the tape, her eyes speaking to me, and my own eyes filled, my breath gone again, on my chest a weight I could feel trying to kill me.

"Thank you," he said. "For taking me down." He paused. "For making sure neither of us blink."

I tried at breathing in, tried at it again, then felt, finally, his hand on my shoulder, him holding me, and then the breath came, and I swallowed, whispered, "It's because I need you," the words as broken as the window behind us, the air out of me just as cold.

"Likewise," he whispered.

13

It wasn't County Road 221 we went for first at all.

It was Hungry Neck.

We left the trailer, headed right back into the land like we'd started out on Saturday morning, headed down Lannear Road toward the levee, around us the heavy shroud of oak and pine, everywhere a cold kind of lushness, winter on its way. We were headed back, Unc informed me only once we were in the Luv, to try and find precisely where Cleve Ravenel lost his way.

Cherish your momma, Constance'd told me, when all I'd done was abandon her back to the house in North Charleston, led her out here only to get kidnapped, sucked in deeper than Unc and me both.

Cherish your momma. Good advice. But it'd been given to me, an idiot. Just me. Just nothing.

We reached the levee, where Lannear hits Levee Road going to the right and left. To the left, the road headed back toward those stands we'd been letting men off at on Saturday morning. Unc said, "Stop here."

Here was beside that clear-cut field, not far from where Patrick and Reynold had let out the dogs.

I looked out across the field, dry white weeds no different from the ones I'd parked the Luv in last night, and the levee itself to the right of it all, a twenty-foot rise of dirt.

Unc said, "What time was it when Cleve left?"

I looked at him. "You mean when you sent him off?"

"Yep."

I shrugged. "I don't know. Maybe six-fifteen? Six-thirty?"

"Turn right."

I turned to the right, followed the back side of the levee. We rotated which parcels we used for hunts and were headed back deep now onto the property, back to parcels we wouldn't be using until near Christmas.

If ever again, I thought.

"Six-fifteen would have been no more than an hour off high tide," Unc said as we bucked through a low spot, that shroud even heavier, the lane narrower the deeper we got. "Go toward the river when we hit Trestle Road, then take the fork off to the right."

I had an idea now what he was thinking, and here came Trestle, Levee Road dead-ending into it.

It was called Trestle Road because it led up to the trestle, though it was gone now, taken down by the WPA, Unc told me once, in some sort of project supposed to keep people working, never mind it was dismantling and not building. But by the 1930s the lumber trains were long gone anyway, the land stripped bare. The track bed still ran through the property, only the gravel left, the tracks themselves hauled away as well for scrap by the same boys took down the trestle.

This was one of my favorite places when I was a kid, where the track bed started its slow rise up to where the trestle used to be. I'd ride my bike all the way back here and on that track bed, and then, at the top, there where the bed ended in a man-made bluff on the bank of the Ashepoo, I'd stop, look both ways up and down the river bending away from me on both sides, the trees right up to the edge of the river like giant men on horseback, I used to think, watching over all the marsh.

Hungry Neck. Our land.

But that didn't matter now. They had Mom. They had her.

Straight across from the bluff and on the other side of the river was the marsh, stretching wide all the way to Edisto, littered across it all those green islands, nameless, empty, the only remains of the trestle out in the marsh the black tips of pylons now and again stretching off into the distance, like the spine of some huge dead animal. Nothing more.

"Stop," Unc said, and I hit the brakes. We were parallel to the tracks, the dead end of this fork of Trestle Road another quarter mile or so.

Unc climbed out, stick in hand, and I followed.

Not ten yards in front of the Luv was where the road dipped lowest, where at high tide a finger off the Ashepoo found its way in, covered the road in a good six inches of water.

He'd found it blind, ticked off in his head the distance as we drove, the directions I'd turned, worked out in his head even the tide tables.

Hungry Neck was his.

We knelt at the low spot, the road muddy still, twice a day covered with water. And there, clear and clean and obvious as a message in lipstick or a homemade tattoo, were the tracks: two of them, big tires, perfect for a Ram 2500 four-by-four.

"There you go," I said. "Tire tracks right on through." I stood. Up ahead the trees started to thin, past them the river, I knew, and the marsh. "Here's where he went through," I said.

But then it came to me: What did this prove? Where was he headed?

Unc still hadn't stood, only touched at the low spot with his hand, the stick beside him on the ground. "Tracks, you say."

"Yessir," I said. "Four tire tracks, two for each side, right and left, front and rear." I paused. "But what does this prove? Where was he headed?"

"Damned if I know," Unc whispered, and now he took hold of the stick and stood. "And you say there's tracks, four of them."

"Yessir."

"Well, then," he said, "what *else* do we not know?" He turned, seemed to look up to the track bed, then behind him, like he was hearing something.

"About what?" I said. "There's a whole lot I don't know."

"About, for instance, these tracks." He looked at me. "Think, Huger."

I looked down, saw the tracks, four of them for four tires, leading on down into the low spot and back out the other side.

Four tracks. One for each tire.

There should have been eight. Four for on the way in, four for on the way out. Trestle Road dead-ended right up ahead.

I looked up at Unc, still with his head turning one way and the other, listening, smelling. I said, "He never came back through here."

"You got that right," he said. "There's hope for you yet."

We drove the quarter mile on to the end, climbed out, looked around. No tracks anywhere, the ground hard packed. The road widened into a cul-de-sac of sorts, a turnaround for after we'd dropped off men at the stands leading out here. The track bed was here right next to us, a good thirty feet high. There were only a few trees between us and the river, and I walked to it, stood there on the bank.

Here they were, those giants on horseback, watching, waiting.

And the marsh, all the colors of spartina and yellow grass, of salt-marsh hay and bulrushes: greens, yellows, browns, reds, all under an afternoon sky, cool and crisp.

My mom was gone.

I turned, went for the Luv, climbed in, saw only once I was settled in that Unc was halfway up the track bed, his hand feeling the ground, feeling it.

I hollered, "Only way he made it out of here was with his four-wheel-drive. I ain't got that, so there's no use, Unc." I paused. "It's almost two o'clock. We got places to go."

Unc started down through the weeds straight to the Luv and climbed in. He said, "County Road 221 is on the way to Walterboro. That's handy."

"Walterboro?" I said.

"Yandle Real Estate and Development, Delbert Yandle, Proprietor," he said. "We're going to pay a visit to a two-bit shitass with a son after his own heart."

I wheeled the Luv around, started back.

"Forgive me," he said, and I looked at him. Shadows in through his window flew across him, the afternoon sun in a November sky quick on its way down.

I said nothing, because there was no blaming him for all of this. I had my own to ask for as well, I knew, and I gave it the gas, gunned it even through that low spot, mud on our quarter panels now, too, I was certain. We had places to go.

14

Pigboy Roost turned out to be nothing, only a spot on a road that led out of Jacksonboro proper, the road between the fire station and the Road to Emmaeus AME Church. But it was thirteen miles we had to head back on it, for nothing. We got there, saw only wet-lands, the upper end of Snuggedy Swamp. Not even a dead refriger-ator or washing machine.

We cruised a mile beyond it, then a couple miles back toward Jacksonboro, just in case my odometer wasn't working right, me the whole while looking, looking. But there was nothing. Only swamp.

"Should've known," Unc said finally, and slapped hard his knee, shook his head. "Just a place to pick up goods. Just a drop site, nothing else."

I drove.

I had no clue what it was had been big about Walterboro once, whether it was cotton or if there was a mill here or if it was some ma-jor lumbering operation, a depot for all the wood taken off Hungry Neck and everywhere else down here.

But it'd been a hub, which accounted for the big pillared homes on the main street through town, all of them perfect and manicured, like sooner or later Scarlett was going to ride up in her buggy.

And the land, too, was strange, suddenly these small hills beside 64, a small twist to the blacktop, geography out of nowhere here in the middle of the Lowcountry.

Now, as we pulled into town, the blacktop twisting, those weeny hills picking up around us, these pillared homes reminded me of the waste of time a thirteen-mile drive into swampland was. The day was quick on its way to dying, my mom somewhere and scared to death while we took a drive in the country.

"Past the stores and whatnot after the light. First house on the right past the light," Unc said. "White pillars. May be a sign hanging out front."

We pulled up to the light at the main intersection, all yellow brick storefronts: a tailor, an ABC store, an Ace Hardware. The light changed, and I pulled through.

There it was, just past Jax Lawn Mower Repair and Snapper Store: YANDLE REAL ESTATE AND DEVELOPMENT in red and blue letters on a white background, hanging from a white signpost.

A pillared house, perfect lawn, rocking chairs on the porch. Live oaks.

"Don't look two-bit to me," I said, and turned into the circular drive.

"Two-bit," Unc said, his hand to the dash, "is a matter of the heart." He nodded, agreeing with himself. "We went to school together. Might have been a friend of Delbert's, if the Lord hadn't been so kind to me as He has." I stopped the car, square in front of the brick steps up to the porch.

He turned to me. "I don't know what we'll turn up in here. But you don't say word one. Don't." He put his hand on my arm. "It don't matter if he knows something about your momma or not. It don't matter. What matters is what we can get this man to volunteer without thinking he's volunteered a whit. So you just keep quiet."

I said, "Yessir," and turned off the engine. I turned to him. "Should I bring in the gun?"

He looked out the windshield. "Today, you're carrying," he said. "If it was any other day, I wouldn't let you do this. But today." He stopped, slowly turned to me. "Today." He popped open his door, climbed out.

I led him up the steps and to the door, a big oak thing with an oval pane of glass set into the middle, etched in it a huge medieval *R*. I let go Unc's arm, made to reach for the doorknob, but Unc pushed it open before I could even touch it.

He walked right in, me behind him, the stick never touching ground.

"Oh," a woman said, her voice a little chirp of sound. "Oh. Oh."

She had on a low-cut blouse and sat at a huge desk, eyes open wide. She had orangish blond hair, boofed out frizzy and long, the bangs sticking straight up in a kind of spray across her forehead. A big-hair gal. Then she stood, and I could see the low-cut blouse was also one of those white see-through-but-not-really-see-through kinds. She had on a flowered bra, pink leather miniskirt.

"Leland Dillard to see Delbert Yandle," Unc said, and walked forward until he touched the desk.

"Oh." I could tell she knew who he was, her mouth all pursed up, eyebrows together: she'd been warned about him.

The desk sat in the middle of what'd once been the foyer, the wood floor shining. Behind the desk was a staircase that led to a window, turned, disappeared on up. The desktop was nearly empty, on it only a lamp, a phone, a tablet of paper on a green blotter. Next to the tablet sat an open bottle of nail-polish remover, three or four cotton balls.

"Ma'am?" Unc said. "Will you tell him I'm here, or will I simply have to intrude upon his highness?"

"Um," she said, and picked up the phone, pushed a button. Three nails on the hand with the receiver were still red.

She listened, her eyes going from Unc to me for a second, then back to Unc. "Uh-huh," she said, then hung up. "He's in there." She nodded to our left.

Unc nodded. "Thank you, ma'am."

I led him to a door to our left, black oak, crystal doorknob. Beside it stood one of those rotating real estate signs, the kind with photographs of places and a line or two about each tacked on. I only saw it for a second, but it looked like every property on there was a trailer.

I pushed open the door, let Unc in first.

There, leaning against the front of his desk, arms crossed, head tilted to one side, stood a man with hair as boofed out as the woman's, only his looked shellacked into place. He was tan, had on a pink button-down and striped tie, black pants, leather suspenders. Slowly he shook his head, smiling.

"Brought the Cub Scouts today, I see," this Delbert Yandle said, and laughed, like he'd actually said something funny.

Unc walked to the middle of the room, stopped. He let the stick touch the ground, and I turned, pushed the door closed.

And heard a commotion, papers tossed, something heavy hit the floor, a grunt and tussle. I turned around, saw Unc had Delbert Yandle on his back on the floor, the stick across his throat, Unc sitting on Yandle's chest, his knees pinning down Yandle's shoulders.

Unc's face was right down in Yandle's, the bill of his cap jammed into Yandle's forehead. "You get your boy and Thigpen out of my affairs now, or I'll kill you," Unc hissed, and I could see Yandle's face screw up, him trying to get air.

I took a couple steps toward them, wondered what it was I was supposed to do. Unc'd told me not to say a word. But now Yandle's face was turning too red, the sound he was giving out something past a gasp.

I said, "Unc. He's not breathing."

"Seems a personal problem to me," Unc said.

"Unc," I said. "This won't get Mom here."

Unc held him there, held him. Then, finally, he eased off, but only a little, and Yandle drew in shallow breaths. "I don't know what the fuck you're talking about," he whispered.

"I'm talking about Eugenie," Unc said, his voice all normal now, calm.

"I don't know what you mean."

Unc put the stick into his throat again, leaned again into it, maybe even a little harder. "Eugenie Dillard," he hissed again. "Eugenie."

And now Delbert Yandle was looking at me, and here came that red again. Only this time there wasn't even any sound coming out of him, not even that sound past a gasp. Nothing, and the color was going to purple now, and then a kind of blue started in.

I don't know, I don't know, he mouthed again and again.

"Unc," I said, touched his shoulder.

Unc held him that way a second more, then let him go altogether, stood up, all in a second. He took the tip of the stick, put it straight to Yandle's jaw, jammed it in the flesh beneath it.

Yandle only lay there, arms flat on the floor, his chest heaving in and out. He whispered, "All's I want to do is buy your fucking property, Leland. I offered you a good deal more than it's worth, and that offer still stands." He grabbed another breath. "Even if you come in here and try to kill me over my own dickhead of a son. And I know a dozen Thigpens."

"Where'd you get money?" I said, and Unc jerked a little toward me, surprised at my voice. But here was the man wanted to buy Hungry Neck, and Unc had him by the throat. How many more chances would I have?

"Where'd you get all this money," I went on, "when all you sell is trailers?"

Delbert Yandle glanced at me, couldn't move his head for the tip of the stick at his jaw.

He swallowed, or tried to. "Investors," he said, and swallowed again. "Want to make it a preserve. Want to make it a wildlife refuge and a—"

Unc jammed the tip a little deeper.

"Want to make it another Hilton Head," Yandle whispered. "Like what they're doing to Daufuskee. Golf courses, condominiums."

Unc looked at me over his shoulder. "Does anybody ever have a *new* idea about what to do with land, except pave it over?" He turned back to Yandle. "And who might these investors be?"

"I don't know," he whispered. "I get faxes from Nashville, Atlanta, Miami, Charlotte." He pulled in a breath again, whispered again, "I don't know," then, "Ain't you ever seen a patsy before?"

Unc leaned the tip a little harder into him. "One more time. Does your son have Eugenie, and where are they?"

"I disowned him three years ago," he choked out.

Unc froze, eased off the stick.

I said, "Disowned him?"

Unc'd given up most all pressure on the man's throat, lost on the news, and slowly Yandle reached up, took hold of the tip, pushed it away. He looked at me, then Unc. "Like I said, he's a dipshit. Haven't talked to him in five years. Still owes me over twenty-two thousand dollars, spent on what I have no clue." He swallowed. "Look at his career decision. You yourself can testify what a losing proposition law enforcement is. And of the dozen or so Thigpens I know, not a one of them will speak to me or to my son. But if the one you're after is any acquaintance of Doug's, he's got to be a dickhead too."

He sat all the way up now, hands in his lap, his chest still going. "This is going to be the hardest six percent I ever come by," he said, his eyes right on Unc. "But it's coming, Leland Dillard. And when it comes, I'm going to be the signing agent, whether you give a damn or not."

Unc turned to him, broken out of whatever thought it was going on in him with the news Yandle junior'd been disowned.

Unc whispered, "Over my dead body."

Yandle chuckled, touched at his throat. The pink button-down collar'd lost a button, the tie all twisted and pulled. A suspender'd popped off his pants, too, for Unc on top of him.

He chuckled again, said, "You just never know, now, do you?"

The door burst open then, and in came the woman. "Oh," she chirped again, and "Oh, oh, oh." She knelt to Yandle, touched at his collar, his shoulder, his tie, then looked up at Unc, said, "Sue the bastard, Del. Just sue this cracker white-trash cripple. Assault and battery, Del. Sue him."

Unc nodded at her. "Ma'am," he said, and headed for the door.

But there was something about the two of them, there on the floor, and in the way she'd talked to Unc that made me want to finish this. It was a temptation, I knew, but I gave in to it.

I looked at them, shook my head. "Won't look good in the papers," I said. "You having Unc arrested. TRAILER SALESMAN WITH HELMET HAIR BEAT UP BY BLIND MAN." I shrugged. "It just won't look good."

Yandle chuckled again. "You ain't as stupid as everybody says you are," he said, and rubbed at his throat again.

Then Unc had hold of my sleeve, pulled me through the doorway, and we were gone.

15

"Disowned the boy," Unc said. He took a sip off his drink, set it between his feet on the floorboard, then found the burger where he'd set it on the dash, took a bite. "I wonder if he even has anything to do with this."

We were on 64 headed out of town, had stopped at a Hardee's, where a black girl took our order: a Frisco Burger, a small fries, and two Mr. Pibbs.

I wasn't eating, though Unc'd told me I needed to. My stomach was gone, Mom somewhere. Somewhere. And I wondered what that Hardee's girl would think of the story I could tell her: murder, kidnapping, suicide.

And now Unc was thinking maybe Yandle wasn't a part of the story we couldn't tell anybody.

I said, "But Unc, he was there at the hospital." I took a sip of my Mr. Pibb, set it in the cup holder hanging from the window well. "Pointed at me like he was shooting me."

"So he's an idiot. So what? Thinks he's Chuck Connors as the Rifleman." He took a few fries from the box wedged between his legs.

"Likes to hang out with the big dogs, hoping someday they'll throw him a bone. Maybe let him wear one of their windbreakers."

He chewed, said, "These need salt," and slapped open the glove box. He reached in, moved around napkins, a map, an old history paper I'd gotten an F on and didn't want to show to Mom.

Mom.

I looked at my watch: three-thirty.

"Gotcha," Unc said, and pulled out one of those salt packets they give you when you ask for them. He held it between his thumb and second finger, carefully broke it open by bending the top down with his first finger, then tipped it over, shook it out.

But he missed the fries, instead salted the seat above the box.

The packet empty, he dropped it in the empty Hardee's bag on the floorboard, then took up another couple of fries.

"Much better," he said. "On to Beverly Hills South: Mount Pleasant."

I shook my head. Even Unc missed the mark now and again. And, I knew, he was missing it with Yandle.

Walterboro to Mount Pleasant is a little over sixty miles one end to the other, and once we were through Parker's Ferry and Rantowles and Red Top, houses and shops and car dealerships picking up and picking up, we were there, right there: stopped at a light beside the Amoco station where a black woman in a red smock with an orange wave in her hair hadn't seen a thing.

Then we were at Citadel Mall, tooling right back up the Mark Clark in the opposite direction I'd come only last night, and I drove on up the ramp and onto the freeway north like it was my own, because in a way it was. I'd survived this, lived to tell the tale.

But it wasn't over yet. No way.

And then, maybe a mile farther on, I slowed down, looked across the median for some sign of where that yellow Ford pickup'd been rolled by Thigpen in his scab-roofed Plymouth. Just last night.

But there was nothing. Nothing at all, no evidence of those two rednecked peasants.

Two of them. Pigboy and Fatback?

Unc said, "What is it?"

"This is where Thigpen rolled them off. Those two bubbas."

"Maybe that's Fatback and Pigboy."

I turned to him, said, "There's hope for you yet."

He gave a small smile, nodded.

Then we crossed over I-26, and here we were, my neighborhood, just trees from up here, a glimpse now and again of asphalt shingles, a lawn, a car on blocks, all of it forty feet below and looking as simple and homey as can be.

But down there was Marie Street, and an empty house that smelled like dog shit when the wind blew right.

Marie Street, and my house. Mine and my mom's, and now, for the first time I could ever remember, I thought of it for a second as my home.

Empty. Mom nowhere I knew. Me on my way somewhere else.

I didn't even slow down. There were things to do.

We came down off the Mark Clark, there where it ended onto Old Georgetown Highway, and even me, a fifteen-year-old kid who had reason to be over here to Mount Pleasant maybe once or twice a year, remembered when Old Georgetown was a two-lane nothing, trees heavy down around it, dogs sitting on the shoulder and scratching.

Now.

Now there was a Super Lowe's hardware warehouse, a Wal-Mart with a McDonald's inside, a Piggly Wiggly the size of our high school, not to mention the Harris Teeter and Food Lion and Publix just as big. Art galleries, golf courses, a tenplex movie theater, twenty or thirty restaurants.

And Old Georgetown: five lanes, all those oaks taken down for it.

We turned off Old Georgetown at the first light and onto Bowman next to the big K mart, and here we were, where Unc'd led me with his directions: Imaging Network Services.

It was a low brick building, had a sign out front, IMAGING NET-
WORK SERVICES and the logo of a man lying on his back inside a circle, beneath that DR. JOE CRAY, M.D.

He hadn't told me who we were going to see, and I hadn't
asked, only followed where he told me to go. But I knew who this
guy was as soon as I saw his name: the fat radiologist with the unlit black cigar he was chewing on all the time. I knew his name because of how Unc picked on him and that cigar every deer-hunt
Saturday morning, after breakfast was over, Miss Dinah and Tabitha
cleaning up the paper plates and what have you, preparing already
for fried-chicken lunch. That was when the men'd gather around
the fire in a circle, then I'd usher Unc into the circle, and he'd ask
for a count-off. Each time he came to Dr. Cray he'd say, "Now,
don't get any big ideas on lighting up that cigar out on the stand,
you hear, Brother Cray?" and he'd answer, "Yes, Pappy," or some
such as this.

He was a good one, far as any of them went, in that if he talked
to me he made eye contact, smiled. Most all the others I was lucky
if I got a grunt out of when I helped haul in the deer they got.

I'd always wondered, too, if that cigar, even if he never lit it, ever
gave off enough smell to scare a deer. But then he'd shot that
fourteen-pointer New Year's Day of this year. End of that concern.

And then he'd quit the club.

"This one know we're coming in?" I asked. "Because it seems like
you caught Mr. Yandle back there a little off guard." I cut the engine. "And that was a nice job, too, of getting him to volunteer what
he didn't think he was volunteering. A stick to the throat. Who
would suspect a thing?"

"Called Dr. Cray this morning," Unc said, and climbed out.
"When I was at Miss Dinah's. While you were off sleeping and
dreaming on a sweet little black girl."

He knew.

How? What had Tabitha told him?

I climbed out, slammed shut my door. "There a problem with
that?"

"Not if you don't get a skillet to the head by her momma. And don't think for a minute she won't try." He reached in, got the stick. "No momma wants her daughter to marry beneath her. So get to studying for that SAT, Huger." He nodded, smiled.

"Married!" I said, too loud. "All I did was kiss her!"

"You did?" he said. He stood across the hood from me, looking at me. "I didn't know that."

"But you said—"

"I floated an idea at you. Run it up the flagpole, see if someone salutes. Damned if you didn't salute. In full dress uniform, no less." He paused, turned for the building. "Thanks for volunteering."

I watched him start up the steps of the place, tap out the ground with the stick. The steps were a couple feet deep, only rose the width of a brick on each one. He was having trouble, his steps small, a little fearful.

I wanted to make him do it himself, but I quick walked up to him, took his arm.

"Don't be expecting any tip," he said, and we started up.

"Brother Cray?" Unc hollered out. He'd pulled open the frosted glass panel, the waiting room empty, nobody in the reception area.

"Back here, you old fart," came Cray's answer.

I brought Unc into the office space back there, the walls on either side lined with color-coded files. At the end of the hall was a door standing open, the room it led into dark.

"Keep going," he called, and I could hear he was chomping down on a cigar, his words squeezed down tight. "Geez, you'd think you were blind or something," he said, and Unc laughed.

He sat on a roller chair at the far end of the room, in front of him a wall lit up, clipped all the way across X ray after X ray. Then he turned, still in the chair, rolled toward us.

"Brother Cray," Unc said, and put out his hand.

"Another membership drive?" Cray said, and shook Unc's hand hard. "You know I won't come back to your godforsaken Club Med for the blueblood bubba set. I don't work at the medical university anymore. Got my own digs now, got my own practice. Gave up that teaching stuff when I gave up my membership."

He stood, took the cigar out, slapped Unc's shoulder. "Good to see you, Leland." He was heavy with black hair disappearing on him, a beard, round wire-rimmed glasses, and it seemed strange to see him here, when the only place I'd ever seen him was out to Hungry Neck, him in his camos and orange cap like everybody else.

"You too," Unc said. "Though it looks like you been puttin' on a few since last you been down."

He jabbed at Cray's middle, made him flinch.

"That's what happens," he said, sitting back down and rolling himself back to the lighted wall, "when you don't get out and exercise regular like I used to down to Hungry Neck Hunt Club." He reached into his lab coat, pulled out a little thing looked like a monocular, pressed it up against one of the X rays. "What I need's a strict regimen like the one I used to get out your way: bacon and eggs before daylight, then piling into a pickup, then hopping out, sitting on a stump shivering my butt off, then picked up three hours later for a lunch of fried chicken and biscuits and gravy." He brought the thing down, moved to the next one. "Used to break a sweat just looking at those piles of bacon." Then he wheeled around to us again, said, "But enough about me. Tell me, what do *you* think of me?"

"I think we miss you down there."

"Maybe *you* do," he said, and now he scribbled something on the clipboard, looked up at the next X ray down. "But I know nobody else does. Except maybe for Tonto here. The silent one."

He glanced over his shoulder at me, went back to scribbling.

"You're the only one pulled in a fourteen-pointer in nine years," I said. "That counts in my book."

I looked to Unc, wanted to see if it'd been all right for me to talk to the man, if I hadn't disobeyed in this.

He was smiling at me, shaking his head.

"My bon voyage," Cray said. "My farewell performance. And do you think one of those turds could come up and congratulate me?

Not on your life." He looked at another X ray, scribbled, then at another. "And now you want me to be a mole."

"A what?" Unc said. He hadn't moved. I looked around for chairs, saw none. This was his room, and his only, I figured. I leaned against the doorjamb.

"A mole," he said. "Don't you read?"

"Haven't been able to get my hands on anything good lately," Unc said.

Cray laughed again, said, "That's a bad one. But a mole. Like in those John le Carré books. A mole is somebody on the inside willing to give info so long as nobody knows who he is."

He turned, took the cigar out of his mouth, leaned back, all in the near dark of the room, so that I wasn't quite sure whether he was smiling or not, silhouetted by the light behind him.

"Then I guess you're a mole," Unc said.

"Yes, I am," he said, and now he put his hands behind his head. He bit down on the cigar, made it angle up, like in that picture of FDR. "And do you know why it doesn't bother me a bit to be a mole?"

"Why?" Unc said.

"Because of what I delightfully refer to as the barium ceiling." He looked from Unc to me to Unc again. "You've heard of the glass ceiling, that point on the corporate ladder of American business beyond which women can't go? The barium ceiling is the point on the ladder of corporate medicine beyond which the radiologist cannot go. I found it over at the medical university, and realized with that fourteen-point buck and the fact not a single one of those turds even congratulated me that I'd met it. No hard feelings, Leland, but the whole reason I joined Hungry Neck in the first place was because everybody of any importance on the upper echelon at the medical university was a member, and I had my eye on the prize, so to speak: a seat on the board at some point. But no. A radiologist is not a real doctor, see? A radiologist looks at films all day, nothing more than a glorified copyboy to everyone on the board over there, no matter it took me eight years past med school to learn all I needed to learn about MRI and nuclear and all else. That doesn't matter. What matters is do you have a monogrammed scalpel and a striped bow tie? It doesn't matter you turn in billable accounts of over a million a year for eleven years straight, keep all those board members in their Lexi—is that plural for Lexus?—and when I took out that fourteen-pointer and you and Tonto were the only ones put up a fuss over there, I decided then and there to bail. Tendered my resignation January third from the South Carolina Medical University, surrendered my tenured associate professorship. And here we are."

He pulled the cigar from his mouth, spread his arms wide, looked at the place, then gave himself a spin in the chair. "Now what gets billed gets paid to me."

He stood then, leaned against the counter, crossed his arms. "And the irony of it all is the sword of Damocles over at the Med U is about to fall. That fine little hair is raggedy as all getout, frizzed to the max, and it's about to fall. And do you know who it's about to fall on?"

"Who?" Unc said. He was smiling, nodding, eating this up. He hadn't even had to run a thing up the flagpole.

"It's about to fall on the board itself. Because there's been an investigation going on for over two years now, an investigation into the ethics and finances of the University Medical Consortium, which is about to get nasty, because now there's been a senate committee set up in Columbia to explore the possibility that things stink in Charleston. Which they do."

Cray turned to the wall, found on the desktop a Magic Marker, and started drawing, right onto the glass. "It's like this," he said, and drew a triangle. He stopped, took a step back from it, took the cigar from his mouth, put it back in. "No," he said, "it's like this," and he rubbed out the triangle with his lab-coat sleeve, drew a square. "No, it's not like that either," he said, and then Unc cut in.

"Just say it, brother. We're listening."

Cray turned. His face'd gone blank, and it looked for a moment like he didn't recognize us. He let out a breath, then sat down, elbows on his knees, hands loose between his legs.

"It's not like I'm holding a grudge or anything," he said, and looked up at Unc. "It's just that I hate the sons of bitches. That whole crew."

He looked at me, took the cigar out. "You see the news the other night, that footage they ran about Charles Middleton Simons?"

I nodded. Of course I did. I'd watched it with the man's wife.

"That whole head table," he said, and pointed the cigar at me. "That whole crew there is what it's about. Every one of them sons of bitches is about to fall flat on his ass and out of money, or at least out of money like they've been used to making."

"How's that?" Unc asked. His head was tilted now, him listening. He'd sensed something in Cray now, this turn. Something was coming.

Cray took a deep breath, put his hands on his knees. "It works like this: you join the faculty at the medical university, you have to join the University Medical Consortium. But being on the faculty at a medical university isn't like being on one at a regular school. You don't go in, talk to your class, and go home. No, you're a doctor, and your students are interns following you around while you handle your patients. And those patients, like everybody else, have to pay. Simple as that. They pay. To be precise, their insurance pays, or Uncle Sam, one." He sighed again, shook his head. "And they pay the University Medical Consortium. That's who takes in the money. My million-plus a year for eleven years. Reading films and billing over a million a year, all billed to the consortium."

He smiled, took out that cigar again, looked at it. "Reason I never light these up is because this way I get all the pleasure of smoking a cigar, without any of the pleasure of smoking a cigar." He looked up at me, smiled. "Figure that one out."

I glanced at Unc, who stood frozen, leaned toward him just the slightest way. "Keep going," he said.

"Don't worry." He tossed the cigar into a wastebasket beneath the desk, reached into his shirt pocket, pulled out another. "But the thing of it is, you're still a faculty member. And you're still on salary. Assistant professor, associate, full. You get your raises, everybody gets a bonus. When I quit I was pulling in a hundred fifty a year, got a fifteen-thousand-dollar bonus."

"Sounds like plenty to me," I said, and as soon as I'd said it I was sorry. Unc turned toward me, his mouth closed tight: this was the kind of talk he didn't want me giving.

Cray looked up at me, gave a single *ha*, shook his head. "Greed is an ugly thing, I'm here to tell you, Tonto. You make that much, and you're right, you ought to be happy. You ought to. But then. Then you see the big dogs on the porch. Those boys—that whole head table, Carter Campbell, Buddy Rose, Franklin Cooper, Trey Morrison, Judd Bishop, Cleve Ravenel, Trey Royall—all those boys are pulling down around eight hundred grand a year. All of it because they're the directors of the medical university. *And* because they're the directors of the University Medical Consortium." He paused, shook his head. "Coming and going they're getting it. On salary, and senior partners in an association you got no choice but to join if you want to be employed at the medical university. And it's all about to fall. The senate committee starts its hearings, and the boys up in Columbia find out there's this skimming of millions to a handful of bluebloods, and that sword is going to fall. Something's rotten in Charleston." He looked up at Unc. "What it looks like to me, too, if you want my considered and professional opinion, is that Hungry Neck Hunt Club's very own Charles Middleton Simons has already taken his fall. For what reason I'm not sure, and probably not as he'd envisioned it might occur. But he's taken it. He was in the thick of that gang. Don't forget," he said, and turned to me, "that file footage was of a dinner honoring the late Doc Simons himself, everybody at that head table a member of the consortium."

He looked back at the lighted wall, at the square he'd drawn there. "And now here I am, pulling down two-fifty a year, but I get weekends free and I'm my own boss." He reached to the desktop, pushed a button there, and the row of X rays started up, the lighted wall rolling into the wall itself, and now here came another row of X rays from beneath, already clipped into place. "No barium ceiling here," he said. "Sky's the limit!"

He pulled out the monocular, said, "Here's your hat, what's your hurry?" and leaned up against the first row. "Too bad I'm here till eleven most nights, and my daughter is going to Yale without a scholarship, and I'm still paying off my own student loans, and my lovely wife won't let me hang a set of fourteen-point antlers in the house, afraid they might carry Lyme disease, no matter how much I try to dissuade her of this ill-founded fear. And yes, we too have a Lexus. Otherwise I'd join you boys on whatever expedition you're on. Whatever fact-finding mission you're on." He leaned away from the X ray, looked at me, then Unc. "Ahh, greed," he said. "It's an invigorating but lonely drug." He put the monocular to the next X ray, leaned in.

I pushed myself away from the doorjamb, went to Unc, hooked my arm in his. Cray was done.

But Unc wouldn't move, only stood there, facing Cray, leaned in just like he had for the whole thing. Listening.

He turned to me, on his face the same look as Cray'd had when he'd turned from his drawings: it seemed he didn't know me, as though the touch of me on his arm were something brand-new, and he was scared.

And I was, too. Mom was out there.

"Unc," I said. "It's getting late."

He swallowed, took a breath, and reached, touched my cheek with the back of his fingers, in his fist the stick. It was next to nothing, that touch, and I could smell the wood of the stick in just that second. Then his hand was down. "Yes," he said. "It's getting late."

He was struck by this all, I could see. Struck by something I wasn't able to see. Not yet.

He started for the door, and I turned, looked back at Cray, close up on the screen. I said, "Thank you, doc."

"Yes," Unc said, though quieter. He paused, half-turned to Cray, but I could see he wasn't thinking on manners, on thanks and good-bye. "Thank you, Brother Cray. You have been of the utmost help."

"Think nothing of it," he said, still with his eye to the screen. I watched him a moment longer, wondered if he'd look at us, wave, something. But he didn't.

And Unc was already gone, out to the front office.

I caught up with him in the waiting room, and we headed out the front door. The sign, IMAGING NETWORK SERVICES and the man lying flat inside a circle, was lit now, the sun down and gone, the sky above us blue and purple and orange. No stars yet.

16

"Keep going on down Old Georgetown," he said. "Turn right at the second street." These were the first words he'd said since we were inside the MRI place, and his voice was low, near a whisper. "Won't take but a second. Then we need to head downtown. To the Battery."

I looked at him. We were at the light at Bowman and Old Georgetown, a few cars back, traffic heavy down from the Mark Clark for rush hour, everybody hurrying home to their neat houses with neat lawns here in Mount Pleasant.

"Where're we going?" I asked. "And when are we going back to Hungry Neck?" I paused. "Or did you forget about my mother?"

I knew I was being smart-mouthed. But that's what I'd intended. I wanted a rise out of him, wanted to wake him up out of whatever stupor he was in.

He didn't even look at me.

I turned right at the light, drove down Old Georgetown away from the Mark Clark, and took the second right.

It was a neighborhood, nothing else. On either corner, right where we'd turned in, were brick stands a couple feet wide, five feet tall and painted white, the words HICKORY PLANTATION painted on both of them, entryway into a tract of homes.

There were trees, yards, brick houses and vinyl-siding houses. There were driveways with RV's and jon boats parked in them, some with bikes just dumped, kids in a hurry to get in the house for supper.

"Turn left," Unc said, and here was a street on the left, and I turned.

"Fourth house on the right," he whispered.

I slowed down, pulled to the curb in front of the fourth house on the right. A mailbox stood out front, the numbers 2032 on the side in those reflective stickers.

I turned my headlights off and looked at him. "We going in?"

He was turned to the house, away from me. "What does it look like?"

"Looks like a house."

Slowly he shook his head, then whispered, "Tell me."

I leaned over the steering wheel to see past him to the house. I said, "There's a green Dodge Caravan parked out front. It's a two-story house, light blue siding. The garage door's open, and there's a workbench in there, no room for a car for all the junk. Two bicycles on the sidewalk up to the front door, both of them flat on the ground."

I leaned back. "It's a family," I said. "A family lives there."

"Two oaks out front," he whispered.

He was right. Two oaks stood off to the left of the front yard, and I saw where somebody'd hung a rope swing off one of the branches, just a loop of rope and a piece of two-by-four.

I said, "Unc, we going in? Because if we are, then we need to go."

He turned to me. He put out his hand for me, and I saw it was shaking.

I took hold of it, squeezed hard. "Unc, what's wrong?"

"Greed," he whispered. "Maybe it's me being greedy." His hand was cold in mine, and I squeezed harder. "Maybe I ought to sell it. Because my wanting it's just the other side of their wanting it."

"Who?" I said. "Who wants what?"

He looked at me a long second, then pulled his hand out of mine, turned and pointed at the house. He said, "This is where we lived."

It took a second, but it sank in.

Aunt Sarah, Unc. Where she died, where Unc lost his eyes. And his life, the first one.

Where the next life, the one out to Hungry Neck, started. The one empty of any real family, just me out on the weekends.

It was a family living in there. Now.

"She killed herself," he whispered, "my Sarah." He touched the glass of his window. "It's my own greed made her do it. My own."

I said nothing, only put both hands to the steering wheel, held on tight.

I wasn't ready for this. Not news of Aunt Sarah, of another suicide.

I gripped and regripped the wheel, tried hard to make some sense out of all this, any of it: my mom, the club, Unc, and Dr. Cray. And this.

But there was nothing for me to make of it, and suddenly the only thing came clear to me was the why behind Mom telling me only of facts that day I'd asked, the trailer choked with boxes, us ready to move to North Charleston, Unc still as a stone on the sofa out in the front room: there was a fire, Aunt Sarah died, Unc's eyes were blinded with exploding glass.

The only thing came clear to me was the veil over it all, a veil of love, black and opaque: love was at the bottom of things, it came to me, always. Unc loved Aunt Sarah, and saw her die. Unc's love of Hungry Neck was at the bottom of why Mom was kidnapped. Now my own love for my mom was why I wanted out of here, away from where another suicide had taken place, why I wanted to get away from Unc and his preoccupations with his own guilt: love was the why of too much.

"Now Eugenie's in it, my greed, and you too. And it's greed killed Constance and Charlie Simons both. Good as killed Cray back there. So I'll sell. To those investors." He paused. "Let them have it. I've had enough."

It sounded good to me. If it meant getting Mom back.

But sell it to who? What did he know now that I didn't?

"Who?" I said again. "Who are the investors? And what does that have to do with what Cray said?"

He looked at me again, on his face now something past disbelief, something past giving up. He said. "The doctors. The members of the club." He swallowed. "My own men. They're the ones trying to buy me out." He slowly shook his head, whispered, "Greed."

He faced forward, put that hand to the dash. "Let's go," he said. "Twenty-six East Battery."

"Unc," I said.

I wanted to tell him I cared for Aunt Sarah, cared about her dying. I wanted to tell him, too, I cared about Hungry Neck, but that selling it, finally, seemed the best way through this all, the best way out. The best way to get back my mom.

I wanted to tell him all this. But I only said, "Unc," again, and nothing came after.

"Let's go," he said, and reached over, touched one of my hands at the wheel. "We have things to do."

I could see a couple stars by the time we made it to the top of the first bridge over the Cooper River. We were on the old one, only two lanes wide, the railing so close out my window I could have reached out, touched it.

But the stars. Only two or three of them, the sky to the west a dark orange, to the east already a blue so deep you almost couldn't tell where the Atlantic stopped and the sky picked up.

And there lay Charleston, to my left and below as we drove down from the first bridge, crossed over Drum Island, the flat piece of land the city used to dump its dredge mud on, then on up the second bridge.

Charleston. Below us now was the wharf, a couple tugboats, a small freighter. Next to that was the railyard, where somewhere a container'd been loaded with goods, whatever that meant.

And past all that were the lights of Charleston, all of them starting up, the spires on the churches lit so that it seemed for a second all that romance and what have you you hear about this place, the charm of the Old South and all, might for a few seconds actually be true.

From up here.

But they lived down there, the members of the club. The sons of bitches, cowards all, trying to buy out Hungry Neck from under Unc in order to bring in the next Hilton Head. The next Myrtle Beach.

Then we started down from the top of the second bridge and into the projects just to the right, those two-story brick rows of apartments with laundry lines strung up between them, to the left the old gray houses about to collapse on themselves.

The best way to East Battery was by going to East Bay Street, the street that paralleled the railyard and then made a straight shot for the Market, and so I turned to the right, followed streets that doubled back, past the projects and the elementary school, and we were on East Bay, above us the bridge we'd just come down.

We drove south, passed the post office and a couple restaurants, then hit the traffic at the Market.

People milled about down here, hanging out, heading into restaurants, buying trash at the open-air stalls all set up and selling varnished seashells glued together to make a palmetto tree, and T-shirts with pictures of sunsets, baseball caps with little fans that blew air in your face. This sort of thing. Gone were the dead buildings now, in their place an Applebee's, a Häagen Dázs, a Smithfield Ham shop, all of it.

And sweetgrass baskets.

On the corners, even in this growing dark, sat the black women in their folding chairs, spread out at their feet the sweetgrass baskets, and sweetgrass trays and cup holders and platters.

Sweetgrass baskets, coiled sweetgrass and bulrushes.

There they sat, in these black women's hands the coils they worked, coils the exact same as the one in my pocket, and it hit me.

There was something else to all this, other than just the greed of doctors ticked they wouldn't be making a million a year much longer, doctors who wanted to go as far around Unc as they could in order to buy him out. There was something more.

Because why would Constance Simons come to me, there in the middle of a hospital, just to hand me this sweetgrass paperweight, a gift to Unc?

I said, "There's something else going on, Unc. Not just selling Hungry Neck. There's something else."

We were past the Market now, beside us more shops—a bookstore, a tobacco shop, a chocolate shop, restaurants. People still everywhere, even on a Monday night.

Unc said nothing.

Then we were at the light for Broad Street, in front of us a horse and carriage tour, the driver standing there with his rebel soldier's cap on and red sash around his waist, pointing at the customs house to the left of us, the huge old building with its porticoes and windows.

"What makes you think this isn't anything other than just stupid greed?" Unc said.

I turned to him. "The paperweight."

He shook his head. "A paperweight. A pine-sap paperweight. The woman's about to commit suicide, and she came to you, because she couldn't find me." He paused. "It's a gift. Her to me. Now me to you."

The light changed, and the carriage started off.

I leaned over, saw no oncoming traffic, drove around them.

"But she told me she didn't do it," I said. "She told me to tell you she didn't do it. Didn't kill her husband."

Now we were south of Broad, East Bay now East Battery, where the mansions were, that layer of shops and trinkets and restaurants, then that layer of slums on top of that gone now, like it'd never existed. Only these homes mattered now, all else forgotten for the piazzas and joggling boards and perfect walled gardens.

"If she didn't kill her husband, which you got to believe is the
truth, then who did? And why?" I glanced at him again, then back
to the street. To the left was the seawall, past it Charleston Harbor
itself, on the right these mansions, and I slowed down, looked for
the number 26.

"Third house past Atlantic Street," Unc whispered.

But there was something different on his voice, that whisper not
the mournful one he'd given when we'd stopped at the place in
Hickory Plantation.

He was thinking on what I'd said.

"So if you think this is all just over who's going to buy the land,"
I said, not quite certain of what I would say, where I was going, "and
if you think she was just handing out a paperweight for fun, then
you think she did it. And you give up."

"He'd gone maverick on them," Unc said. "Charlie did."

"And goods. Goods. They want the land, what has goods got to
do with anything?"

Here was Atlantic Street, a narrow alley off East Battery. I
counted three houses down.

And there was a parking spot, right in front.

"We got to get Mom," I said, and cut the engine. "And we got to
get who killed Simons. I think it's Yandle. Maybe Thigpen. Maybe
one of those shits in the truck Thigpen rolled."

He turned to me, popped open his door. He said, "You keep your
mouth clean. We're here to pay respects."

A black wreath hung on the huge oak door. We were high above
the street, the flight of steps up a good fifteen feet on this three-
story brick house, the porch itself as long and wide as the single-
wide. White pillars, porch painted gray, the ceiling above us a mint
green.

A heavy black woman answered the door. She had on a black

maid's dress, white apron. She looked at us, the door open barely a foot.

Unc'd left the stick in the cab, and he held on to my arm.

She said, "Mrs. Dupree is receiving no more mourners today," and started to close the door.

He quick let go my arm and took off his hat. He bowed a little, said, "My name is Leland Dillard, and I have come to give my condolences to Mrs. Dupree."

"Leland?" came a feeble voice from behind the maid, and she looked to her right, and to Unc, then opened wide the door.

A Persian rug ran from one end of the foyer to the other, what seemed fifty feet, to where a staircase emptied out, big and wide. What parts of the wood floor you could see gleamed in the light from a chandelier above us, and already I could smell the flowers, though I couldn't yet see any. Dark oak went halfway up the walls, above the wood wallpaper thick with a flowered pattern, all golds and reds, the ceiling twelve or fourteen feet in here.

I put a hand to my hair, raked it over, started to tuck in my shirt, one tail hanging out from under my Levi's jacket, and saw the maid looking at me and Unc both, a hand at the door into the room to our right.

I smiled, nodded at her, and she slid the door into the wall.

There at the far end of the room, surrounded by huge arrangements of flowers, sat a shriveled woman in an overstuffed chair. She was tiny, the glasses on her face thick, her eyes bleary behind them. She had white hair, a blue dress, and sat with her hands in her lap.

She had on white gloves.

"Mr. Leland Dillard," she said, and put out a hand.

Unc walked across the room to her. He tucked his Braves cap in his back pocket, and without my telling him her hand was out to him, he put both his out, moved them a few inches one way and the other.

Mrs. Dupree did nothing to help him find hers, only held her white-gloved hand out, steady.

Unc found her hand, bowed to her.

"I am deeply sorrowed at the passing of your daughter," Unc said. I'd never seen him like this, never heard him talk this way: formal, sorry. "She will always hold a special place in my heart," he said, still holding her hand.

"And I am sorry at the passing of your own sweet Sarah," Mrs. Dupree said, "though I am these many years late in offering these words."

"Thank you," Unc said, and it seemed his hands on hers quivered, as though she were holding him together with just that tiny gloved hand of hers.

She let go, said, "Won't you please sit down?" and motioned to the sofa on my right, carved wooden arms and legs, blue-and-gold striped silk material. At either end of it were more flowers, baskets on the floor and on the marble-topped end tables. Across from the sofa was a small, shallow fireplace, baskets of flowers in front of it.

I led Unc to the sofa, where we sat, the two of us on the very edge. We were silent a few moments, and I couldn't help but look at my watch: six forty-five.

"This is the parlor," Mrs. Dupree said, and I looked up. She had a glass in her hand, a dainty one, half filled with a light brown something. "This is the room in which one brought the family member to have passed, let him or her lie in state while mourners could pay their respects. Much as you are doing now, Mr. Leland Dillard."

She took a sip at the glass. "I am afraid my manners have escaped me in the midst of my loss," she said. "May I offer you a glass of sherry?" She held up the glass. "It has certainly helped me to remain calm these last three days. We can have Miss Esther bring you in some, if you wish." She turned, with her free hand reached for a small silver bell on the end table beside her. She picked it up, ready to ring.

"No, thank you, Mrs. Dupree," Unc said, "as we have to be going."

"So soon?" she said, and put the bell back.

And beside it, there on the end table, sat a paperweight. Brown glass, the size of a Coke-bottle bottom, rough edges.

I felt my hands go hot, my palms start to sweat, all in a second.

She took another sip, pinky extended, the other hand set perfectly in her lap. "My mother, when she passed in April of '26, was presented in this room, as was my father, in September of '39."

I glanced at Unc, as though he'd noticed it too.

"I have now outlived my only child," she went on, her voice a sharp, thin fact in the room, her eyes closed. "My daughter, Constance. And my wish for her passing was that she too would have had the honor of lying in state here in the parlor as well. But they tell me these things are no longer allowed. That this is no longer considered proper."

I wanted to hold it up, see if there was inside it a sweetgrass coil. If she kept her eyes closed, then I might be able to stand, just reach over, pick it up.

But then she opened them, tipped up the glass, drained it, turned to the end table.

"It is my desire, indeed will be my last request, to be presented here in this room, and a curse will be upon those who do not honor this request," she said, and now she was looking at me, her mouth straight, eyes open.

She said, "Who is this young upstart, Mr. Leland Dillard?" and nodded at me.

Unc sat up a little straighter. "My apologies, please, for not introducing him," Unc said. "This is my nephew, Master Huger Dillard."

I nodded. "Ma'am."

"Imagine," she said to me, "if I hadn't forced my Constance to marry Charles Middleton Simons, instead had let her marry her love, you might very well be living with me, here. I might very well have been your grandmother." She gave what seemed to be a smile.

I looked to Unc, then to her again. I said, "He's not my dad. He's my uncle." I shrugged. "My dad is—"

"Very well," she said, and nodded, hands still in her lap. Unc sat facing forward, and I could hear the tick of a clock from somewhere.

I looked down, said, "Yes ma'am," and glanced at the paperweight again.

"Mrs. Dupree," Unc said. "With all due respect, we must be going now in order—"

"It seems you have an inordinate interest in this latest keepsake of mine," she said, still looking at me. She picked up the paperweight, held it up to her face.

I said nothing, and Unc turned to me, said, "What's this?"

I whispered, "She has a paperweight."

"A paperweight, is it," she said, and now she was looking at me. "This is a symbol, I was told by my Constance on the day before her passing, of my daughter's transgressions." She turned the paperweight one way and the other, her eyebrows up, inspecting it as though it were an apple she might or might not buy.

She said, "It is a cryptic symbol, I believe, one I cannot yet decipher. But my daughter was given to cryptic behavior, most assuredly when it came to matters of the heart." She looked at Unc, then to the paperweight again.

Unc cleared his throat.

"You call it a paperweight," she said, "when it seems she meant it to carry more sentiment than that. And now my daughter is dead."

We sat there, the ticking between us filling the room.

Cherish your momma, Constance Simons'd said.

I looked at this woman, her momma. Her only child dead.

I stood, crossed the room. She was looking at me, her eyebrows still up, her mouth a small *O* of confusion: Who was this upstart daring to come to her?

I knelt to her and felt at my waist the gun, heavy and sharp. Still with me. Then I pulled from my pocket my own symbol, the one she'd given to Unc through me. It was warm.

"Huger?" Unc said from behind me.

She looked down at mine, and I could see better now the one she held: a small coil of sweetgrass inside, as tiny and delicate as my own. She looked at me, and I saw the watery look in her eyes wasn't the old age I'd figured it was, but grief. Plain and simple.

Her only daughter, giving her her sins.

She said, "How—"

"She came to me Saturday night," I said, my voice low, almost a whisper. "I was in the hospital. At the medical university. She gave me this to give to Unc."

She took in a breath, whispered, "You talked to her."

"Yes ma'am." I nodded.

"And what did she say?"

"She said to tell my uncle she loved him. And she said, 'Cherish your momma.' "

She quick looked at me, and I could see on her face a kind of startled shine. Slowly she brought down her hand, let her paperweight rest in her lap.

She said, "Do you?"

"Yes ma'am," I whispered. "I cherish her."

She looked from one paperweight to the other.

"I can't tell them apart," she said.

That was when I turned to Unc, and as though he knew precisely what I was thinking, knew and could see me looking to him for something I couldn't yet name myself, he nodded. I looked at him a moment longer, then turned to her.

I took her gloved hand, and placed it there. I said, "You can keep it, if you like."

She looked at me, and it seemed she tried to smile, though her chin quivering wouldn't let it happen. She said, "One is sin, and the other is love. And I can't tell the difference." She tried the smile again, looked up at me. "Can you?"

Unc cleared his throat again, him standing now behind me. He said, "We must go now."

"She told you to cherish your mother," she said, that thin fact that was her voice going even thinner now, "because I did not cherish *her.* And as I did not cherish my child, so she did not cherish me."

Then Mrs. Dupree cried, shivered in on herself, grew smaller in only the seconds I looked at her. It was a pitiful sound in this room, cluttered with flowers and the thick smell of them all, a smell, I figured, as close to death as the smell of old blood. It was a pitiful sound, hollow and too late.

"Our condolences," Unc said, and took my arm.

17

What was left?

We'd driven the whole afternoon, like all we'd had to do was run these errands, like we'd just gone to drop off some overdue videos or picked up some TV dinners. And now we were in the trailer, Mom's Stanza still out front, Unc and me waiting.

We'd stopped at the Pantry on 17 almost to Red Top, where Unc climbed out, called Miss Dinah at the open-air pay phone set up in the parking lot. The sky was black by then, the Pantry lit up bright as the Amoco station'd been just last night, and from the cab of the Luv I watched Unc punch at the numbers, watched him talk, his head down, chin to his chest. Then he'd hung up, climbed in, said, "Missy Dorcas got nothing. Still no news on who the sender was of those orders to void Charlie Simons." He shrugged. "But she's still trying." He gave a small smile. "And she says to tell you she's praying for your momma."

But I didn't smile, only put it into gear, pulled out onto 17.

And the only thing we could show for this whole day was that we knew some things.

Deputy Yandle had been disowned. The University Medical Consortium was after buying Hungry Neck to make it another Hilton Head. Goods were involved somehow.

Constance Dupree Simons had given her mother a sweetgrass paperweight.

Aunt Sarah had killed herself.

And my mom had been kidnapped.

It was cold in the front room, the windows broken out, Unc and me sitting on the sofa I'd tackled him on what seemed a year ago. If it had happened at all.

Then I pulled out the Polaroid of Mom from my back pocket.

Fifteen minutes until nine o'clock.

"None of what I've got you into is worth this," Unc said. "The land."

I didn't move, only took in Mom's face, her eyes. "This is over," he said. "And it's not what I'd hoped, Huger." He tried at a smile. "This land. It was for you. Yours." He put out his hand, touched my shoulder again. "This is what family we got. You, Eugenie, me. It's all we got. Not much of a family, I know. Screwed to pieces. But it's all we got." He let go, slowly shook his head. "Not what I hoped, Huger. Selling this place."

So it was over. Just like that: sell the land. That was all. And we'd have Mom back like some sort of collateral against a loan. If they played by their own rules. And then we'd all go home.

But somebody had killed Charles Middleton Simons.

Pigboy and Fatback?

Yandle and Thigpen?

And they'd let us go on *home*?

Then it came to me, the stupid truth of all this too big and dumb for me to keep track of: *nobody knew Constance Dupree Simons had come to me, there in the hospital.*

And nobody knew she'd told me she didn't do it.

Unc sat up on the couch, back straight, head turned just barely away from me. "What time is it?"

I looked from the picture to him. "Unc," I said, "they don't know she came to see me. Constance."

"I said what time is it," he snapped, and moved his head one way, the other, his eyes to the window.

I looked at my watch. "Ten till. Unc, what's wrong?"

"It's Patrick and Reynold coming up. Reynold's pickup." He paused. "Son of a bitch. Hell of a time for them two boys to pay a visit."

Then I heard it, in the same moment saw headlights play through the curtains.

Patrick and Reynold. What did they want? Last time I'd seen them was Saturday morning, when they'd torn off with the dogs and horses, and I thought of that rebel yell, the smell of beer on them before daylight. Patrick, with his filthy ponytail, Reynold's bald head lit with the green light of the dashboard.

And there we'd been, all those members holding on to the dogs so's they wouldn't take in to the body.

Patrick and Reynold. They'd never come back for their dogs. At least not before I'd fallen, hit my head. Forty-five minutes to an hour after they let those dogs loose, when usually there they were on horseback not fifteen minutes behind the dogs.

Patrick and Reynold.

Their engine cut off, and Unc stood, moved for the door.

"Patrick?" he called out. "Reynold? Boys?"

"Leland?" Patrick called out. "You okay? What's with your windows?"

"Unc," I whispered, and reached for him.

Then came the sandpaper sound of boots on cinder blocks. "Huger, Leland?" Reynold said. "You boys all right in there?"

"Unc," I said now. "Unc, it's them," I said.

Fatback and Pigboy.

I reached to my shirt, fumbled with the buttons on my jacket.

"Boys," Unc said, and glanced over his shoulder at me, his eyebrows together, trying to figure out what I was talking about, and in that instant there came to me the picture of Unc salting his seat and missing his fries, and the truth of how sometimes things got past him no matter what.

"Can't be standing around yapping," he said, and pulled the doorknob. "We're expecting company any minute now, and—"

The door burst open, Unc's hand shooting back with the shock of it, his whole body in a half twirl away from the door.

Here was Patrick, that greasy ponytail swinging behind him as he slammed in, then bald Reynold, the two of them smiling, between them five or six front teeth missing.

I got my jacket open, started to pull out the gun. But before I even had it out, Patrick whispered, "Company's here," and punched Unc hard in the face, his sunglasses broken in two in just that second, then Reynold's fist met my own jaw, and I was out.

Mom.

Here she was above me again, her face in close, coming into focus just like she'd come into focus in the hospital room. But this time it wasn't the flowery smell of her perfume I smelled first, but smoke off a fire.

Her skin was a beautiful gold in the light from the fire. Her makeup was all down by her eyes, like in the picture of her, but now there was no duct tape.

Mom.

I reached up to her and felt as much pain as when I'd woken up in the hospital, only this down below my mouth instead of the back of my head, and I let my tongue, fat and hot, go to my jaw, felt three or four loose teeth, and I was cold, my feet granite blocks, and I tried to move them.

They wouldn't, and I heard the sound of a heavy chain, pushed myself up on my elbows.

"Huger," Mom said, and touched at my jacket, pulled it a little tighter to my neck. "You don't get up. You just rest."

"Huger," Unc said from my right, "you just lay still."

But I was looking at my feet, at the leg irons around my ankles, the chain between them spiked into the ground.

"You'd be surprised the sort of things we got on hand down to the station," Yandle said.

I turned to his voice. Mom touched at my jacket again, then my forehead, my shoulder.

Past her on the other side of a small fire sat Yandle on the tail of a Ram 2500 four-by-four. Beyond it, barely visible for Cleve Ravenel's truck, sat Patrick and Reynold's Dodge. Yandle: perfect trim mustache, crew-cut hair.

So it was Cleve Ravenel, the white-haired fat doctor who'd turned too quick to his name, scared. Cleve Ravenel, the man whose e-mail trash Unc had figured out to go through. Cleve Ravenel, member of the Medical University Consortium.

But where was he?

Yandle's arm was still in the sling, and with the other hand he made the gun again, shot me.

"Don't say anything, Huger," Unc said, and his voice sounded different, stuffed up. He sat a few feet to my right, facing the fire. His legs were up to his chest, his arms around them, holding on. He had leg irons, too, spiked to the ground, and in the flicker of light from the fire I could see his eyes were swollen shut, the skin split open between them, blood, black in the firelight, down either side of his face. He still had his hat on.

"Patrick broke his nose," Yandle said. "Did a splendid job at it, too." He paused, gave a little laugh. "Of course Leland here never saw it coming."

Mom touched at my jacket.

We were just out in the woods somewhere. The fire'd been there a while, some big pieces of oak burned down, the canopy of live oak above us dull browns all moving for the flames.

I had no idea where we were.

Yandle took a long swallow off a bottle of beer. He had on jeans and boots, an army jacket, a holster and gun. "But about them leg irons," he said, and burped. "Took those off an Oreo couple over to Gardens Corner, him black, her white. Got a call for a domestic one night—that's a 214—and I pull up, see this naked fat white bitch coming down the porch off her trailer at me, them leg irons on and rattling, her waddling like a duck can't shit. Turns out they use these leg irons for bedroom fun, the two of them locking up and having at it, all the time their video camera on and recording the whole works."

He shook his head, and Mom turned to him, said, "Just shut the hell up, would you, please? Won't you just shut the hell up? Has anybody ever told you you're just an asshole?" She touched my forehead, said, "Excuse my language, but I've been having to listen to this all day long, him and his police-boy stories. And I'm getting sick of it."

"That was a comedy," he went on, "that videotape, which we confiscated too, her with her fat turkey legs chained up and wrapped around his skinny nigger butt." He was just talking, happy at the sound of his voice. "But it turns out they had a fight," he said, "right in the middle of this Mandingo thing they got going, and he up and swallows *her* key. Took two days before that brother let loose of what he was holding, and I'm not the one went pawing through it, I tell you what. No sir. It was the brother himself we made do it." He laughed again. "Now, they were losers. But *you* all." He took another long swallow, emptied it, then pointed the bottle at me. "*You* all are one fucking loser family. The Dillards." He burped again. "A blind man, a snot-nosed runt, and a cracker bitch to boot. One fucking loser family."

"Don't say a word, Huger," Unc said again.

But I wasn't sure if I even could. My tongue had swollen up, the whole left side of my face a sandbag, heavy and fat, and I reached up, touched it.

Nothing. It hadn't swollen, far as I could tell. Just cold flesh, my cheek, my jaw.

"Don't go to moving around," Mom said. "Don't try moving around or anything at all, Huger." Then her chin started to quiver again, all this just like two days before.

But where were we? And why weren't they just letting us go? Hadn't Unc told them they could have the land?

"Unc?" I said, turning to him, my hand still to my dead jaw, the word out of me more a grunt for how big my tongue'd gone.

"Be quiet, boy," Unc said again.

"Might ought to listen to that bad boy Leland Dillard," Yandle said, and burped again. "He's been around the block a time or two." He laughed, pointed the empty bottle at him this time. "Looks like somebody done backed over him a time or two, too." He cocked back his arm, and for a second I thought he meant to throw the bottle at Unc, just for fun.

But he didn't, only shot it out into the woods behind us, and I heard the rush of small sounds through thick branches, the bottle caught a moment or two in the brush before the sounds stopped.

I sat up, though Mom didn't want me to, and pulled myself to my knees, just like Unc. Mom didn't have leg irons on but had a piece of rope tied to her ankle, the other end knotted into a spike, just like what Patrick and Reynold did with the dogs out in their yard.

And I could see way off into the woods behind the truck what looked like a lighted window, the barest glow of a lamp through a window the size of a postage stamp from where I was.

"So once the aforementioned cracker bitch little miss mother of the year here discovered my associates on the premises of Hungry Neck Hunt Club HQ"—Yandle laughed again, shook his head— "namely your fucking trailer, Leland, we had no choice but to apprehend the suspect rather than allow her to escape." His words were sliding together now, a sound I knew was the first slip into being drunk from all those times we'd sat around and drank Colt 45 under the Mark Clark back home. Boxes were piled up in the bed of Ravenel's truck, the boxes catching light now and again from the fire. Yandle reached behind him, pulled up another bottle from an ice chest there. He held it with the arm in the sling, screwed off the cap with his free hand. He sipped at it, wiped his mouth with that good arm. "Seems she'd seen us planting produce around the place, got all hot and bothered, and proceeded to knock shit out of Patrick and Reynold." He took another drink. "Feisty bitch."

"They were carrying equipment into the trailer," Mom said to me, almost in a whisper. "Grow lights and spray bottles and hoses and bags and bags of marijuana and—" She paused. "You know what I mean, grow lights?"

I nodded, closed my eyes for the pain again. Grow lights. Pot. Weed. This was about *weed*?

Goods, of course. They were growing stuff out here. But where was here?

And now here came the doctor himself, Cleve Ravenel up out of the dark, his white hair orange in the light. He had on camos like every other time I'd ever seen him, and he was carrying another box, him breathing heavy. He set it in the bed, pushed it back to the others.

"The doctor of kind bud," Yandle said. "If it hadn't been for that little bastard over there falling down on top of me," Yandle said, and nodded at me, looked back at Ravenel, "I'd be a little more service to you this evening, Cleve Ravenel, DKB. Doctor of Kind Bud." Yandle slowly rubbed his shoulder, the neck of the bottle held between his thumb and first finger. "But life takes its turns, don't it, DKB?" He laughed.

Ravenel shook his head. "Why the hell I have to deal with you is beyond my comprehension," he said, and wiped at his forehead with the sleeve of his jacket.

He looked over at Unc. "I'm sorry about all this, Leland," he said. "This taking you hostage and all. I'll make good for you. I will."

Unc said nothing, didn't move.

"You got to deal with *me*," Yandle went on, too loud, his eyes on Ravenel, "because I'm the only one knows who the hell to distribute to out thisaway, and who knows how to keep anybody wanting in from getting in out thisaway." There was an edge to his voice now, something like what he'd used wanting to take charge of everything at the crime scene. "You fucking pasty-face doctor types living South of Broad wouldn't know how to sell a kilo if a College of Charleston undergrad walked up and waved a thousand-dollar bill in your face. Only kind of work you're comfortable with is putting on your candy-ass latex gloves and giving a finger up the ass of some ninth-generation Pinckney." He stopped, tipped back the bottle, took a swipe at his mouth with his sleeve again. "Truth is, I'd rather be out here and take billy-club hits at trailer trash any day. Any day, you fat motherfucker."

Ravenel stood there, hands on his hips, his eyes on Yandle, staring hard at him. He tilted his head to one side the smallest bit.

I glanced at Unc. He hadn't moved, eyes still swollen shut, those black streaks of blood like some kind of tattoo down his face.

Mom was sitting next to me now, and put her arms around me, held me to her like I was six. But it felt good with what seemed about to turn into something past the ugly it already was, all of it out of our hands not fifteen feet away.

"And so now we have three hostages who know precisely what the hell has gone on here on their own property," Ravenel said. "Three hostages, and not a clue in the entire animal world what we're supposed to do with them, because you and your gap-toothed little minions get it into your heads you're going to go over and frame Leland Dillard, just in case your SLED pals figure out our little enterprise here." He shook his head. "And then the woman shows up, and your boys decide to play take-the-hostage."

"How was they supposed to figure she'd show up?" Yandle said, and put his hand with the bottle to the bed, steadying himself, or holding himself back, I couldn't tell which. "How's they to figure she'd pop up and screw everything to pieces? SLED's showing up tomorrow morning, my man tells me, to go over every square inch of the whole club land, this backwater parcel even Leland Dillard forgets he owns. We ain't got enough time to liquidate and tear it all down, I figure, so why not go ahead and plant evidence at Leland's? Where's the harm in hammering a couple more kilos into that old man's coffin?"

Ravenel stopped shaking his head. "There you go, thinking again. That's your first mistake." He paused. "Big mistake."

"You son of a bitch," Yandle said, and before I could even think of what I was watching, Yandle brought the bottle up from beside him on the bed, and broke it against Ravenel's head.

I jumped, like I'd been shocked, my stomach knotted up and tight, and Mom squeezed down tighter on me, squealed, all in that second.

"Hold on," Unc said, his voice cut low, just for us.

Ravenel gave a sort of failed groan, just a sound like the air in him had no choice but to leave, and fell, back and away from the truck.

Yandle pushed himself off the tail of the Ram, looked down at him. He still had hold of the bottle neck, the broken end ready now for whatever else might piss him off. He put his boot toe to Ravenel's leg, pushed at it. Ravenel moaned, the sound almost nothing.

"Fucking doctors," Yandle said. "The whole reason this whole thing is coming down—doctors."

He turned to us, pointed the broken bottle at Unc. "If it hadn't been for your doctor's wife coming along and blowing away her hubby's head, we could of been set up and operating here from now till kingdom come. But no. Doctors. Fucking doctors."

Mom held me tighter, took in quick breaths, her face to my shoulder, and I held her.

"Good idea," Yandle said. "Just close your eyes and pray this all goes away."

Now came footsteps, a rush of them, pounding through brush and stomping toward us, and Reynold came into the firelight, breathing hard, his bald head like an orange bulb in the light, flannel shirt and jeans on. He bent to Ravenel, took in a breath or two, looked up at Yandle. Patrick showed up behind him, chest moving for the distance they'd run from the greenhouse. He had on a down vest over long underwear, jeans. He gave a big sniff through his nose, rubbed at it, shook his head.

He cut his eyes to Yandle, who'd sat back on the tail.

"This," Patrick said, and took in another breath, "is a fucking twisted way to try and cover our ass."

Reynold stood. "What in the hell did you do that for?" he said, and took in a breath, another. "This is the man who knows the judge, Doug. This is the man who knows the fucking *judge*. And you go and break a bottle on the son of a bitch."

"Just shut up," Yandle said. "Just shut the fuck up and let me think a minute."

He gave what was left of the bottle the same throw he'd given the other empty, the bottle making the same small rush of muffled sounds, then leaned his head down, rubbed at his eyes with his free hand. Patrick said, "But we wasn't supposed to brang down this kind of shit, Doug, we wasn't supposed to go on and smash the fucking moneyman's head."

Yandle shot him a look, and the three of them started to arguing and whining at one another, hollering and pointing back into the woods to that lit window, then at each other, fingers to chests and pounding and how it all wasn't supposed to fall like this.

And yet even with what I'd just seen, a bottle broken on the side of a man's head, a body gone limp, I was thinking on what Yandle'd said just then: *We could of been set up and operating here from now till kingdom come.*

What did that mean? Weren't Cleve Ravenel and his pals supposed to buy Hungry Neck? Wasn't that what this was supposed to be about, our being back at nine o'clock so we could meet up with Thigpen and tell him whatever he and the people he worked for, those men who counted, wanted to hear? That Unc'd sell them the place, then get Mom back, be left alone to try and live the rest of our lives with all that'd happened?

Where was Thigpen?

And marijuana. Stupid *shit* was all this was over. But crated up in popcorn and shipped on a container? The people Yandle knew were nothing more than the lost clods who lived out here in the woods. That black-and-white couple with the leg irons'd probably been his customers, the leg irons some sort of bartering deal. What were they shipping it *away* for? In popcorn?

And why would Yandle think he'd be in business for life, if the plan was to sell Hungry Neck and make it another Hilton Head?

I didn't get it, didn't get any of this: what looked like the tearing down of some kind of pot greenhouse out here in the middle of nowhere, right here on Hungry Neck; Cleve Ravenel taken out by his own man; Mom taken hostage because she'd seen something she ought not to have; and no mention of selling Hungry Neck at all.

I looked to Unc, Mom still pressed to my shoulder, Yandle, Patrick, and Reynold still at it. I whispered, "Unc?"

"Be quiet," he whispered. His head was bowed now, forehead on his knees.

"But Unc," I whispered, "what about selling off Hungry Neck?"

"Boy," he whispered, and on that single word I knew he meant for me just to shut the hell up, that that was the most important thing I might could do at this particular moment.

But I went ahead, asked him what I asked, because I was scared, scared at not knowing a damned thing. I didn't know. I didn't know *anything*, and I knew Unc did, by the way he'd said nothing.

I whispered, "Where is Thigpen?"

Unc lifted his head toward me, and I saw only half his face now, him looking at me, the one half moving and moving in the firelight, the other dark, lost, and I wondered if finally he was going to answer me, even if he'd told me to shut up.

But there was something different about him looking at me, I saw, in the tilt of his head, the line of his chin. He wasn't looking at me, but past me, above my shoulder, and I turned, even with Mom still pressed into my shoulder.

There sat Thigpen on a pale horse, hands on the pommel of the saddle.

"Right here," he said, smiling down at me.

18

He had on a heavy coat, jeans, that straw cowboy hat with the sides folded up, the front end bent down. He had a holster and belt at his waist.

"Leland," he said, and nodded.

I glanced to Unc, saw him nod back. We'd none of us heard him coming up for the noise of the fighting. Only Unc'd heard. Only Unc.

It was a strange moment, his being here, a moment jammed with too much feeling on my part: relief, because this was the man who'd shoved that truck off the road; and there was fear, too, his presence inside all this stuff happening in front of us, none of it I could figure out; and there was in me, too, the feeling this was logical, that all would be revealed to me in a moment, now that the last person in this parade was here. All that just in his smile down at me from up on that pale horse.

Yandle, Patrick, and Reynold stopped hollering, froze.

Mom stiffened up, scooted around to see who was behind her.

"What the fuck you doing with my horse?" Reynold said, and I saw him out of the corner of my eye take a step away from Patrick and Yandle and toward Thigpen. "What the fuck you doing with my Jeb Stuart?"

Yandle said, "Glad you finally showed up, Tommy," and put his free hand to Patrick's chest, pushed him off, and drew his gun, held it on him. His arm was stiff in front of him, just like on TV and in the movies, and he glanced from Thigpen to Patrick, pointed the gun at Reynold, at Patrick, then Reynold. Firelight played off the barrel. "Caught these sons of bitches trying to dismantle a greenhouse back in here. Leland Dillard here and his nephew and the little lady here was in on it, too, and best I can figure they've committed at least a half dozen felonies." His words still had that slur on them, but now his voice was bright, edged up and too quick.

Neither Patrick nor Reynold even looked at him, their eyes on Thigpen.

"Wasn't sure how I was going to get backup in on this one," Yandle went on, "but now you showed up, we can go ahead and—"

"Shut up, Doug," Thigpen said. He was looking at Reynold, still a step closer to him than Yandle and Patrick.

Yandle's gun moved down a bit. He looked at Thigpen. "But Tommy, we got us a 326 and a 372 on our—"

"So, this your horse?" Thigpen said to Reynold. He leaned a little forward, sat back again, the saddle creaking with it all.

"Damn fucking straight it is," Reynold said, and took another step. "Now get the fuck off him right now, before I knock shit out of you, you cocksucking—"

"This the one you take on your drives over to Leland's deer hunts?" Thigpen cut in. He was smiling.

"Who you think you are, you son of a bitch?" Reynold said. "You think 'cause you wear a fucking badge you can go on ahead and steal somebody's horse?" He started around the fire then, his bald head glittering with sweat, his hands in fists.

Pigboy and Fatback. Yandle and Thigpen, showing up at the same time to the club, the two of them back there with us and looking at the body. They were together.

But, no.

No, they weren't.

It was there, in front of me the whole time: *set up and operating till kingdom come.*

And Thigpen's words: *The only way through this all is for him to do what he's been asked to do. You tell him things'll be fixed. All's he got to do is what's been asked.*

Two different stories.

And only now did I understand why Unc just wanted me to shut up: if I opened my mouth, Yandle might figure out something he didn't yet know, namely, that there were other things at stake: the fact Constance Dupree Simons hadn't murdered her husband, that somebody named Pigboy and Fatback had been ordered to void Middleton, that all of Hungry Neck itself was about to be sold off.

Cleve Ravenel, it occurred to me, was just feeding off both sides of the fence.

Greedy.

If it hadn't been for your doctor's wife coming along and blowing away her hubby's head, Yandle said. He didn't know Constance didn't do it.

Reynold stepped past Mom and me, his smell as thick and nasty as the floor of his horse trailer, and moved toward Thigpen, and then, like it wasn't even happening, Thigpen drew the gun from his holster, said, "That's good, because if old Jeb here is the one you take on your deer drives, I don't imagine he's much gun-shy." He pointed the gun at Reynold and fired on him, three shots quick in a row.

I'd heard pistols before. I'd fired them. I'd fired at cans, into trees, into woods I couldn't know were empty. I'd shot squirrels before with a pistol, even shot a crow once for no good reason other than that I had a pistol and here was a crow.

But the sound back then was nothing next to the roar and flash off the barrel of this pistol, the flash reaching like thick red daggers to Reynold, with each dagger the sick thump of a bullet into his chest, the clean, quick whistle of them right on out his back. All three bullets hit the fire, where a nearly burnt-through log split in two, rolled a few inches, sent up sparks.

I saw all this, in just this instant.

He hit ground only a couple feet from Mom and me, his face turned to us, his bald head orange for the light from the fire. He blinked five or six times in a row, his arms still at his side. He was stiff, tensed over, eyes blinking away, and the hand I could see wasn't in a fist anymore, but the fingers were spread wide, wide as they could get. He let go a deep breath from all the way down in him, a sound far away and heavy, like he was drowning in mud.

His hands went limp, his eyes closed, and I saw in the firelight steam up from his mouth, where that breath had let out, and steam up, too, from there in his chest, those holes.

"How old are you, Huger Dillard?" Thigpen said.

I turned. There sat Thigpen, one hand still to the pommel, the gun pointed at the ground.

I opened my mouth. I blinked, felt my throat go dry. I hadn't breathed yet.

"How old?" Thigpen said.

"Leave the boy alone," Unc said. He hadn't moved, his arms around his legs, his face toward Thigpen.

"I said, how old?" Thigpen adjusted himself in the saddle. The saddle creaked, the horse twitched one ear.

I swallowed hard, whispered, "Fifteen."

"Damn," Thigpen said. "I didn't see my first murder till I was twenty-one." He slowly shook his head, smiled. "Must be true what they're saying about how fast kids grow up these days."

"Leave him alone, Tommy," Unc said.

Then Mom screamed.

It started with a rasping breath in, long and hard, and for a second I thought maybe Reynold wasn't dead after all, that here he was trying to breathe in all the air there was to breathe. But then the scream itself came, pierced me and shocked me all at once, Mom finally reacting to what'd happened. Here was a dead man, shot in front of our eyes, fallen at our feet.

I took hold of her and tried to push us away, tried to scramble away from this body, only to find the leg irons were still there on my ankles, that Mom was still tied to her own spike, and we had nowhere to go except here, spiked to the ground. Still Mom screamed.

Then Thigpen fired again, and I turned, saw he'd shot this one off into the air.

I felt my breaths in and in too quick, Mom doing the same. She held on to me, her arms around me too hard, though they were exactly what I wanted: Mom holding me.

"Tommy?" Yandle said.

His gun was down now, his mouth open. He stared up at Thigpen.

Patrick was gone.

"Unlock them," Thigpen said.

"But Tommy," Yandle whispered, "why'd you shoot—"

"Do it," Thigpen said, and cocked the hammer.

Yandle quick shook his head, like he'd been slapped awake. Mom whimpered beside me. Unc looked at Thigpen.

Yandle put his gun back in the holster, reached into the front pocket of his fatigue jacket, pulled out a key chain, all with his eyes on Thigpen.

"We was just running a pot farm back here," Yandle said as he started around the fire, his steps slow, his hand with the keys trying to find the right one without the use of that arm in a sling. His voice had emptied itself of that police-boy pitch, now just a Walterboro nothing. "Cleve Ravenel come to me one afternoon looking to make some money, told me he could bankroll a little operation back here." He nodded toward Unc, still without taking his eyes off Thigpen. "Figured Hungry Neck'd be the smartest place, what with a blind man watching over the place." He paused. "And a snot-nose runt his only helper." He tried a laugh. Still his hand fumbled with the keys. "This parcel back here's tough as hell to get into, so we set up in here."

He stopped altogether, forgot the keys, like something had occurred to him, a big idea. "Then the fucking doctor's wife come in and killed the son of a bitch, which of course makes this land hotter'n shit, what with SLED crawling around, looking for whatever the hell it is they may want to find, chief among it all maybe, we're thinking, our little operation. I hear tell from Mitch over to the office SLED is coming in here tomorrow morning, going to give Hungry Neck a comb-through."

He was just jabbering now, talking and talking, trying to reach something in Thigpen.

"So we're liquidating. Getting the hell out of Atlanta before it burns to the ground." He tried the same laugh again.

"Unlock them," Thigpen said.

Yandle stood there a second longer, then looked down at the key chain in his hand, shook his head, finally found the right one.

He went to Unc first, knelt in front of him, slipped the key into the clamp on Unc's left foot, and the clamp fell open. He pulled the key out, opened the other, his eyes always on Thigpen.

Now both Unc's feet were free, but he didn't move, only held his legs with his arms.

Yandle stood. He was coming toward us and had to step over Reynold's body, there between us and the fire.

He knelt at Mom's feet, took the rope her ankles were tied with, and started working the knot at the spike with his one hand until Mom's left ankle was free. He was looking up at Thigpen, scared shitless, his hand shaking, his face wet with sweat that glistened in the firelight. Mom pulled her foot away from him hard, jammed herself into me deeper to get away from that body there and at the same time trying to hold on to me, like she might be able to protect me from something.

"Tommy, you can't arrest me," Yandle said. "You can't."

"Finish up," Thigpen said.

"Tommy," Yandle said, "Tommy, we can work this together. We can figure out how to make it look like Reynold and—"

"Finish," he said, and now the saddle creaked again, the horse's ear twitched.

Yandle turned to my leg irons, put the key in. He fished it one way and another, and then mine fell open, and I pushed back and away from him, Mom with me, the two of us scooting hard and fast and away.

Yandle stood, faced Thigpen. His good hand was out to his side, palm up, the key chain hanging from a finger. He said, "You can't arrest me, Tommy. I got enough shit on you to sink a ship. Now." He lifted his hand up a little higher. "Either we work this together and figure out a way through this that's going to be mutually beneficial to the both of us, or—"

"I ain't going to arrest you," Thigpen said. He was smiling now, and I caught a glint of firelight off that gold tooth of his. He leaned his head to one side. "Way I see it, you come out a hero. You out here solo stumble on Reynold, and Leland and Eugenie and the boy out here to their Mary Jane hideaway. Patrick's got to be halfway to Jacksonville by now, the chickenshit." He chuckled. "Then all hell breaks loose, and in the ensuing gun battle everybody, Dr. Cleve Ravenel included, just plain gets killed." He leaned his head the other way. "This, of course, includes you."

"What?" Yandle said, and he gave the little shake of his head again, like he'd been slapped one more time.

"Get out your gun."

"What you mean, Tommy?" Yandle whispered. He took a step back, then another.

Unc moved then, his head turned to the fire, looking past it to the other side and Ravenel's truck. It was the smallest move, only his head turning, his back straightening a bit.

He heard something.

"Tommy, you don't mean to—" Yandle started.

Then it all happened, all of it in four seconds, maybe five.

Patrick stood from behind the tail of the pickup, there where Cleve Ravenel lay. He had a shotgun, quick leveled it at Thigpen. "You fucking killed my brother!" he shouted, the words tight and wild and broken, and he fired.

Here was another flash, this one bigger, the roar louder, and he worked the action on the gun, fired again.

But in the piece of time between the action being worked and him firing, Thigpen fired, and the next flash off Patrick's shotgun went up at a crazy angle, and I saw Patrick's forehead burst, the way a melon will burst when fired upon. Just like that, and he fell, disappeared behind the pickup.

Now Yandle's whole body was shaking, I saw in this same second, but he still pulled his gun out, held it up, pointed at Thigpen.

I looked up to Thigpen and the horse. The horse sat there, stone still, Thigpen leaned way over to his left in the saddle, his left shoulder hunched up, that smile twisted tight into a grimace. He'd been hit.

His gun was on Yandle, and he fired.

Yandle screamed. I flinched, and Mom too.

It was a scream beside us and in us, a scream twisted and clotted up and too loud, Yandle sprawled on the ground. His boots were there at Reynold's head, almost kicked it for how his feet twisted and turned, like he was climbing a set of stairs.

Then I saw his right arm, the one he'd held the gun in. The fingers were splayed out, just like Reynold's had been, but they were moving, twitching, one finger and another and another, twitching. The gun lay about a foot away from his hand, just right there, on the ground.

And there, about halfway up the sleeve of his fatigue jacket, was what looked like a splintered piece of wood poking up through the material, the material ripped open, that piece of white splintered wood shiny in the firelight.

It was bone.

All this in four seconds, maybe five. The time it takes to breathe in and breathe out.

Yandle stopped the scream a moment. His head snapped back and hit the ground, and he swallowed in quick breaths, his arm in the sling there across his chest.

"One-in-a-million shot," Thigpen said, on his words the fact he'd been hit: his voice was hard, sharp, no air to it. He still held the gun on Yandle. "You idiot rednecks have made this harder than it had to be." He took in a breath, held it a moment, let it out. "One in a million. That bullet tunneled right down the bone in your forearm, blew out the whole thing." He took another breath, held it, let it out. "One in a million."

Thigpen lay over the pommel, sort of rolled down the side of the horse until his feet hit ground, all with the gun out in front of him, aimed at Yandle. Still the horse hadn't moved.

Mom pinched down on my arms and chest, holding me, her face in my shoulder. She took in a thousand short breaths, inside each one a shard of a whimper. Still Unc sat there, his face to Thigpen, who took a step toward Yandle.

Yandle was groaning now, a dark sound full of itself and this night and that shiny bone, and the fact he knew he was dead. The fingers of his right hand still twitched each on their own, but the arm itself lay there, dead already, and now he started to try and roll himself toward the gun, as though he might use that hand in the sling with it, and as though Thigpen with the gun pointed down at him weren't walking toward him. He rocked himself, his eyes darting again and again at Thigpen, then to the gun, with each rocking of his body a short, sharp gasp coming out of him for the pain and the knowledge of what was to come.

And here I was, only watching. I thought for an instant to grab the gun, there only three or four feet from me, but I let that instant go, because I was afraid, and I saw in Yandle's eyes that, in fact, the same thing was going to happen to us, that we were going to die, too, and that trying to grab up a gun would just bring it all about quicker than it would otherwise.

"You always were nothing but an asshole," Thigpen said to Yandle. He stood beside Reynold's body now. The left arm of Thigpen's coat, just below the shoulder, was torn up, a spot no bigger than a small pinecone. Patrick'd only nicked him.

He brought up the gun, cocked it. Still Yandle rocked, faster now, the arm in the sling reaching across his body, reaching, that dead arm in the way, its fingers still twitching.

"But I like your idea about letting this greenhouse back here serve to convict the good Leland and company. We'll do that, leave it up, so when they come back here and find all these bodies, you'll still be the hero. It'll be only me here to testify to your strength and courage."

Still Yandle rocked, harder and faster, the gasps gone, only him moving fast for a gun he had to know he'd never get hold of.

"And the funny thing about all this, the real hoot of it," Thigpen said, drawing a bead on Yandle, "is that you're going to die and don't have a flying fucking clue what you stumbled in on."

Finally Yandle stopped, his chest heaving, with each breath in the same shard of a whimper Mom gave out.

Thigpen pulled the trigger.

Yandle screamed.

But nothing fired. Only the empty click of a gun out of bullets.

"Hah!" Thigpen shouted, and shook his head, looked at the gun. "Forgot I shot off six rounds." He chuckled again, though he had to take in a breath for it. "Guess this ain't much like some old TV show," he said, and lowered the gun, shook open the chamber. He grimaced again as he lifted the arm that'd been shot, put that hand into his coat pocket, pulled out a handful of bullets.

Then Unc was up, took two fast steps, all movement coming toward us, one solid shot of himself from where he'd been sitting all this while, and he clipped Thigpen from behind, his shoulder lowered, head down, all of him aiming at only what he heard, distance and position gained just from sitting there, listening.

Thigpen fell onto Yandle's legs, the bullets flying from his hand, and now Unc rolled across Reynold's body and toward Mom and me.

"Run!" Unc whispered hard, teeth together, him scrambling to stand.

But I was only looking at him, Unc right here in my face, black blood down both his cheeks, white eyes open wide, empty and hollow and dead, dead as we were going to be a few seconds from now.

Thigpen pushed himself up from Yandle, but Yandle kicked him now, his legs furious into Thigpen's stomach, who doubled over, Yandle's boots into his middle again and again.

"Run!" Unc whispered again, though this time it was loud as a shout.

Still Yandle kicked at Thigpen, who finally rolled over and away from him, almost into the fire. He was on his knees now, the gun still in his hand, but he was leaned over, coughing hard.

I looked at Unc, at those eyes, eyes that seemed even in how hollow they were to hold out some hope.

I stood.

Mom came up with me, still holding tight to my arm, still whimpering, and Unc grabbed up my other arm, and I turned, ran, the three of us heading off into a darkness I couldn't see into, the thin blanket of light cast from the fire gone in a matter of four or five strides.

But we were running, away from all this.

"Catch up to you in a few!" Thigpen called out, and coughed, then laughed, coughed again.

And though I know I shouldn't have, know it only slowed us down a moment or three, I turned, looked back. Already the woods were folding in on us, my feet ripping through growth, the trees and vines and all else pulling closed like a curtain between us and the fire.

There stood Thigpen, Yandle back to rocking. Thigpen pushed in a bullet, then snapped shut the chamber. He took a step up, only a silhouette now for the fire behind him, and stood over Yandle, who stopped rocking, lifted his head, as though he might be able to sit up. He was crying now, giving out this small, high-pitched sound.

Thigpen said something to him, something I couldn't hear, then fired, one shot to Yandle's head.

His head slammed back, and for a second in the silence there came the echo of that shot.

Thigpen looked up, still only a silhouette.

"On my way!" he called out.

Unc pushed me from behind.

"Run," he whispered, "or we die."

19

We ran.

Mom held my right hand with both hers, still took in quick breaths, whimpering. Unc had hold of the back of my jeans jacket, held on, and we ran.

It was black, all of it, the ground and sky and trees, my eyes not yet adjusted to whatever light that same half-moon'd given out last night when Tabitha and I had walked back to Benjamin's shack, and now it wasn't just Unc was blind anymore. It was me, blind to everything that'd been going on at Hungry Neck, this place like some sort of ugly cancer of a sudden, filled with shit and death, when all these years of my life I'd thought it perfect, a place to get away from all the shit of North Charleston, shit that was right there where you could see it, the carjackings and BP minimart shootings and innocent-bystander kids shot down in the high school parking lot. Shit right there on the surface, I'd always known. But only now, tonight, did I finally realize there was shit even in the most perfect places you could imagine.

Hungry Neck.

My heart pounded for the running, branches brushing against my face and legs, weeds and palmetto fronds and saplings and dead branches at my feet all taking a piece of time with having to make our way through, no trails anywhere, not even a deer path I might find and follow.

Then slowly the shadows started making their way into my eyes, light and dark giving in to let me see, while still Mom whimpered, stumbled, pulled at me, and while Unc pushed, him right behind me like I was some battering ram through it all, and I realized in this growing light of shadows and night that this was what my life had always been: the pull of Mom to some life she'd seen might be better for us close in to Charleston proper, and Unc pushing me deeper into Hungry Neck, deeper and deeper, so that with the stump my foot hit then, me losing balance a second or so but still staying up and still running, I saw that even Unc's tossing me those keys last April, the gift of a beat-up Luv once owned by a man killed in a cafeteria half the world away, was just another way to get me deeper into this life, and into whatever it was he wanted me in it for: chauffeur, errand boy.

His eyes.

And though that afternoon I'd gotten the Luv I drove this land for hours, drove it like I'd known the land better than my own bedroom, then parked it out on Cemetery, where the road goes close to the Ashepoo, and where I'd looked out over the marsh and all those nameless squat islands scattered around, I didn't know any of it.

I'd watched the sun set that night, the marsh going that green you couldn't name, mixed in and down inside it browns and reds and a color like bone, and I'd believed that night I knew something: what the world was about for a few seconds, maybe, and how beautiful it could be.

But now I'd seen bone, seen it splintered up and through a man's arm, seen the fingers twitch, the eyes flutter, the head snap back.

I ran, and Unc pushed at me and Mom pulled at me, and here now were branches low off a live oak, and I ducked down, whispered hard, "Look out," and dipped down, half turned to Mom, and put my hand to her head, pushed her down so she wouldn't hit, Unc ducking too, and we made it, and started to running again.

And here was my job with my mother as well: protector of some sort, the boy meant to shepherd his mom through a night of the shit smell off a paper mill, through an empty Sunday after Thanksgiving, through a life trying to find another life, away from the one she'd left back here at Hungry Neck.

Hungry Neck. It all came back to here.

I heard a gunshot, far behind us, and Unc yanked hard on my jacket, stopped. I almost fell, my feet headed away from here, but I caught my balance, Mom going a little ahead with me.

The echo off the shot still hung in the air, a whisper of sound next to nothing, dying just as quick.

I thought Unc'd been hit.

"Unc," I whispered, "you okay?"

He nodded, I could see in the shadows and moonlight. We were all breathing hard, Mom with her hands to her knees, bent over, Unc half turned from us, listening, the only sound now all of us breathing in and out, in and out.

We were in a clearing of sorts, big as the trailer, live oaks lying low all around. A screen of growth surrounded us, this empty piece of land where the wetlands surged up, the ground soft and spongy, puddles now and again, and I wondered if we were off to the north, anywhere near Cemetery Road, or Baldwin, or Lannear.

"We have to go," I whispered, and heard how it was me that'd made this decision, not Unc pushing from behind, not Mom pulling because she couldn't keep up.

It was me. Huger Dillard.

I took a deep breath, grabbed up Mom's hand, Unc's arm, and I started off across the clearing.

They said nothing, and we splashed through water as we crossed, then ducked beneath more limbs, Unc's hand back on the tail of my jacket, me a divining rod of some kind, telling him exactly which way to turn as we came to a palmetto and rounded it, then a fallen log, the three of us up and over it and going again in a second, all of it in the best way I could gauge as being in the opposite direction of that gunshot.

We ran, the screen of trees not a screen at all, but just growth without end, a wall as deep as the woods with only a moment or three now and again of clear woods, of tree trunks around us like the twisted skeletons of animals too big to believe, then came the growth again, mixed-in rotted stumps and more dead branches, all of it only slowing us down and slowing us down so that, though it seemed we'd run for miles, I knew that gunshot a few minutes before was just a hundred yards or so away.

It was Mom this time to stop. She let go my hand, just let it go, and stopped.

She had her hands to her knees again, her shoulders up and down for the breaths she was trying to grab. Slowly she shook her head.

"We can't stop," I whispered, and put a hand to her back, saw in the dark only the blurred image of my mother's face: her mouth, her nose, her eyes.

"All y'all!" came Thigpen's voice, far off and muffled for the woods it had to travel through to find us. "Ollie ollie oxen in come free!"

Mom let out a single, small sob. Just a cry, nearly silent, but here with us.

I whispered, "Let's go," and took her hand, turned to find Unc.

He was right there, his face as close to mine as when he'd told me to run.

He whispered, "Find the North Star," his whisper next to nothing, even less than Mom's cry. But I'd heard him.

"What?" I whispered.

"Got some business with y'all," Thigpen called out.

He was out there, on horseback, with a gun.

"I woke up when the truck stopped back there," Unc whispered. "When we got here." He paused. "I don't know where we are. But you find Polaris, we might have a clue."

Mom was beside me now, stood close. She held my hand tight.

I looked up. We were beneath a canopy of branches, the only

piece of sky I could make sense of that half-moon, broken up for leaves.

I whispered, "I can't see much. We have to get to a clearing."

Unc nodded once, and we turned, started away from where that voice had come.

The next clearing came a minute or so later, past a patch of dead blackberry bushes we had to step through, the thorns tugging at sleeves and legs and ankles, until we were there, in a piece of land covered over in white grass knee high.

I stopped, looked up. This time Unc didn't let go of my jacket, and turned with me as I scanned the sky.

The moon was clear now of leaves, the stars thin for that moonlight but still there. I turned slowly, the sound of my heart beating too loud in my ears, and for a second I was afraid that sound would give us away and scare off these stars, both.

I turned slowly, looking, looking. Then there it was: Polaris, straight ahead, almost touching the tree line, but there.

I took in a breath, whispered, "Got it."

"Had to polish off ol' Doc Ravenel," Thigpen hollered. "Case you wondered what that last shot was about."

He was closer now, the words clearer, sharper.

"Turn me," Unc whispered. "Turn me to it."

His eyes were closed now. He'd let go my jacket, stood there, waiting for me to touch him.

I looked up at the star, at him, the star again. Then I stood behind him, put my hands to his shoulders, turned him toward it. He was a quarter turn from it, his feet taking small steps, his whole body under my strength, as though if I were to let go his shoulders at this instant he would topple. Then his shoulders were squared to it.

He whispered, "Lift my face to it."

I brought my hands from his shoulders, placed them along either side of his jaw. I could feel the stubble on his face, the hard bone right there under skin.

I lifted his jaw, his head leaning back in front of me, that Braves cap still on. I looked up at the star, his head tilting back, until it seemed we were both staring up along the same imaginary line, some tangent off planet Earth that could draw us in the right direction, and I stopped.

My uncle. A blind man, our compass.

I let go his chin, set my hands on his shoulders again, his face to the North Star. Then slowly, slowly, his chin came down, until finally he faced the ground, and I wondered what pictures played through him right then, in this silence, this black. I wondered what memories of Hungry Neck he held, what maps he knew, maps drawn not on paper but on his heart.

Mom touched my shoulder then, and the three of us stood there, above us a black night sky, as black as any idea of what might happen next to us might be.

I heard movement to our right, leaves moving underfoot, and my hands tightened a second on Unc's shoulders in fear.

Then he shot his arm out to his side, pointed off into woods.

Here were more sounds: leaves, a branch crack.

He turned toward where he pointed, reached to me, this time grabbed hold of my belt at the small of my back, and pushed me away in front of him, and we were running. I looked back a moment for Mom, saw her running, reaching for my hand, reaching for it, then I felt it, and I turned, ran harder into the wall of woods.

"No problem your running off like this," Thigpen called. "Only makes it a little more interesting is all."

The growth went thick on us, me slowing down and ducking and pushing away and ducking again, Unc tight on my belt, Mom letting go now and again to handle herself on her own. Shadows down and around us moved quick, darted in and out, became the horse he was on, became Thigpen himself swirling up and in while still we ran, and while still I didn't know where we were headed.

"Don't worry how I'll explain this one to SLED," Thigpen called again. "Got four or five different guns on me." He paused. "Including that one you got last night, Huger. Turns out Reynold had hold of that bad boy." He let out a laugh. "Each of y'all's going to be shot by a different one. This whole thing'll look like one big redneck-on-redneck crime spree, everybody firing on everybody else."

The ground dipped down a moment, a puddle splashed through, back up to level ground.

Then came the hard thrashing of something on us from behind, the heavy pounding of a horse through woods. It was a sound I'd heard a million times before: Patrick and Reynold coming up after the dogs'd run through.

We came to a fallen oak, the trunk of it four feet high, and I started over it, felt Unc let go and Mom both, all of us up and scrambling.

I slipped down the other side, felt Unc take hold. But Mom's hand wasn't there, and I'd already taken a couple steps away when I turned, saw her behind us, bent over.

I turned back to her, Unc going with me, and moved to grab her, to pull her with us, and still the thrashing came through the woods, a crash and tumble of broken sounds coming right for us, and I glanced over the top of the trunk, saw way back in the woods a shape, big and hulking, black and lumbering inside all the shadows and black, headed for us.

I crouched, hoped he hadn't seen me, and reached for Mom, reached for her, ready to spin, to keep running.

But then she quick lay down, rolled away and beneath the log, and she was gone.

I squatted, looked for her, Unc coming down with me. He pulled hard on my belt, his signal to get us out of here, get us going and away.

Mom's hand came out from beneath the log, that jacket sleeve like some thick and jittery snake, waving frantic at us, and I took it, lay flat on the ground, rolled like she'd done, and suddenly I was inside total black save for a couple-foot-wide swath of gray, that slip of space we'd rolled down through, my back pressed into Mom.

Now the pounding was even thicker, heavier, right here in my ears, us down beneath the ground, the horse hard on us, nearly here, and now Unc was squatted down, and I reached out, pulled hard on his hand, and he rolled toward me and Mom, his body pressed into mine, the three of us smashed together in this washed-out space, cold and damp.

And just as Unc fell into place in front of me, the whole trunk shook, a huge shock of sound and movement, and in the next instant the whole world was fixed in a perfect silence, no sound at all, and now here came the horse, I could see over Unc's shoulder, the whole of Jeb Stuart flying off in front of us from above, then the shock of it landing, the heavy strike of the hooves on the ground out there enough to send down on us wet rotten wood, and there sat Thigpen, riding away, in his silhouette a shotgun out to one side, him ducked low in the saddle, riding hard.

Riding away from us, into the woods.

I pushed at Unc, wanted up and out of here to head back the other way. But Unc didn't move, reached back his hand and touched at my face with it, found my lips, and put his hand to them a moment: *Stay put.*

Thigpen kept heading away from us, the hoofbeats thinner, farther away. I could see him, still low, the trees about to swallow him.

But then he stopped, pulled the horse up, nosed him this way, and they were standing sideways to us, maybe thirty yards off. That silhouette again, shrouded and choked by the silhouettes of limbs and trees.

Mom moved behind me, put her arm over my shoulder, clutched at my jacket. She was breathing hard.

Thigpen wheeled the horse around, started back at us, walking it slow.

I whispered, "He's coming back."

Unc and Mom froze.

"Don't make this any harder than it already is," Thigpen called out. "Larry, Moe, and Yandle back there went easy. No need to make it tough on yourselves, considering you got to know by now there ain't no way out of this thing." He paused, stopped the horse. Mom still breathed hard behind me, though I could feel she was trying hard to hold it in, keep it slow. Unc didn't seem even to breathe.

"Shame about Doc Ravenel," Thigpen said. "Something of a surprise, that one. What you might call a nigger in the woodpile."

He started toward us again, and I could feel the cold ground working on me, digging in, and I shivered.

Mom pulled me closer to her.

"Sort of like that Dr. Joe Cray over to Mount Pleasant y'all paid a visit to," he said. "Something of a surprise to me you ended up over there. Or did you think I wouldn't follow you, Leland?" He stopped the horse again, this time maybe twenty yards off. He was talking normal, just his voice out in the night. He knew we were out here.

He moved a bit, then came a flare of orange at his face, a match lit up. He held it in front of him, the match nearly going out, then flaring up, out and up. Finally he shook the match, dropped it, and turned his head, his profile to us now.

He was smoking a cigar.

The tip went bright, and he leaned his head back, brought it from his mouth, held it out. "These black cigars taste like horse shit," he said, and laughed. He settled the shotgun back into place, the barrel out to his left. "Got this as a gift from the good doctor, once you boys left him alone in there."

Mom pulled at me, breathed right there at my ear, and I thought I could hear the smallest edge of a whimper on each breath she let out.

"Guess that'd be lying, calling it a gift, though. More like a perk. Perk of the profession. Kind of like watching Yandle back there squirm. Listening to him squeal." He brought the cigar back to his mouth, drew on it. "Now, that's a perk."

He started toward us.

"Same kind of squeal Dr. Cray give out when I popped him. Didn't particularly need to do it, other than the fact he'd talked to you two, and he'd be able to testify at some point to something. Which explains why it took me so long to catch up with you boys, why I didn't just head things off at the pass at the trailer." He chuckled, his shoulders moving up. "Then again, we'd never have discovered this little gold mine set up in the woods. Worked out nice. This way there's no backing out of agreeing to sell Hungry Neck, because all y'all, the whole Dillard clan, will be long dead and gone, and the land'll be seized by the state, and the wonders of the greased palm will serve this whole stinking patch of land up to the people who want it, Leland."

He stopped suddenly, looked quick off to his right, the tip of the cigar gone a dull red. He'd heard a squirrel, maybe. Still, he sat there, listening, looking, while my heart beat, banged in me too loud, my breaths thin and empty.

He'd killed Cray.

Slowly he looked away from his right, turned to the left. He drew on the cigar, the tip going bright orange. "Course that bad boy with no head nor skin to his hands didn't squeal a bit when he met up with the working end of a shotgun."

He gave the reins a shake, and Jeb moved a few feet before Thigpen gave a pull, stopped him again. "Not him," he said, and now I could feel Mom shivering, clutching my shoulder, breathing shallow and quick. "That man had testicular fortitude when it come to meeting his maker." He took the cigar from his mouth. "Testicular fortitude. Like none I ever seen."

Unc lay still as a stone, Mom's shivering behind me heavier, that edge of a whimper too close on her, ready to break out.

"Them shitheads of Delbert Yandle's squealed out, too, when I rolled that Ford of theirs. Couple of flunkies, them. Just like Delbert. No need even to waste a shell on them. Though it turns out I had to lose two on his boy back there."

He started Jeb toward us again, the horse moving slow, step on step.

He was closer now, and I thought maybe I could see his face, some kind of grin on it, barely lit by the tiny jewel of orange on the cigar. He looked either way again, leaned forward in the saddle, back again.

"But the headless hunter didn't squeal before he went, and I admire him for that." He let out another laugh, shook his head. "Son of a bitch winked at me just before I did it. A man after my own heart. Then pop, he's gone, my job to shovel him up, haul him over to Hungry Neck, and prop up that sign at his feet, see what happens and when." He laughed. "And I'm getting paid for all this!"

Mom was shivering full on now, her breath hard and sharp in my ear. Still he heard nothing, no movements at all in these woods, so he knew we were here, somewhere. He knew. And talking was a way to flush us out.

He shook the reins, the horse moved toward us, and now I could hear Jeb breathing, head down, then up. "The bargain I cut with the main man is to see to it Mrs. Constance Dupree got taken care of too. And the funny thing is, she didn't squeal, neither." The horse came toward us a few more feet, Thigpen looking one way and the other, that cigar there in his mouth. "She didn't squeal. Weird one, that bitch. Didn't complain word one, once she figured out what her now dead hubby's request was. Checked herself in to the Rantowles Motel, me out in the car, watching to make sure she didn't pull anything on me. Then she just walked right into the room, wrapped that electrical cord round the shower rung and her neck both. All's I had to do was watch her step off the edge of the tub." He paused, slowly shook his head. "Can't say she winked at me. But she was smiling, looking at me just before she took that little step, and then her eyes commenced to bulging out big, her tongue too." He gave out another laugh. "Quite a charge, I tell you, watching a woman do that to herself. I see now how that Kevorkian fuck gets his kicks."

Unc was trembling now, both my hands on his shoulders, and I could feel my throat welling up hard, felt my eyes going wet and my heart pounding too loud for all this, all this. That was the night she'd come to me, that was the night she'd told me she loved Unc, that was the night she'd told me to cherish my momma.

My mom, behind me, shivered too, us here and almost dead. Us, here.

"Y'all got to move sometime," Thigpen shouted now. "You got to move sometime, might as well be now." He put his boots to the horse, and the horse moved toward us again, now ten feet off, and I knew he could hear my heart pounding.

"But them two was out of the ordinary, them not squealing on me," he said, and pulled hard on the cigar. He was close enough now to where I could see his eyes and nose when the tip flared, there above us, silhouetted by the night behind and around him, the pale light off that moon above us all. He brought down the cigar, let out the smoke. "Most of them go squealing away. Kind of like the sound a woman'll make when you're poking her good." He put the cigar back up. "Now, ain't that right, Leland?"

Unc still trembled, and Mom trembled, and my heart banged loud enough to be heard a mile away, and the horse brought down his head, held it low a moment: Jeb smelled us.

"Just like that sound a woman makes when you're poking her good, and she's wailing like it's hurting her too much but there ain't a chance in hell she wants you to stop." He pulled on the cigar again, took it out. He put his hands to the pommel, leaned forward, the leather creaking.

Jeb shook his head.

"Maybe ol' Constance used to give out that squeal I was hoping for, Leland, back when you was poking her for sport." He settled himself back into the saddle. "Or maybe," he said, and gave a short laugh, "that's the kind of squeal Eugenie give out one night a long long time ago."

Unc was breathing hard now, Mom still on the edge of whimpering, and now she pushed herself into me even closer than before, and I felt her chin on my shoulder, heard her breaths quick in and out, and felt the heat of her breath, too, right there at my ear.

She whispered, "Huger, no."

They were next to nothing, words maybe I didn't really hear.

"Hey, Huger!" Thigpen shouted now, "Huger, you know-it-all shit, I'll wager I know something you don't!"

"No, Huger, no," Mom whispered.

Unc stopped breathing, stopped trembling. He reached with his hand up to my hand on his shoulder. It was cold, that hand.

But I was watching Thigpen, there in the dark.

Something was happening.

"Huger," Thigpen said, no longer shouting. He gave Jeb a small kick, and he came even closer, Jeb's front hooves almost close enough to touch.

"Huger Dillard," he said, even quieter now, "this here news I'm going to let you in on is what you call dead-man talk. Words just between us, not meant for nobody else." He paused. "Dead-man talk. You tell, you're dead." He chuckled again, stopped the horse. "But I guess that point is moot. You're dead any way you cut it." He stopped the horse, and I could hear in the quiet him draw in on the cigar, let it out.

He said, "Ain't you ever wondered why your auntie burned herself alive, and why your daddy hauled ass out of Dodge not too long after?"

Here was Jeb's head again, down at the ground. I couldn't see Thigpen anymore for how close he was. Only Jeb's hooves, his head, looking at us.

And now it was me trembling, me breathing hard, me falling deeper into this hole under a log, this hole of my life, because there was something happening here, Unc with a cold hand on mine, Mom pressed into me and whispering words I wasn't sure were words at all, maybe dreams of words circling me, circling me like that buzzard'd circled the body of Charles Middleton Simons, M.D., good riddance to bad rubbish, that dead body leading me finally here to solve a problem I'd not wanted to solve my entire life: why my daddy left me and Mom and Unc here at Hungry Neck. Added now was the news my Aunt Sarah killed herself, the burning of Unc's house never explained to me, a mystery neither my mom nor Unc ever thought to make clear to me. Only that she'd died, Unc injured for life.

She killed herself, my Sarah, Unc'd said at that house in Mount Pleasant. Their home.

It's my own greed made her do it, he'd said. *My own.*

My mom and dad, howling at each other out to the kitchen.

Leland, Eugenie.

And me.

Something I'd known before I even knew. But something I never wanted to know.

"Huger," Thigpen said, nearly in a whisper. Jeb's head shot up, and I couldn't see him at all anymore, just his legs, four stalks in the darkness, a darkness closing around me, closing and closing as tight around my heart as what I knew, finally, was coming next.

What was happening, and had already happened.

Who I was. No news at all.

"Huger, if your momma's at all like most every fuck I ever had, the night Leland give it to her she squealed like a rabbit in a trap."

"Huger," Mom whispered again, then cried, air out of her like knives into my back, my neck.

"Imagine that, Huger: your momma and your uncle fucking to beat the band, making what turned out to be you, you little shit. A love child. Kind of makes you think twice on that word *bastard* now, don't it?"

Unc clutched my hand in his.

The world went tighter, the hole I could see out of, this thin slip of night, going smaller and smaller.

"Huger Dillard," Thigpen said. "Bastard child of Eugenie and her husband's brother, Leland Dillard."

What I'd known, and never knew.

I broke my hand free of Unc's, pushed at him and pushed over him and to that hole closing down over me now, before me only the legs of this horse, and then the horse reared, and I was out of that hole, my own legs kicking against Unc behind me, and I could taste my heart pounding in my throat, the source of all the dark red metal on earth in my throat and pounding, and the horse reared higher, whinnied, and now I was standing, above me this horse, Tommy Thigpen falling back in the saddle, startled, one hand with the reins, the other with the shotgun, and I saw his eyes as clear as any day, saw him looking down at me, saw the cigar fall from his lips, saw that mouth turn into a smile, all this while the horse reared up, all of this in the dark, all of this surrounded by trees and stars and this night, and I jumped at him, grabbed his arm, the one Patrick'd shot, and pulled at him, pulled at him, because I wanted to kill him.

He screamed out when I pulled that arm, lost his balance a moment while the horse came down for the first time, and he dropped the shotgun.

"Huger!" Mom cried out from behind me, and even in this instant of all things happening I didn't recognize the word as meaning anything I could know.

And the horse reared again, this time higher, and I held hard Thigpen's arm, pulled at him, pulled at him, while he still tried to hold on to the saddle, and I could feel my feet off the ground, me hanging on to only that arm, him hanging on to the pommel and trying to stay on, the horse turning and turning, and then I reached high as I could, and punched his arm, punched it again and again, felt the bone through the flesh of his arm, felt the wet cloth of the jacket, felt this all, and heard, too, his own scream, a low-pitched growl, and I heard only then, too, the sound I made: my mouth was open wide, screaming out of me all the air my lungs could hold.

Finally he pulled that arm free of me, and I fell to the ground, my feet gone from beneath me, and I was on my back, Jeb reared up above me, above him those stars, and then he came down, Thigpen now with a hand to the inside of his coat and fumbling, Jeb's hooves an inch from my legs, and here was the glint of moonlight off the steel of another gun, him leaning toward me, his good arm raised, the one I pulled slack at his side like a man's arm hanging from a pickup window: dead, hanging.

He brought the gun up, the horse still scared, jangled up and dancing, aware of his hooves too close to me, Thigpen jostled and trying to get a bead.

It didn't matter. The gun, these stars, the ground beneath me.

Huger Dillard. Bastard son of a blind uncle and a mother who figured she could run from whatever truth of her life the trailer at Hungry Neck reminded her of every day.

Me. The truth of what I reminded her of every day.

Me. Nobody.

"Go ahead," I said up to Thigpen, and I meant it.

"My pleasure," Thigpen said, and smiled again, the gun out at me hard and straight.

"*Yah!*" Unc shouted from the other side of him, and I heard a hard slap, saw Jeb rear up again, Thigpen lose his balance again, then Jeb charge off and away.

"*Yah!*" Unc shouted again there in the dark, his head turned to the sound of hoofbeats away from us, and I turned, saw Thigpen in his saddle, facing us, the gun up, the dead arm still slack at his side, the reins given up for him bent on killing us rather than gain control of the horse.

He was aiming at Unc.

And Unc had to know this, had to know Thigpen would go first for him, no matter the horse was at a full gallop away from us, and no matter Unc was blind.

But Unc only stood there, hands to his hips, like he was waiting to get hit. Like there was nothing left for him but this.

He was my father.

I stood and rushed him, tackled him flat out and heard the pistol fire, heard the split of sound the bullet made into the log, heard another shot and another, me rolling with Unc and rolling in the brush of this clearing.

Then came a hard and heavy chunk of sound, sharp and cold, with it and inside it a cry out of Thigpen, a shriek of pain, and I looked up, saw the horse already swallowed by the woods, saw, too, the live-oak branch he must've passed under, that sharp piece of sound Thigpen slamming into it, turned in his saddle and firing on us.

I lay back down, still holding Unc, him and me both breathing hard. All I could hear now was a horse galloping away from us.

I pushed him away, pushed him, heard him whisper, "Huger," and then I was on my knees, looking back where Jeb's sounds grew fainter and fainter.

Only then did I feel the wet on my face, feel the tears coming out of me and streaming now, my breaths too quick in and out, and I knew I was crying, and that I needed to kill this man, Tommy Thigpen, and that I had to get away from Unc and away from Mom.

Unc was beside me, breathing hard. He took my arm, whispered, "We have to go. We have to get Eugenie and go."

I shook him off, swallowed down a breath and turned, stepped away from him.

He looked for me, his head weaving like it did when he wasn't sure what might happen next, or who it was coming near to him.

Here were those white marble eyes, small pieces of moonlight in his face and in the dark.

Who was he?

He put his hand up, whispered, "Huger?"

What did this word *father* mean?

The horse's gallop was gone now, the night sounds back: treetops moving in the wind up there.

But then, beneath that sound, came Mom's crying, and I looked to the log, saw she hadn't come out.

Unc turned to the sound, too, looked back to me. He said, "You got to get her, Huger. We got to go." He took in a breath, let it out. "I'm sorry, Huger."

"You get her," I said, and took another step back.

"Huger, we have to—"

"You get her!" I shouted. "You get her!" and I took another step away.

Unc stood there a moment, that hand out to me, the air between us filled with the muffled cries of my mother, and then that hand dropped, and he turned, made his way toward the log, felt along the trunk a few feet, then squatted, reached in.

"Come on, Eugenie," he whispered. "It'll be all right, girl. Come on."

I turned from them, felt my jaw tight, felt the wet on my face, my heart still pounding but that pounding now a hollow sound, nothing in me, and I looked up, saw shimmer in my tears the thin stars up there, that moon, saw it dance in a way I had no control over. Just dancing, shimmering.

"He'll be back," Unc whispered to Mom. "Just give me your hand, Eugenie. Give me your hand."

Still she cried, a sound as soft as the wind in these trees, but sharp enough to cut through them in the same moment. My mom, crying, and I turned, my eyes to the sky, searching.

Here was Polaris, dancing.

I shivered, shivered hard and deep, shoulders to legs, through me some cold current, and I turned, walked toward where Unc knelt beside the log, his hand down inside, the sound of Mom's crying up from beneath it.

Unc looked up at me.

I said, "We have to go," and though I'd tried to hold it in, tried to make my words sound like they had some authority to them, they came out broken.

That was when she crawled out, quick breaths in and in, took Unc's hand, struggled up, and stood.

She wiped at her eyes with the backs of her hands, still crying. "I'm sorry, Huger," she managed, her words more broken than mine. She took a step toward me, and I could see her face crumpled up in the dark, her two arms out to me, her wanting to hold me.

I stepped away, turned from her, with my boot pushed through the weeds, toed at them. Then my foot hit it: the shotgun.

I leaned over, picked it up, cold in my hand, but nothing. There was no weight to it. Only that cold steel of the barrel.

I took in a deep breath, tried hard to settle myself and the tremble in my throat. I said, "This way," and looked back up at the North Star.

And here was her hand taking up mine, the hand of a woman

who'd kept truth from me my entire life, the hand of a woman who called herself my mother. And I took it, through no choice of my own, only that there was a man with a gun on horseback, bent on killing us.

Next came Unc's hand at the small of my back, and I felt him loop his fingers around my belt again. The man who'd kept the same truth from me my whole life.

I started off, running.

20

Mom wasn't whimpering any longer, and Unc wasn't pushing. It was me, leading, and running, holding tight her hand, Unc right there behind me and holding on, right there.

I didn't ask him where we were going, because I knew it was best never to ask him or Mom anything ever again, seeing as how they would lie to me on it, too scared to tell the truth, however ugly it might be. The truth for them was me, I knew: this kid they'd made, this kid who'd thought it was his own life he was living.

And now I started to thinking on the fact maybe my father, that man I'd always thought of as my father, the one who'd left once Unc'd moved in to lick his wounds, hadn't done any wrong. Maybe he'd known all along who this kid was in his house. Maybe he'd known all along his wife'd cheated on him, so that the day his brother came hobbling back to Hungry Neck to start on healing the wounds inflicted by a woman who'd finally dealt with the truth of her husband's fucking his brother's wife, maybe that was the day my father'd finally made the decision to go: here, in his own trailer, was his wife and her lover, his own brother.

Maybe this man I'd always thought of as my father deserved still to be thought of as my father, because he'd looked at the truth, taken it in, dealt with it.

I didn't want her hand in mine, didn't want it there as we splashed through a low spot, didn't want her here beside me as we made it over another fallen tree, didn't want her holding on through more wild blackberry, the dry sticks sharp and snagging our clothes, the shotgun in my hand still nothing. I didn't want her here.

And I didn't want Unc holding on from behind, because he was a liar, too, scared of the truth, scared of telling me what I was: his bastard son.

Unc. Even the name was a lie.

We came through the blackberry thicket, ducked beneath another low live-oak branch, and then the ground changed, rose up at a sharp incline before us, and I saw past and above it the tops of trees on the other side.

The railroad track bed.

We were on the other side of it from where we'd been yesterday, looking at Cleve Ravenel's tire tracks, trying to figure where they'd gone once they disappeared.

He'd gone over the track bed, of course. Then down to this parcel of land on Hungry Neck, and now I knew where we were, my bearings turning and falling into line, and all of it hit me: Trestle Road was on the other side of the track bed, and we could make our way from there to Levee and to Lannear, and back to the trailer.

Two and a half miles.

"What is it?" Unc whispered, and I heard him behind me take a deep breath in through his nose, smelling.

"The track bed," I said. Mom bent over, took in breaths, but kept her hand in mine.

I let it go.

"Now we know where we are," Unc whispered, his hand still on my belt. He paused, breathed hard a couple times. "Let's go on up."

We made it to the top, a good thirty feet up, and here we were, on the flat track, rails all gone. Just this strange piece of ground in the middle of the woods, no trees, no bushes. Only gravel, stretching away to either side of us.

To the left the track bed led off into woods, the bed a straight line shrouded by trees on either side and finally disappearing in the black.

I looked to the right. There a few yards away stood Mom, breathing hard, hands to her knees again. She didn't look up at me, only breathed.

And not fifty yards past her was where the track bed ended at the bluff on the bank of the Ashepoo, the view from here like a window away from my life.

The bluff, where I'd ridden my bike when I was little, back when I'd believed myself to be somebody else. Somebody I wasn't, and'd never been. The Ashepoo, where I'd stop, look both ways up and down the river bending away from me on both sides, the trees right up to this side of the river like giant men on horseback watching over all the marsh.

The bluff, where just yesterday Unc and I'd been, me somebody else.

Dead-man talk, Thigpen'd called it, and I knew that was me, the dead man. Dead to who I thought I'd been, and dead to who I knew I was: Unc's son, all along.

"Huger!" Unc whispered hard, and pulled at me, that hand on my belt. "Run!"

I heard next the sound Unc'd already heard, the distant crash through brush back to my left, where now Thigpen and the horse rose up from the woods maybe a hundred yards away. Here they were, the dark figure of that horse mounting the incline, on it the slumped figure of Thigpen, still with an arm out, that gun pointed toward us, and they were coming at us.

Run where? We were here, and I was dead already. I was dead.

So I turned to him, full on. I held up the shotgun, still nothing in my hands save for the cold of it, and I fired.

The sound and flash were nothing, too, nor was the slam against my shoulder, the kick once fired. It was a pump-action .410, the kick at any other time in my life enough to jar my spine. But nothing happened. Only blast, light, kick, all in this instant.

Mom screamed, and Unc pulled hard at my belt, because still here came Thigpen, and I'd missed altogether.

I pumped it, felt the action only go halfway down, then stop. The gun jammed, the cartridge caught on its way out of the chamber.

Thigpen laughed. "Got the clutch way open," he called out. "For targets close in!"

Unc pulled harder on my belt again, and now he was leading, me nearly stumbling for the angle he held me at, and now here was Mom running, too, running and running, and I was running, too, and only now did I figure it: we were running toward the bluff, and I dropped the shotgun, heard the clatter of it on the gravel, me through with it.

And now Mom was falling behind, and I saw her face in the moonlight out here, heard a cry on her heavy breaths, and I put my hand out to her.

Thigpen fired, a spit of gravel splashing up beside me.

I turned from Unc pulling harder at me, harder, trying to move forward. I slowed down, held out my hand, and Mom's hand was up, and she was running, and I could hear in this dark her crying.

There they were, horse and rider at full gallop, Thigpen low, arm out, a solid black shape hurtling toward us, seventy-five yards now.

"Mom!" I screamed, and held out my hand.

He fired again, another spray of gravel, this time beside Mom, the rocks flying up and hitting me and Mom.

She let out a startled yelp, stumbled, her arms going wild to keep her balance, but she didn't fall, reached that hand out again.

Thigpen was fifty yards behind, the gun still up.

Then Mom's hand was in mine, and I grabbed hold hard, pulled at her, Unc holding hard to me, pulling.

Here was the bluff, and the marsh.

We were running full blown now, faster than we'd run any time this night, Unc pushing hard from behind, Mom holding tight my hand. But here was the edge, and the answer to the question I'd wondered a moment ago—*Run where?*—came to me.

The river. This was where Unc'd wanted us to go all along. If you went east off Polaris from anywhere you stood on Hungry Neck, I finally saw, you came to the Ashepoo.

I stopped as best I could, Unc still pushing from behind, Mom still holding tight, so that when we hit the edge of the bluff it was all I could do to keep us all from falling in.

Thigpen fired again, another bullet past us and above, and I looked back at him: thirty yards now.

"Jump," Unc said.

I looked at him. He was facing the river, and I turned, looked at what he couldn't see.

The Ashepoo at high tide, black water thirty feet or so below us and fifty feet wide, on the other side of it the marsh all the way to Edisto, in a straight line across it the black tips of those empty pylons more than ever like the spine of some huge dead animal. And spread across it all those tiny nameless islands.

Above it all these stars, the moon.

"Jump!" Unc shouted, and now he pushed at me, and in the last second I laced the fingers of my hand in Mom's, held it tight, and jumped, because there was nothing else to do, and no one else to die with.

Huger Dillard, I thought on our way down toward that black water, and still the words were new, and meant nothing.

It was a cold I couldn't prepare for, a cold so black and cold it seemed to split me open, the wind knocked out of me, and I let go Mom's hand to get to the air above me, everything black and cold.

I kicked my legs, the water thick with the cold, my eyes open to black and stinging, and I reached up, hoped my hand would break the surface, but it didn't, and for an instant I thought maybe I'd twisted upside down somehow, that I was reaching down and away from what I needed.

But then an arm had hold around me, beneath my own arm, and I was being pulled up, and still I was kicking.

Here was air, and I pulled it in, pulled at it like I could swallow down all the air there ever was, and I knew it was Unc's arm around me, knew that touch even here in this cold and black.

"Huger," he whispered, "Huger, stay still, and just float."

I took in more breaths, more breaths, and finally opened my eyes, saw the bluff, the dark shape up there of a man on horseback, stopped, slumped forward, an arm out toward us.

We were moving, the tide on its way out, him growing smaller, and then he fired, a sharp shard of light out at us.

Where was Mom?

I turned, Unc's arm still around me, and looked for her, saw a shape on the water only a few feet downriver, a head just floating, beside us on the right the Hungry Neck side of the Ashepoo, those trees right up to the bank, to the left the wall of grasses where the marsh began.

I tried to make my breaths go small, tried to keep from shivering into a ball and sinking. Unc still had his hand beneath my arm, and I could feel his legs treading water, the small whip of cold water around my legs as his moved and moved beside me, and then I started treading, started kicking.

Thigpen fired again, our backs to him so I couldn't see the flash off the barrel, but I heard in the instant he fired the swallowed *snap* the bullet made into the water between Mom and us, and Mom yelped, kicked hard her legs, her arms out of the water, I could see, and she was whimpering again, splashing and kicking, and he fired again.

Then Unc let go of me, slapped the water hard with his hand, shouted out, "Right here! Over here!" and kicked his legs at the surface, slapped again.

He was turned to the bluff and was kicking back toward Thigpen, away from me and away from Mom.

He wanted to draw Thigpen's fire.

He wanted to save us.

I saw that arm up off Thigpen, saw Unc splashing, saw that piece of moon above them both, saw it all moving away from me, the tide

working to carry me out and away from this: the place and time—
the Ashepoo, tide turning—Unc had in mind since he'd had me turn
him to Polaris, put him in the line of sight of that star, in him the
knowledge of tides and time and placement of constellations in the
sky. He knew this was where we'd end up, knew the tide would carry
us away. He knew.

Thigpen had his gun up, Unc slapped the water.

And then because I was no one, because my name carried on it no
meaning, me no one I knew, I shouted, too. "Hey, Thigpen!" I
shouted. "Hey, Thigpen!" I slapped at the water.

Thigpen's silhouette moved, that arm jumping up, lining up with
me now, me floating away from Unc, downriver.

Here came light skittering across the water from behind me, the
quick and perfect sweep of it there on the water, in that sweep the
surface of the river and the Hungry Neck bank of the Ashepoo, its
branches casting twisted shadows that moved with the light moving,
then came the back of Unc's head lit up, his arm moving, the light
illuminating for an instant bits of water like broken white glass
falling from his arm as he raised it and lowered it again, splashing,
the light nothing to him, invisible as the rest of his world, and now
this piece of light slipped past him and up to the bluff, and to Thigpen to light him up, give detail where none had been the entire
night so far: the bright figure of a man in blue jeans and an army fatigue jacket sitting on a gray horse, one arm limp, the spot where
he'd been hit by Patrick and where I'd punched him dark with
blood, his other arm up, the gun pointed now at the light, ready to
fire.

His face was pale, his mouth open. The hat was gone, and he
seemed in this moment for all the world some deer caught in the
headlights of a pickup, about to be hit.

"Hold your fire!" a voice came from behind me, and I turned, finally, saw where the beam off a flashlight pointed up from the water: it was a boat down there.

And there in the light off that flashlight was Mom, her head in the
water facing the boat and this voice, the boat coming toward her.

204 • Bret Lott

"Thank God!" she shouted, her head a silhouette to me, her hair flat, and she turned to me, looking for me.

"Huger," she said, but I looked to Thigpen to see what he would do. This wasn't over yet.

Unc'd stopped at that voice. "Who's there?" he called out, too loud, then, "Huger!"

"Right here," I said, but I was looking at Thigpen.

He still held the gun out, pointed toward that light.

But then he let the hammer back with his thumb, let his arm drop, and he seemed to let out a breath he'd been holding all night.

"Who's there?" Unc called again, his head moving, looking, listening.

"Thank God!" Mom said again, and now the boat was near on her, the flashlight beam falling from the bluff to shine on her full blast, and she turned to me again, called, "Huger, come on!" and then the beam was in my face, and everything went white.

"Who's there?" Unc said again. "Who is that?" and the light was off me.

"One guess, Leland," the voice said.

Unc's mouth fell open.

I turned to the boat. The beam was on Unc, and I could see it was a man sitting at the stern of a jon boat, and two people were sitting in the bow, and now Mom was at the side of it. One of those two stood, moved to the gunnel, and reached down, helped Mom get a foot up, pulled her in.

I looked at Unc. Still his mouth hung open, him caught back in the tide now, all of us slipping away and slipping away from Thigpen back on the bluff.

Then, like whoever was holding that flashlight knew what I was thinking on, the beam swung back up to him on the horse, growing smaller each second. He was looking at us, the gun still down.

"You were supposed to have handled all this before we met up over here," the voice called out to him.

I thought maybe I knew this voice, and I started thinking on doctors at the club: those investors Yandle senior represented.

"Good God," Unc whispered, his face to the voice.

"Ran up on some problems is all," Thigpen called back, shook his head. "Busted a couple ribs back there," he said. "Took a hit off a shotgun too." He let out another breath, reined the horse around so they were facing the woods. "Nothing I can't handle. Meet with you in a few." He let Jeb go a few feet, then stopped him, turned. "Do what you want with the niggers and the boy and his momma. But you leave Leland for me. Hear?"

"You work for me," the voice said, and the flashlight clicked off, and now we were back in darkness.

But it was only a second or so before the shadows came back, and now the boat was near on me, and I heard the trolling motor on it, the little electric job on the tail, bringing the boat here in silence.

There was the man, sitting at the motor, and Mom was in there, too, next to the person who hadn't stood, and that person who'd helped Mom in was reaching down now for me, the boat right next to me.

Tabitha.

"He got a gun, Leland," Miss Dinah said, and now I could see only Tabitha in the dark, the shape of her hair, what little light off the moon giving in to the whites of her eyes, a shadow to her nose.

Here was her hand, and I took it, brought my leg up to the gunnel, pulled myself up and rolled into the boat. I landed on something hard, long sticks, it felt like, and I saw they were shovels, two of them, laid out in the bottom.

Miss Dinah was on the bench next to Mom in the bow, Mom with a jacket around her shoulders and crying, Miss Dinah with her arms around her.

Tabitha crouched in front of her momma and took off her jacket, that same one she'd worn last night when I'd followed her through the woods.

She held it out to me, and I looked at her.

Tabitha. Miss Dinah.

I heard the hammer pulled back on a gun, turned, saw this man held a pistol out at me.

He was looking past me at the water. He had on a baseball cap, I could see, dark jacket and pants, heavy rubber boots to his knees. But I couldn't make out his face for the black shadow cast by the bill.

"Let's go, Leland," he said, and here was that voice.

Tabitha lay her jacket over my shoulders, and I realized I was shivering for the cold. I looked at her, nodded, and she nodded back. But her eyes were on the man.

"Help him in," the man said, and I knew that voice from deer-hunt Saturdays standing at the campfire, Unc parceling out the men, who would go with who on whose truck.

I knew that voice, knew *him:* forest-green Range Rover.

Now Unc was in the water beside us, and I leaned over the gunnel, said, "Unc," so he'd know where I was, and held out my hand. He took hold of it, put a leg up to the gunnel, and I pulled him over and in.

He was breathing hard, and sat up fast, his face to the man.

Forest-green Range Rover.

It came to me.

Unc whispered, "Charlie Simons."

"Back from the dead," the man said.

21

He was dead. I'd seen the body, seen what little of the head was left, and those skinned hands like squirrels, the dark red and glistening muscle, the white tendons of his hands. I'd seen it.

Here he was, the one from the file footage on the news the night his wife came in and told me to cherish my momma.

My mom: no one I knew.

Or was she? Thigpen'd lied about killing Simons. Or he'd made us think he'd killed him. So why wouldn't he lie about me, about Mom and Unc, just to get me to run like I did, get me to blink?

I'd blinked. And maybe Thigpen was lying.

But he wasn't. I knew. I'd known forever.

I shivered from the cold and wet, even with Tabitha's jacket around me.

"Timing is everything, now isn't it, Leland?" Simons said. We were headed upriver, the bluff already past. We sat facing him in the stern, Mom and Miss Dinah still on the bench at the bow, Unc and me on the middle bench, Tabitha next to Simons, facing us. He had one hand to the engine, the other with the pistol pointed at Unc.

The boat was moving slow, headed into the current, and I wondered where we were going, and I knew in the same moment it didn't matter. Nothing mattered.

"I hope our little interruption of the festivities between you three and Deputy Thigpen hasn't disappointed you much," he said. "Of course, Miss Gaillard and her daughter's cameo appearances this evening have certainly put a crimp in their day, a day otherwise filled with information gathering. But once one finds intruders rummaging though one's e-mail, of course it behooves one to go to the source, as it were, and prune the offending branches." He paused. "As I said, timing is everything, and the coincidence of our crossing paths in this manner has the ring of Providence about it."

Unc was silent.

Simons shrugged. "Or maybe not. Maybe quite the opposite. I guess we'll find out once we rendezvous with Deputy Thigpen. We'll see whether Providence plays a hand or not."

"Dorcas found what station he sending mail from," Miss Dinah said from behind me, her voice low, steady. "She found out he sending from Miss Constance address at the museum." She paused. "But he found us out."

"I am sorry, Miss Dinah," Unc said. "I placed you in this, and I am truly sorry."

"Sweet sentiment," Simons said. "And it may sadden you even more when I inform you the mail was nothing. Only cosmetic, in case someone came knocking where he ought not, figuring out what is best left a mystery." He paused. "To paraphrase Mr. Clemens, e-mail as regards my demise has been greatly exaggerated." He laughed. "This way it appears as though messages sent from Constance to Cleve Ravenel incriminate the two of them, implicating them in my death as well as yours, LD."

Unc let out a breath. "And Pigboy and Fatback don't even exist."

"Precisely," Simons said.

The river widened out here, a clearing coming up on the Hungry Neck side, and we would be right where I'd parked the Luv that first day I had it, the marsh stretching away for miles. "Almost to the cut," he said, and looked at the motor a second. "If this troller will get us there. Truth be known, I hadn't expected all this company, even though we'll be packing out a great deal of material this evening. Even so, the engine I've got will do the work, I'm certain." He looked past Unc now. "Truth be known," he said. "Truth be known. Now there's an oxymoron if ever I encountered one."

He turned the engine, and we were heading out into the marsh and off the Ashepoo, beside us the gray walls of marsh grass, the channel suddenly narrow, twelve feet across, and now Hungry Neck was what I could see behind him and Tabitha: trees growing smaller as we pulled deeper into the marsh.

Unc said, "If you'd wanted the land, you could have come to me."

"Hah!" Simons let out quick, his head tipping back a moment, and Tabitha flinched at his move. Without thinking, I reached a hand out to her, touched her knee a moment.

She did nothing.

Simons hadn't seen it. He shook his head, looked at Unc, then past us again, maneuvered us deeper into the marsh, the walls swallowing up the trace of the Ashepoo I'd been able to see behind us. "Your lack of vision, Leland—and I apologize for the bad pun— though precisely what I've come to expect from you, still astounds me," he said, his words perfect the way South-of-Broaders made them perfect: to remind you of who they were, and of who you weren't.

"Land," he said, and steered this time to his left, those walls still around us. "If it had been only the land, there would have been no need for all these forensic pyrotechnics. No need for the degloving of hands and the blasting away of any dental records an indigent male of my approximate height, weight, and skin coloring might have revealed, rounded up with no questions from me by my loyal sidekick, Deputy Thigpen. I could have simply gone in with the rest of the boys and made an offer to you. But you and I both know what good that's done. Delbert Yandle as front man? Come now. Even you're not going to give in for that."

"Let them go," Unc said. "Let them all go. You want me. It's only me, Charlie."

"Noble, certainly," Simons said. I still couldn't make out his face for the shadow across it, only pictured that file footage, him standing at a podium and waving in triumph, his wife seated beside him, looking up at him.

"Noble, unto death. But if you believe I'm merely after a blood sacrifice, you are mistaken, and prove yet again you haven't the ability to grasp the scope of things around you. To my way of thinking"—and now he turned us again, the moon swinging through the sky above us, the walls of marsh grass the same, all of us weaving deeper and deeper into the marsh—"there is a vast array of information that has been disseminated by hook or by crook to each one of you, including the deaf-and-mute young virgin beside me." He nudged Tabitha, and she flinched again. She had no idea what was being said here, her eyes on us. "Even Miss Dorcas here possesses information quite detrimental to my endeavors, and though you, Leland Dillard, are responsible for her sifting through cybertrash, that responsibility isn't enough to have you serve as stand-in at her execution."

"Goddamn you, sir," Miss Dinah said, and I heard on the words a tremble, and heard steel at the same time.

"There is no God, Miss Gaillard," Simons said, in his voice a kind of laugh. "But if it gives you a certain semblance of comfort to call down on me the wrath of your empty faith, please do so."

"No need," she said, that tremble gone now. "You done that work yourself."

"Quick-witted to the end," Simons said, "and just in case I forget later on when things will get ugly between us, let me say thank you for all those biscuits and eggs and bacon and grits and fried chicken you've served me over the years Saturday mornings at Hungry Neck." He turned the boat again, that moon moving once more, and now in my line of sight fell one of those nameless islands, a small one, a rough rise of brush and a single palmetto, black and silhouetted in black above the marsh. It was maybe a hundred yards off, the snake of this cut maybe headed there, maybe not, and I wondered if the plan was just to kill us all and bury us out on one of these islands and be done with it, head back to Hungry Neck and whatever was so valuable even the land itself was taking a backseat.

"What do you want?" Unc said, his voice low, too hard and sharp for a whisper but nearly silent all the same.

"What you don't know will kill you, Leland," Simons said, and gave that same sort of laugh. "But if you must know, it's money. Hate to be as vulgar as all that, and as predictable, but it's money. And with the money to which I am laying claim comes all its attendant joys, chief among them a new life. Born again, as it were, Miss Gaillard." He leaned to his left, looked past us and nodded at her.

She said nothing. Mom had stopped her crying, was breathing quick and shallow.

He looked back at Unc, that gun still out and pointed. "It occurred to me only a few years ago," he said, "after having lost a patient to anaphylactic shock, that there were certain fiduciary amenities available only to the dead, Leland. This was a woman of great standing in Charleston society, a fervent supporter of Spoleto, a Junior League charter member." He gave a shake of his head. "In for a breast implant and liposuction, two birds with one stone. But with her cadaver there on the table before me, what had only moments before been a South of Broad force of culture, I realized that there were great luxuries she had initiated simply with passing on, chief among them her life insurance. For the first time, believe it or not, it occurred to me that a graying cadaver could suddenly, in its passing, become worth whatever policy had been taken out on it, and that all that money would be given to someone else." He laughed. "A travesty, certainly. And it was at this point I began taking measures that have brought us to this moonlit evening in the marshlands of the Carolina coast."

"And to killing Constance," Unc said, his voice the same low and cold whisper. He moved his hand from the bench beside him to his lap.

"Constance, Constance, Constance," Simons said, in it nothing.

Only three words. "A necessary evil, to my way of thinking. Of course she never quite got over you, Leland, and many were the times amidst tears shed at bedtime that your name was offered up as a sort of votive. There was no love lost between us, as I'm not quite certain there had ever been any to begin with. But the harridan of a mother she had was, chiefly because of my middle and last names, on my side from the beginning: a Dupree-Middleton union by way of the Simons family. What greater cachet hereabouts, Leland?"

Unc was quiet a moment, the only sound the dull, empty hum of the engine. Unc moved, settled himself, his hand on his knee now. He said, "You are evil."

"But as there is no God," Simons said, and turned the boat again, "then there is no evil, simply each organism for itself. This organism—namely, Charles Middleton Simons, M.D.—with the wheeling away of a dead, still lipidinally and mammarially challenged South of Broad matron, immediately set about upgrading his insurance and adapting his will to plans set in motion. When I died, all proceeds were to go directly to poor, devoted Constance, who, as an aside, wrote out her death confession with no more prompting from me than three whiskey sours and a Magic Marker one night not a month ago." He chuckled, his shoulders up and down with it, and Tabitha pulled away from him an inch, squirmed a moment beside him. "The degloving, of course, was a touch anvil-like in its irony, the wife of a plastic surgeon having skinned her murdered husband's hands. But it served as well to eliminate any corroboration of fingerprints."

He turned us again, that island I'd seen now gone. "And were Constance to die," he went on, "all benefits go directly to the Christian Children's Reconstructive Surgery Foundation, a charitable organization I set up that treats needy children with cleft palates and harelips in Third World countries, headquarters of which is nestled in the pleasant little town of Lucerne, Switzerland, which feeds a branch office in Bangkok, which in turn wires funds to its satellite facility in the Cayman Islands." He shrugged. "As warned, Leland, this is awfully predictable: filthy lucre and all that. But now that I am dead, and as this foundation exists only on paper, and as my murder has been solved by a signed confession and the murderer's suicide to boot, there will be waiting for me in a matter of weeks the tidy sum of six million dollars at that branch office, this in addition to thirty-three million I've managed to sock away one way and another. Not bad for a four-year setup. A sort of business-administration project for the passed-away, proving that yes, indeed, Miss Gaillard"—and now he leaned left again, nodded behind me again—"there is life after death, but also dispelling that nasty rumor you can't take it with you. I can."

"But why now?" Unc said. His hand was still on his knee, but I could feel him begin to lean forward in the smallest way, felt his leg touching mine tense up. He was getting ready for something.

"Things have been pushed toward fruition on this day, Leland, because of a change of heart our dear departed Constance had in the last few weeks, culminating with her telephone call to you last Wednesday. A change of heart our late Carolina Museum of History trustee undertook once our buried treasure yielded a bit of history for which she hadn't prepared her emotions. Trinkets, really, two of them."

He looked past us again and stood in the boat, the tiller still in hand, but now he put the gun to Tabitha's head, held it there as he looked forward.

Tabitha's hard breaths came back, and that high-pitched shard of sound from deep inside her.

"By the way, Leland, I realize you are about to try and jump me, thereby sacrificing yourself in Jesus fashion, one death for all. But the gun is now at Little Eva's head for the duration, the destination of our clandestine junket not far ahead. So don't try." He paused, turned the tiller. There behind him was another island, smaller, farther away. Or maybe it was the same one. "In a few moments all will be made clear. Unexpected gravy. Buried treasure. The pièce de résistance, as it were. The *pièce d'Africain*." He laughed. "And though Miss Gaillard and the nubile nubian here are not on the original guest list, it seems most apropos they are with us nonetheless."

Unc eased off, let his head drop, leaned back. He let out a breath.

And then the bow scratched bottom, a sound like sandpaper from beneath us, and we stopped.

"Everyone out," Simons said.

I turned, looked forward. There sat Miss Gaillard and Mom, both turned, too, looking.

The bow was nosed into marsh grass, just beyond it an island, black trees and bushes, a single palmetto, all silhouetted against a black sky. One of those nameless ones, way off and small, you could see from Hungry Neck.

Buried treasure, I thought. Two trinkets.

One is sin, and the other is love. And I can't tell the difference.

The paperweights.

But I was thinking, too, of Eugenie and Leland. My mother, and my father.

22

Pluff mud went to my shins, and I used the shovel to keep my balance.

Here was the same smell as that first night in North Charleston, and the same smell as had started up off the body between stands 17 and 18 the second time we went back there, Thigpen and Yandle with us.

Charles Middleton Simons, M.D., hadn't been anywhere near. We'd stood at only a body with next to no head, the hands degloved, he called it. A body nameless as this island.

In front of me was Miss Dinah with the other shovel, Mom in the lead. We stepped through the mud, arms or shovels out for balance as the mud swallowed our feet, let them go, swallowed them.

"Huger," Unc said from behind me.

"Leland, you have anything to say, you need to say it to me," Simons said, and I turned, saw Unc reached toward me. Past him were Tabitha and Simons, the gun now to her neck, his other hand holding tight her arm.

"Don't," Simons said, and I knew it was to me, and I turned around, kept going.

Mom stepped up out of the mud and onto the island itself, put a hand to the palmetto, leaned on it, and now Miss Dinah stood beside her, and it was my turn to step up and onto ground.

It was ground. An island, maybe an acre or so, thick with growth, like all of them, so thick there was nothing to see into, only black, pieces of shadow here and there, all of it thicker than the woods we'd run through for half the night.

Unc struggled through the last two steps of mud, then fell forward. His hands hit the ground, and I watched those pale hands in the moonlight search for something to hold, to help him pull himself up onto ground.

There was nothing, only weeds, and he was on his knees now, his feet finally free of the mud. He touched the base of the palmetto, got to one knee, the other, and stood.

Tabitha still gave out that sound, the gun still to her neck, and the two of them stepped up, all of us crowded now at this piece-of-dirt landing, and I stepped toward the black of the growth, looked into it.

Something cold took my free hand, and I turned, saw Mom, holding mine in hers.

"Give your mother the shovel, Lord Huger," Simons said. "Then lead us to the Promised Land."

I looked at him. The canopy of growth above us, all I could see was a silhouette holding something to the neck of a silhouette, behind them both stars, gray marsh.

"I can't see anything," I said.

"Sounds like something Leland might say," Simons said, and laughed. He moved an arm to his side, brought it up. Then here was light: sharp, white, pointed at me.

He let the beam go to the ground, reached toward me with it, a circle of light moving over our feet, weeds. "Take this," he said, "and do not imagine there is room here for heroics. Simply follow the trail."

I stood there a moment, still. Light was with us, and I could see things, and I could feel my heart beat, and I could smell this mud, and I could feel the cold of my legs and feet, my arms, my mother's cold hand in my cold hand.

This was all there was, I saw. Only this.

I let go her hand, gave her the shovel, then took the flashlight.

But before I turned away, I let the beam fall below Tabitha a moment, enough light to let me see her face full on. She was looking at me and breathing hard, the dull glint of gun at her throat.

Then she nodded. It was small, near nothing. But she'd nodded.

I brought the flashlight down, and it seemed she was the only one in the world who might know me.

I turned, started away.

The flashlight filled up the world after all this time in so much dark, a world lit only with moonlight and black, the fingers of branches and feathers of weeds and lines and angles and all those black shadows the only thing I knew all night long. Before this night I thought I knew about darkness, thought I knew how to make my way through it, whether it was climbing out my bedroom window into a dark in which waited Jessup or Tyrone or Deevonne, or if it was only driving the Luv before dawn back on Cemetery and dropping off men at the next stand and the next, my headlights off the whole time because I just wanted to see the gray and black world of Hungry Neck, and thought maybe it helped somehow to keep the deer down and at ease not to have all this light cutting up the place. I thought I knew how to make my way through dark.

But I didn't. All I knew this night was a moon, Polaris, and that Mom and Unc had together betrayed me. Now here I was with a flashlight, the ugly power of it—with its light all those stars were gone now, all those shadows built on their own shadows disappeared—and now even the place I wanted to grow old on and die, Hungry Neck, seemed to betray me, too, that land a half mile away and standing alone, empty.

Land. Just land.

The flashlight seemed to ignite the vines and crepe myrtle and all else, the browns and greens all washed clean of most color for the light, like a body drained of blood. But Simons was right: here was a trail, and I followed it.

Growth hung over us, the trail almost a tunnel, and we walked slowly, the flashlight first on the ground at my feet, then on the ground ahead, at my feet again. I turned around a time or two, shone it on the ground behind me for the others, Mom next, Miss Dinah, Unc, then Tabitha and Simons.

Mom teetered for a moment, the shovel in her hand, Miss Dinah's jacket on; Miss Dinah put out her hand to Mom's shoulder a moment when it seemed she might fall forward, the other with the shovel; Unc took one step, paused, took another, with each measured step a hand reaching hard for the next hold on a branch or vine.

Then there was Tabitha, her arm still held by Simons, and I saw she had on only a long-sleeve T-shirt.

I stopped, held the flashlight in one hand while I slipped off the sleeve, then swapped hands with the light, the jungle suddenly flying with light, quick sharpened shadows here and gone as it moved, and then the jacket was off, and I stepped back among them, held it out to her.

"Those noble Dillards," Simons said, the gun down from Tabitha's neck, pointed now at me. She glanced up at Simons, then took the jacket, carefully shrugged it on, her eyes cutting from him to me to him.

"Move," he said. "Deputy Thigpen will be here soon, and the festivities will continue. But there's work to be done first." He put the gun back to her neck.

I turned, started through the growth.

But this time it was me to teeter forward, my right foot caught for a second in a root or vine, and I put my hands in front of me, the flashlight flipping out of my hand, that beam flying again, bleeding color and forcing shadows out of everything in an instant, and I fell.

I was on my hands and knees, the flashlight a couple feet ahead of me, pointed up and away inside the tangle of growth. It was shining on something down here, something black and solid, no shadow to it but for those cast by the dead vines that shrouded it: nothing more than black rock, like a piece of wall two feet wide in front of me.

"My dear Lord," Miss Dinah whispered. And Mom quick whispered, "Oh, oh."

I got to my knees, looked up.

The flashlight shone on it from below, like a spotlight: a head, carved in this stone; the piece of black rock I'd seen was its base, the whole thing one piece of rock six feet tall.

I picked up the flashlight, stepped back, shone it at the head, and as I brought up the beam, it seemed for a moment it had eyes, eyes that sparked and took me in, moved over me, green light from in them.

It had eyes.

"My dear Lord in Heaven," Miss Dinah whispered out again. "I know where we are."

"What?" Unc said. "What is it?"

They were glass. Green glass eyes set into the black stone head of a black man. Eyes that swallowed up the beam and sent it back at me, at all of us.

It was a black man: lips, nose, jaw, all worn, soft with time, and though I believed in this moment that I ought to be afraid, I wasn't.

It was those eyes, I knew, that kept me from being afraid. Something in them—the way they took in the light from the flashlight, the flicker of them, the way they moved without moving—gave me no fear.

"We have arrived," Simons said. "But tell me, Miss Gaillard, where is it we have arrived?"

I stared at the eyes.

"Huger?" Unc whispered.

"Quiet, Leland," Simons said. "Miss Gaillard?"

"The Mothers and Fathers," she whispered.

"Precisely," Simons said. "The fabled place."

No one moved, made a sound.

I turned to him, still with the light on the statue.

They were all looking past me, all these ghosts, white and black both, all of them lost in the wash of light shining at that head.

I'd heard of this place. Everyone down here had. The Mothers and Fathers. But it wasn't anything anybody ever talked about, because it was just a story. Like Miss Dinah painting her house haint purple to keep the demons away. Campfire stories. Just stories.

Slowly Unc's head moved, no more than the nod Tabitha had given me. It was a move of emptiness and knowledge at once: he couldn't see this, but he knew what it was. And here were his white marble eyes, swallowing the little light given up by a flashlight pointed away.

"Right where we're standing, home of the Mothers and Fathers. Stumbled upon a few months ago by surveyors I dispatched to take stock of precisely what made up Hungry Neck. Back when I was with the boys, still thinking small: the next Hilton Head."

I turned back to it, looked at those eyes.

Maybe this was what made me unafraid: his eyes and Unc's: both empty, both seeing everything.

"As doctors are wont to do, no one of them could make the decision to send out surveyors for fear of a lawsuit from Unc, though we were each of us, I must admit, salivating over this place, with the senate about to plow under the University Medical Consortium, our cash cow about to be sacrificed. And so it fell to me to send them out, unbeknownst to any of the others." He paused. "Jackson Filliault, my surveyor, reported back to me he wasn't able to finish the job, that his boy Jimmy Horry slipped a cog or three when he saw what we're looking at."

"Jimmy Horry," Miss Dinah said. "He dead."

Simons sighed. "As is Jackson Filliault. June twelfth, a roadside accident, two surveyors killed off 17 South, hit and run. This, after I'd told dear Constance of what Filliault relayed to me, and after my late wife, trustee and former director of Acquisitions for the Carolina Museum of History, informed me of who the Mothers and Fathers were, and of the legend of these heads with eyes. And the potential value of such items on the black market." He laughed. "Listen to me. Legends, buried treasure. It's as though this were one grand bedtime story for all involved. But there is no bedtime story in the amount of money this bust will bring. Though it appears to be rock, it's actually black tabby, circa 1690. I've already accepted a bid of three and a half million for it." He laughed again. "On the black market. Yet another bad pun. But a certain West African potentate has placed a sizable deposit on it in the guise of a check made out to the CCRSF in Lucerne. A black West African purchasing with his impoverished nation's dwindling funds a piece of black tabby made by the first Africans to land here. The first slaves in the Lowcountry."

I looked back at them. Miss Dinah had a hand to her mouth now, Mom leaned into her. Unc said, "Tell me, Huger."

I turned back to it. I was quiet, then said, "The head of a black man. On a six-foot pedestal, kind of. And he's got green glass eyes."

"My God," he whispered. "It's true."

"Of course it's true, Leland," Simons said. "Everything Constance told you Wednesday night on the telephone was and is terrifically true, beginning with her confessing to you her role in fencing our finds through her contacts with curators across the country." He paused. "A delightful technological toy, the tapping of a phone. Even if it's your own."

Unc quick turned to him, said, "She did it only because you, you bastard, drove her to it."

Simons laughed, his head back with it. He pointed the gun at Unc. "Surreptitiously sock away enough hard-earned dollars to the right charitable foundation without your wife knowing, then blame your apparently decreasing income on the health-care industry and looming senate-committee hearings, and your wife will believe the life to which she has been accustomed is soon to disappear. Next dangle a small temptation—perhaps a mythical plot of ground never before excavated—and the revenues one might gain were one to sell off a piece here, a piece there. Promise her, of course, only a piece here and a piece there will be sold, and promise her as well that all else will be presented to her beloved museum, and there you have it: a sort of archaeological bait-and-switch. She participates in the sale of one item to the black market, I then threaten to divulge this tid-bit to the proper authorities, and her life as a South-of-Broad Dupree-Middleton-Simons is over. She must keep her mouth shut while we salvage what we can, or her life is over." He paused, shook his head, still smiling. "As well you know, Leland, as regards your in-ability to inform Lord Huger of your sordid soirée with his delight-ful mother here some sixteen years ago, pride is a frightening thing, powerful unto paralysis. And unto death."

Mom cried again, let go the shovel. She moved to me, held me. But I did nothing. I kept my hands at my side, let her cry, hold me.

I said, "Guess everybody on earth knows."

"You imagine true," Simons said.

And still Unc said nothing.

Tabitha gave out a sharp cry, just one, and Miss Dinah turned, looked at her. Tabitha moved her hands, looked at her momma, nodded now and again at the statue.

Miss Dinah slowly nodded back. That was all, and turned back to it. "Where the rest of them?" she asked. "The other three?"

"I'm afraid the other three have already been crated and shipped out of Charleston Terminal, though of course we don't cart from here the entire structure, only the bust itself. Deputy Thigpen has the most delightful diamond-bit cable saw that slices through tabby like a scalpel through skin, and uses only the muscles in one's arms so as not to arouse undue suspicion; no whine of a power saw ema-nating from a nighttime island. This is the last one, this night's har-vest our last on the island. This particular one," Simons said, and looked back at the bust, "according to the information Constance, bless her heart, amassed for this project, and as states the lore no doubt handed down to you by your ancestors, Miss Dinah, is the Son, set facing due west. And set exactly forty-two feet due east was the Mother, facing south; forty-two feet due north of her was Fa-ther, facing east; and forty-two feet due west of him stood Daugh-ter, facing north. The Family, each statue at a corner of a perfect square, measured in cubits. And, of course, inside the square is—"

He paused, turned Tabitha to face him. "Miss Dorcas, can you tell us what's inside the square these statues make up?"

Tabitha looked up at him. She knew what he'd asked. She looked from him to Miss Dinah, and I thought maybe she'd glanced at me.

She moved her hands.

Simons looked at Miss Dinah. "Translation, please?"

She was quiet, slowly turned back to the statue.

"Miss Dinah?" he said again.

But it was me to answer. "The first slaves here," I said. "Their burial plot."

"My dear Jesus," Miss Dinah breathed out.

"Very good, Lord Huger." He held the gun out at me. He smiled, said, "We've work to do. Let's go," and motioned with the gun for me to turn, move on.

There to the left of the statue led that trail, even more a tunnel now the deeper we went on the island.

He'd found the Mothers and Fathers. Here. A story, something just a lie kids told to scare one another, now truth. The place the first slaves were buried, but not just the first slaves—the holy ones, a family of kings, we'd been told.

A family.

"The shovel, Miss Eugenie?" Simons said.

Mom let go of me, stepped back and away, her eyes on me. Then she knelt, picked it up. I could see in the light her face twisted up, her looking at me, and I turned, walked.

But it was only a few feet before the trail ended altogether at a curtain of growth, the flashlight penetrating no farther, only giving me washed-out wax myrtle, thick brown tendrils of wisteria vine.

It looked odd, even given the ugly shadows the flashlight cast. The wax myrtle was dead, I could see, the leaves drooping, some gone brown, and I shone the beam to the ground. No base, no trunk. Only dead leaves, and the bottom of this curtain.

I reached to it, heard Simons chuckle behind me. "That's right, heir apparent. Just give it a push."

The curtain fell back, twisted away and to the right to show it was a kind of doorway propped up to keep what was past it hidden.

I leaned in, swept the flashlight beam from one side to the other.

There lay cleared ground, a large patch of low weeds, spread about it wooden stakes driven into the ground, each a foot or so high, and in the play of light across it all I saw, too, strings between them all, strips of cloth hung here and there on them.

Together the strings and stakes made a large, rough circle, walled all around by the same growth as everywhere, and from the circle led more strings and stakes to the center, like spokes on a wheel. But they stopped at a set of stakes in the middle of the circle, making another, smaller circle in the center, all of it cleared.

"The hallowed ground," Simons said. "A kind of North American Tomb of Tutankhamen, a burial site untouched for nearly three hundred years, only now yielding its bounty, the spoils most lucrative, though those busts have made the greatest contribution to the lives of the harelipped in Bangladesh."

I started in, stepped over a string, shone the light on it for the others. "There's a string up," I said to Unc once Mom and Miss Dinah were in, "about a foot high. Step over it."

Unc bent down, touched it, and stepped over, and then came Simons and Tabitha.

I shone the light around again, looking. The ground where we stood was soft, as though we were in a carpeted, hollowed-out cavern, above us the moon again.

"Museums never pay enough," Simons said, "and demand clean bills of sale as well as germ-free documentation. Of course were anyone, from the National Historic Trust on down to those mewling Wetlands Commission prisses, to find a single potsherd out here, things would be sealed off immediately, grand proclamations made, museums erected. Not what I have in mind."

"And what you have in mind," Unc said, "is just to kill us all, haul out what you can, and get away with it."

"Why, what else, Leland? In a few minutes, Deputy Thigpen will arrive with a second boat. Tonight's 'haul,' as you so trailer-trashedly put it, will prove, I believe, to be an astonishing event. We'll let you help, of course, as a means of expediting the recovery of our quarry, and then do as the Egyptians did at the burial of their pharaohs: simply kill the slaves who dug the graves. In this case, we'll kill the slaves who dug *up* the graves." He laughed, let go of Tabitha's arm, the gun on me. "The flashlight, please."

I looked at him a moment longer, thought to shine it in his eyes, blind him a second.

And then what? Dive for him?

"Your reticence, Lord Huger, at giving back the flashlight signals me you are mulling things over. Let me remind you, I have the gun." He pointed it from me to Mom. "I'm hazarding you'll choose not to let me kill your mother, regardless of her wayward past and your questionable lineage."

"Huger," Mom whispered, and took in a quick breath. "Don't."

"Wise woman," Simons said.

I brought down the light, handed it over.

"Good boy. Now take a shovel, you and the virgin both, and go to the center of the circle." He shone the light past me, to where the stakes came together, that small circle. "If Constance's research proves correct, the center hub is where the Father of Fathers lies, waiting. We've saved him for last, though this night was not in our plans. We're here only because of poor Constance's gambit, calling you, Leland. For the last five months we've been here at new moon, as little light as possible so that no one might see us heading here, Thigpen and myself. But in our last episode, a mere week and a half ago, we brought Constance along, who had, I'd believed, begun finally to warm to the opportunity being afforded us. Unfortunately, we turned up something quite unexpected." He shone the light to my left now, to a wedge of the circle on the far side. There the ground, I could see, had no growth, only bare dirt.

"Whereas we had ascertained there were twelve sites here, we stumbled upon a thirteenth." He paused. "That of a child, its rude sarcophagus perhaps three feet long. And when we opened it up, there lay the perfect remains of a female child, interred along with

her, as with all the rest of the Fathers and Mothers, her earthly possessions, each crafted by her own hands, items entombed for the
long voyage home."

I looked at the ground. Nothing, only dirt.

"Of course the precious child's possessions were few, but two
pieces—those trinkets I mentioned—captured the heart and imagi-
nation of dear Constance: two small, unfinished sweetgrass baskets,
resin-encased." He stopped, filled with himself, I could hear on his
voice, pleased at his words, this explanation of all things before he
killed us. "In a weak moment, one designed nonetheless to ensure
she stayed happy with our arrangement, I gave them to her. Though
each might have garnered a contribution somewhere between fifty
and seventy-five thousand dollars, nevertheless I made the sacrifice.
A sacrifice that, as you now know, has precipitated our being here
tonight."

The paperweight I'd thought nothing of, worth that much
money.

But it wasn't the money that mattered, I saw. It wasn't that at all.
It was that she'd thought enough to risk heading into a hospital to
give it to me. To give to Unc, the one she loved.

Cherish your mother, she'd said, and I saw even she knew who my
mother was, and knew who my father was, and knew something
about love, and about death.

She knew enough to give the other to her own mother, upon it
the disclaimer of sin, on Unc's the curse of love.

"Curiously intelligent, these first savages," Simons said. "We've
found in each casket—carved out of oak, lined inside and out with
pitch—a perfect sort of mummification, both bodies and possessions. Each item with which they have been interred, and believe me
there are troves in each casket, has been encased in resin, rendering
everything, from the shields and spears the men are buried with to
the sweetgrass baskets the women bear, a delightful perfection,
yielding top dollar again and again. Ingenious, actually, using this
resin, every item intact. Especially considering the capital gains I'm
making from their own world of the dead. Imagine that." He

laughed, the beam falling from the bare ground there to the weeds at my feet. "I've become a contemporary of theirs with passing through the great veil. And not only am I taking *mine* with me, but I'm taking theirs as well."

I heard crying from behind me, turned to see Miss Dinah now leaning on Mom, her hands to her face, shoulders shivering.

Tabitha moved then, took a step away from Simons and toward her mother. But Simons reached out, took hold her arm, pushed her toward me. He stepped to Miss Dinah, the gun still pointed at me, and took from her hand a shovel, with the same hand took the other shovel from Mom's hand, and held them both out to Tabitha. She looked at them, at him, and took them.

"Lord Huger, the two of you will be our excavators for the evening, and we'll see what the Father of Fathers himself yields up. A trove beyond troves, I am certain."

I looked at Tabitha, slowly held my hand out to her.

She looked at Miss Dinah, still weeping, then at me, at Simons. She took a step away from him, put out her hand to me. I took it, then took one of the shovels.

Her hand was cold.

I stepped through the low grass toward that center, Simons shining the beam past us so that our shadows were big enough, it seemed, to move past all this, move away and to some other life. Somewhere else.

Here was the string of the center circle. Only string between two stakes, and a rag. But something else, a circle into which we'd step, and start digging the hole where we'd pull up a coffin, replace it with our own bodies once the harvest had been completed.

Unc said, "Constance came to Huger in the hospital, gave him one of those baskets. Told him to give it to me."

I stopped, looked at him.

He was facing Simons, his back to me, his head moving, listening. He'd heard something again, something none of us heard. Mom was looking at him, too, Miss Dinah still with a hand to her face.

"And?" Simons said.

"I told him to give it to Mrs. Dupree," he said. "Your harridan. He did."

I let go of Tabitha's hand. She looked at me, turned with me.

"Thigpen reported to me he lost the missus for an hour or so the evening in question," Simons said, matter-of-fact. "But he rounded her up in time for her reservation at the Rantowles Motel. So, as I see it, no harm, no foul. Mrs. Dupree has them, she can keep them."

"Someone will see them," Unc said. "Evidence of something. Someone will ask one thing, another."

"Let me kill him," a thin voice said from the darkness past Simons. "Let me kill the fucker now."

Thigpen came into the backwash of light off the flashlight, there beside Simons. Unc'd heard him coming up and'd started talking in the hopes of stirring something up.

Thigpen looked dead, his face white, his breathing shallow and small for the broken ribs. His jacket was off, his left arm tied round with an old towel up near his shoulder. A pistol was tucked into his jeans.

Simons hadn't moved, only laughed. "What, and surrender too soon to the great beyond the love of my late wife's life? A blind trailerman on social security and policeman's compensation? The latter-day saint of the redneck set? And besides, were you to kill him, I'm afraid we'd have something of a morale problem in the meantime." He paused, looked at Thigpen, down and up. "You're in no condition to work, it appears to me. We need them. But we don't need them looking at their dead patriarch all the while."

Thigpen took a couple of breaths, said, "He's just stalling. Talking about them damned tiny pieces she took off with." He took a step toward Unc, who tensed up, stood taller, his head weaving, listening.

"Unc," I said.

But it was too late, and meant nothing besides: Thigpen swung at Unc, his fist buried into Unc's stomach, and Unc bent in half, met with Thigpen's knee in his chest, and hit the ground.

I took a step to him but heard the hammer cocked on Simons's gun, and I stopped.

He said, "You would do well, Lord Huger the bastard son, to dig rather than tend to the weak of eye."

Thigpen stood straight, his free hand holding his side. He was winded with the effort, grimaced with the pain. Unc lay twisted on the ground, his back to the flashlight so that his face was in shadow, lost. He groaned, coughed out a breath.

"And talk, dear Leland, of items missing will do nothing to stop work here. Though a child's knickknacks proved the undoing of barren, sterile Constance, they have no genuine discernible consequence this evening. The king's ransom we are about to unearth will make each cache of African memorabilia thus far sold pale in comparison. Each coffin is filled to the brim, each item fetching prices one might not believe, were it not for the fact of the vogue value these items seem to carry. Carved wooden pomegranates at two hundred thousand a set, a quiver of arrows for two hundred fifty, a cowhide shield for five hundred, a full-sized sweetgrass rice basket for eight hundred thousand dollars. And imagine, these sums multiplied by twelve! So much disposable income, so many buyers: Hollywood types, dignitaries, foreign statesmen like our potentate. Why, one of the busts, the Daughter herself, is owned by a former Grand Dragon and failed gubernatorial candidate from a sister state of ours, which will go unnamed here, for obvious embarrassing reasons. He keeps it, I am told, in the foyer of his summer home on the Gulf. A kind of slave ownership, I imagine, without all the fuss of civil rights and its attendant—"

"Will you just shut the fuck up?" Thigpen said, and looked at Simons. He took in a quick breath, grimaced for it again. "Fucking doctors. Every one of you thinks he knows everything, and thinks people really want to hear it." He looked back at Unc. "So just shut up."

Simons quick looked at Mom, at me, at Unc on the ground. "You are correct, in that this is a waste of time. Daylight will be upon us in a matter of two hours." He let the hammer back, brought the gun down.

Unc got to his knees now, coughed again, slowly stood.

He said, "Tommy, you know all about Charlie's money in Grand Cayman? About his insurance?" He was trying to stand up straight again. He wouldn't give up.

"Don't even try," Thigpen said, and I thought I could see him smile. "I know what he's making, and what he's paying me. I've got things on him, he's got things on me." He shook his head, then squinted hard, held his breath a moment. "I don't get my money, or I disappear, I've got things rigged, and the world knows about him. And I let on what I know about him, I'm sure he's got things rigged to take care of me. Right, doc?" He looked back to Simons.

"As rain, my fellow malefactor. Honor among thieves, this sort of thing."

"So you just shut the fuck up, too, Leland," Thigpen said, trying at the smile again. "Just shut the fuck up, and know you'll be dead before the sun's up."

"To business," Simons said, and shone the beam on Tabitha and me. "Dig?" he said, and laughed.

There were things I thought of while we worked, the ground like everywhere down at the water, more clay than sand, heavy. But with each turn of the shovel, each lift of it out and onto the ground to my right, things came to me: the months Unc lay in bed in the trailer, and the nest, the antler, the feather I'd brought him. I thought of the way his hand'd wrapped itself around the paperweight in the warm dark of Benjamin Gaillard's shack, and how he'd then given it up to me, and I thought of a minivan out front of a house with two oaks, and of the smell of that dead body. I thought of my mother curled up on a cot beside my bed, and the way the sun set just this evening on Charleston Harbor as we drove over the bridge from Mount Pleasant, and the light on the water, the red in the sky, the last sunset I'd see.

And of course I still hadn't yet thought it was true, any of this: our being killed.

It had to do, maybe, with the way Tabitha worked at shoveling, like this was what, finally, we'd been born to do, our only job: dig up a coffin, lay ourselves to rest in the hole we'd made. We faced each other, stood a few feet from each other, and when she put the shovel to the ground, she stepped on the edge with both feet each time, slicing as best she could through the roots we'd come on now and again, and then she'd lift it up, a shovelful of black earth, and lift it, lift it, let it fall on the pile growing to my right, and start again.

Each time, too, she looked at me, her eyes glancing up at me to see if I was doing the same, working to do what had to be done. She wanted to see, I knew, that I was moving too, that I hadn't yet died. That I was alive, like her, and doing something, because everything else had shut down on us, and there came a shovelful again and again when I had to remember to breathe in and out, everything so near being done around us. This whole world, over and done with.

Simons was back at the statue with the cable saw, Thigpen too broken to do anything except watch over us. Mom and Miss Dinah sat on the ground to my left, their wrists tied behind their backs; Unc, beside Tabitha's end of the hole, had his hands tied to his ankles. Behind them stood Thigpen with the flashlight, the shadow heads and shoulders of Mom and Miss Dinah and Unc falling down on us, watching over us, so that each shovelful of dirt came from the black hole at our feet, then up through their lives, these shadows, and into the beam, and onto that pile.

And still I thought of things: of the lights off the paper mill and how sometimes when I woke up at night I thought for a second it was daytime, my eyes so adjusted to the pale dark in my room, and I thought of the way moss hung from the branches of live oak here at Hungry Neck two nights ago, and I thought of Mrs. Dupree and her white-gloved hands holding the paperweights, looking at them, unable to tell any difference between sin and love, and I thought of when I kissed Tabitha, not because it was a sin to kiss a black girl or because it was love between us, but because it'd been a moment when someone had been close to me, and our lips had touched and there'd seemed something past meaning I could know as a fifteen-year-old with a learner's permit, a nothing kid who knew nothing and would die knowing nothing of love, really, except for a mother who'd spent her life lying to me because of her own sin, and an uncle who'd accompanied her right along with it, who'd led me to love him as I'd love my own father, though I'd not thought of him as that because he wasn't, because my father had left, and I didn't want, ever, to love someone who could leave.

It was my uncle I loved, not my father. It was my uncle.

The beam down on us moved now and again with Thigpen's being near dead, I figured, broken ribs, arm shot. And between shovelfuls I could hear behind us and away the rhythm of the cable saw, the quiet and perfect empty whisper of it in the night, and I pictured the doctor the world thought dead pulling that saw back and forth through tabby three hundred years old just for the money it'd give, pictured him sweating for it, his arms aching for the pull and pull, and still I dug, even though I knew that when it was over, when I'd finished digging, there would come all our deaths, just as when the doctor finally cut through that statue and this last grave had been robbed, there'd be an end to the evidence the Mothers and Fathers had ever been here, and the Dillards would be gone, too, and the Gaillards, and I thought of the deer I'd butchered, and of the does, and of the fetus I'd pulled from them, white ghost deer no bigger than the palm of your hand, perfect hooves and ears and closed eyes, and I thought of how they'd never been born, and how they'd been killed even before they were born, and I wanted again and again only to be a deer, maybe these deer, these deer that'd never been born and'd been killed even before that, wanted more than anything to be them, and knew at the same time I was alive and that as long as I kept digging, and as long as Tabitha kept digging, we were alive. We were alive, and so I dug.

But it was me to hit it first.

My shovel stopped hard, made a thick scratch of sound, jolted through my arm.

I looked up at Tabitha, her eyes already on me. Her mouth was closed tight, a thin line, and I could see she knew what I knew: once we finished this job, we were dead.

Thigpen moved, the beam suddenly over us from a different angle. He was behind Tabitha now, and I couldn't see her anymore.

He shone it down into the hole. The hole was about four feet deep, the beam falling on only black dirt, the tip of my shovel a few inches in.

"Keep going," Thigpen said, his voice even shallower now.

Still the cable saw worked, off and away from us.

We were here.

"Huger," Unc said.

The word came to me as if from across water, like some shadow of itself, light from behind it.

"You shut the fuck up, old man," Thigpen said, and shone the light on Unc.

But I looked at Tabitha.

Huger. My name.

"You just keep your fucking mouth shut, Leland, or I'll kill you now."

"Son," Unc said, on it the same distance, the same depth.

"Last warning," Thigpen said.

And now I closed my eyes.

I could see things: this hole, four feet deep. Thigpen above and behind Tabitha, Mom and Miss Dinah, and Unc. I could see it all.

I heard the cable saw stop, heard Simons call out, "You find it?" and then I saw him, too, saw the distance from the statue to here, the narrow path he'd have to walk to get here, the time it would take, and I saw the gun tucked into Thigpen's waist, saw one arm useless at his side, in the other the flashlight, pointed at Unc.

And still with my eyes closed I saw two shovels, one in Tabitha's hands, the other in mine, and I saw behind her Thigpen turned a moment from us, saw he was close enough, close enough, and saw Simons start from the statue, and toward us, here, now.

Now.

I opened my eyes. There was light, more than I could need, more than the world of this night could ever need, all of it from a flashlight held on a man who could not see it.

I'd seen all of this, all of it, in an instant.

Son, he'd said.

I put my hand out in front of me, held it out to Tabitha, my index and middle fingers together, held them out for her to see, then brought them to my chest.

Trust me.

"Don't blink, son," Unc said.

She looked at my hand, looked at me. She nodded.

"That's it, you fuck," Thigpen said, and turned from behind Tabitha, took a step toward Unc.

I held my shovel handle with both hands like a baseball bat, nodded hard at her, with my eyes looked up at Thigpen.

She knew.

I saw Simons, still on the trail, still moving.

Tabitha turned, swung the shovel at Thigpen, caught him hard behind the knees, and he fell back, slammed full on the ground, and with it let out a jagged and deep cry, the air out of him in a moment, the flashlight flying like it'd done when I'd fallen, sending shadows and light everywhere, confused and torn light that made no sense.

But I didn't need it. I'd seen what I had to do, seen how we might live.

I was out of the hole in the same moment Unc rolled to his side, tried hard to kick at Thigpen, though his hands were tied to his ankles, and in the same moment Mom and Miss Dinah cried out, the light finally settling, pointing away, and then I was on Thigpen, and pulled from his waist the gun, and turned, backed away from him and away from the hole, looking toward where in a moment I knew Simons would emerge.

Tabitha was up from the hole now, too, held the shovel above Thigpen's head, ready to hit him.

I cocked the hammer and saw in the new angle of light Charles Middleton Simons, his own pistol drawn, step through the green and into the circle.

"Clever," he said, and stopped.

He had the gun up, his arm straight and stiff, pointing at me, and slowly started toward us. Between him and me lay them all, watching him: Mom, Miss Dinah, Unc. Tabitha with the shovel.

Thigpen groaned, rolled his head back and forth, and Tabitha lifted the shovel, ready.

Simons pointed the gun at her, arm still out stiff, and Mom and Miss Dinah gave out quick yelps. "Her first?" he said, and stepped over a string.

Tabitha stood frozen.

"Or Mother?" Simons said, and quick moved the gun toward Mom.

She winced, her eyes on me, leaned hard away, and Simons took another step.

I'd seen what I would do. I'd seen it. But I hadn't seen him with the gun at her. Only on me. That's what I'd seen with my eyes closed, with that gift of sight I'd been given by my uncle.

My father.

Yet I'd seen the gun on *me,* the one to shoot or be shot.

"But of course," Simons said, and now swung the gun to Unc, there in front of him, twenty feet away. "It will have to be Leland. Unc." He paused, took another step. "Daddy. Of course it will have to be him, because he's the only one I fear." He took another step, another. "A wild card. He's willing to die, willing to kill or be killed. All because of this land, this place." He took another step, now stood only a few feet from Mom and Miss Dinah, huddled into each other. "And because he carries with him some guilt over the life he's led, from squiring you to the suicide of his wife to the bum deal lost eyesight can be." He took another step, leveled the gun at Unc sitting there on the ground. "And logic would dictate I would kill him first for Constance, for the fact that she loved him more than me."

Still he looked at me. "As I said, Leland, all of this is horribly predictable. For money, yes. And unrequited love. Predictable." He paused. "And so you ought to die first, for predictability's sake, for the symmetry of it."

He held his arm even straighter, angled it level with Unc's head.

Then he swung it to me.

I fired, and felt fire inside me, saw the flash and smoke from off his gun.

It was the deer that came to me in this instant, their settling into woods for the night, one of them gone—me—and none of them knowing the difference, my absence among them no absence at all, me nothing, and in this instant I felt the rush of night sky through me, felt all the ghosts of all the dead on Hungry Neck there'd ever been, and I knew them each, knew them black and white, old and newborn, these people what made the land this land, made a nameless island where I would die more than nameless, made it something to keep, to *cherish,* I knew, and I knew only then the difference between sin and love, knew only then both could be one and the same at any given moment, as life and death become the same in the moment between high tide and its beginning to wane, that moment when all the world holds its breath for the next thing to come, and then it comes, the tide letting out, the sea edging away to leave its debris behind. Sin and love could be the same, I knew, a fact maybe only knowable in the moment you stepped off the edge of a tub, a cord around your neck for the way your life had unwound before you, or maybe only knowable in the moment of the middle of your first night in a new town, the smell of death and decay summoning you from sleep, only to find here it is outside your back door, that smell of decay swallowing you whole, while here at your leg stands your only child, the hem of your nightgown bunched in his fist, him comforting you, telling you not to cry. Sin and love could be the same, a fact maybe only knowable in seeing your burning wife in her bed just before the explosion of hot glass, searing into your eyes the image for the rest of your life. Burned there, like the burning in me the instant he fired on me, the moment between sin and love as distant and close as a mother and father hidden from you your whole life, and yet present beside you every moment you breathed.

It was the deer that came to me, and these ghosts, and this land, all of it swept into me and around me and through me, the way my blood swept through me with each heartbeat, blood mine and in the same moment my mother's and father's both, me a part of them but only and always me, and then slowly, slowly, I fell away, and I disappeared into the black night above me, and into the ground beneath me, my blood carried out to sea, I knew, on this tide, beneath this moon, me the debris of this day, dead.

I saw things.

I saw a buzzard above a dawn sky, a jay's nest, a hickory stick. I saw deer tracks, saw raccoon prints at a river's edge, saw spartina green in a breeze. I saw these things.

And then I was cold, and I saw nothing, only black, and I heard the wash of water beneath me, felt fingers of wind pick at me, cold.

"Huger, we got you," I heard Mom say. "We got you, baby," and I opened my eyes.

We were moving, above me Mom, past her a dawn sky still too close to night.

But there was color to it. Violet to one side of Mom, pale gray to the other.

I felt nothing, only cold.

"Huger," she said, and now she cried above me, her mouth crumpled to nothing, eyebrows knotted, and she said, "Huger, you okay?" The wind pulled at her hair, moved it and moved it. "Oh, Huger," she said, then glanced up and away. "He's awake," she cried, and there was movement, rocking with that movement.

I whispered, "Mom," and she looked back down at me, smiled, cried, and leaned in close, kissed me.

I was on my back, and we were in a boat, and I was cold, and now Tabitha was beside Mom, and touched my face with her hand. She smiled, and I could see her face with this daylight coming on. She smiled, put her hand up close to my face, her first two fingers together, and brought them to her lips.

"Now," Miss Dinah said from above and behind me. "Stop that."

Then here was Unc, Tabitha moving away for him, Mom still here.

His nose was swollen up, his thin hair whipped by the wind. His marble eyes, the gnarled flesh above them.

Then he cried, his mouth going wide and crumbling, his eyes creasing closed, tears going.

"Huger," he gave out. "Son."

And I whispered, "Daddy," though I was not certain he might hear it on the wind here on the marsh, and on the light coming up around us.

He leaned down, kissed me as Mom had, and as he pulled away I saw above us now the creeping edge of live-oak branches out over water, the green of them in a sky starting yellow.

We were home.

Epilogue

We left the trailer when it was still dark, got here before light. Three miles, about, the two of us walking. He wouldn't tell me where we were going, and I didn't ask.

There was no moon out, only stars.

New Year's Day, closing day of deer season, a day bigger than the Saturdays after Thanksgiving. But this year it was only Unc and me, and we walked our dirt roads, Unc's arm looped in my right arm, me with my left still in a sling.

But in my hand I carried the hickory stick.

He'd made coffee before I was even up, and bacon, eggs. We'd sat at the counter in the kitchen, the only light that from the stove hood, and said nothing, only ate.

Mom was still asleep, back in her old room. She had to work later today, and'd stayed up long past midnight. Tabitha had been here, and Miss Dinah too. But now it was only Unc and me.

And just before he'd closed my door last night—he was sleeping on the couch in the front room, me in his room—he'd told me he'd wake me early, that he had somewhere he wanted to show me.

Things have happened.

Thigpen hasn't said anything, is only in the county facility while the sorting of charges continues. He's got a pile of money somewhere, we're sure. But we've told our side, all five of us.

And there's the island, already cordoned off.

Like Simons said would happen, there's plans already for a museum of what's left, and there's been proclamations made, state archaeologists out for measurements and photographs, probes into smuggled goods and their recipients. There is debate, too, on whether or not to dig up the Father of Fathers, put on display the treasures inside, or to leave him alone, there in the ground.

Someday something will happen here, and Hungry Neck will no longer be as empty as I or Unc needs it. But Unc has told me already he'll donate the island, whenever they get to setting something up.

The senate-committee hearings haven't started, but Delbert Yandle still calls every other day, representing the board without hiding the fact anymore. He asks how I'm doing, wants to make sure I'm feeling fine, and that Unc is feeling fine, and that this next bid might be enough to make us feel fine for the rest of our lives.

Mom has been here more nights than not. And one night a week or so ago, when they thought I was asleep in Unc's room, I heard them talking out in the kitchen, and heard Mom's laughter, heard it from Unc, too. The two of them, and laughter.

I haven't been back to school yet, and Tabitha brings books over, or I go over there, and we read, and we talk.

Dr. Joe Cray's MRI shop is empty, a FOR LEASE sign set up out front, and Mrs. Dupree has somewhere in her house two paperweights.

And I killed a man.

But what's strange is that killing Simons isn't what comes to me nights, when I am alone and trying to sleep. Nor is it a body with hardly any head, or the killings of Yandle and Ravenel and Patrick and Reynold, though there are moments when those things sneak up on me, make my pulse pick up, my hands go hot.

What comes to me is the statue. The Son, and his eyes, green glass, the years those eyes have seen come and go, every one of them spent here at Hungry Neck, seasons in and out and in again.

And the Father of Fathers, that sound when my shovel hit the coffin. Just that sound, the thick scratch of the tip into pitch-painted oak, the jolt through my arm.

They're the only ones left out there. The father and the son. That's what comes to me when I am alone, and in the dark.

I had a Thermos of coffee in the daypack I wore, and on our way here Unc told me which roads to follow, which way to turn. And when we came to the sweet gum he'd told me to watch for, the one with a perfect elbow parallel to the road, he let go my arm, hooked his hand on my belt, and pushed me off the road and into the woods.

The sky had gone violet by this time, still too dark to see the hands on a watch. But Unc led me, as best he could, by pushing, and subtle pulls, a kind of blind tack through a woods he seemed to know better even than the roads we'd walked on our way here.

And as we steered through the woods, I came to know what I'd begun to feel that night on the island: there is another kind of seeing, a way of looking in front of you and seeing maybe what you can't really see, a way of knowing something without knowing it. There is a kind of darkness that allows you to see itself, and the trees are suddenly there before you, and the leaves, the fallen branches and low places where water fills in, all of it there before you and shrouded in a kind of knowledge you can only get with being inside the dark of it.

There's no way to tell you about it. Only that it's a kind of seeing when there is light and no light, and that I came to it, finally, through no one but Unc.

And then here we were, Unc and me, at an old tree stand deep inside Hungry Neck, two-by-four steps up the trunk of a live oak, a platform fifteen feet up, the wood weathered the same gray as the trunk itself, gray melted into gray in the light before dawn.

I'd never seen this one before.

He let go the belt, and I turned to him. He smiled, nodded.

I went first, like every time we ever climbed one of these, so that once on the platform I could reach down to him at the last, take hold a hand, and pull him up.

But this morning was different: I had my arm in the sling, and I put my foot to the first two-by-four, took hold of the board above me with my right hand, and pulled, the flesh in my left shoulder still tender just beneath my collarbone, where the bullet went through.

But it was a good pain I felt, and I stepped up, leaned into the trunk, let go my hand, reached to the next board up, pulled, so that climbing the tree stand became a series of holding tight and letting go, holding tight and letting go, and it seemed in doing this there was something larger than what I was doing.

Then I was at the platform itself, and pulled myself up to it, brought up my legs.

I turned, sat with my legs hanging off, and looked down from the platform to him: that baseball cap, the sunglasses.

He leaned the stick against the trunk, then started up, and I reached to him, whispered, "Unc," and he took my hand. I pulled, pulled, felt the pain in my shoulder again, a pain I would take, I knew, and he was beside me, brought here by his own strength and mine.

His hand stayed in mine then, and we sat.

"We built this one together," Unc said. "Your daddy and me. And we never hunted off it. Only came here, to sit."

I said nothing for a moment, only took in a breath, whispered, "I remember you two talking about this place one time. When I was little."

It was all I knew to say, but it seemed enough, because now I saw what he was giving me by taking me here on this new day, in a new year, the next one of a new life I'd been given:

Before us lay the land, daylight coming up, a perfect daylight that gave color to everything.

They'd built it, brother and brother, for what they could see: land thick with palmetto and loblolly pine, oak and hickory, dogwood and wax myrtle and wisteria vine.

And there, through a curtain of two ancient live oaks it seemed spread open just for us, lay the Ashepoo, maybe a hundred yards off, the wide cold blue of it, past it the spartina and yellow grass and salt-marsh hay, all the way to Edisto.

Spread across it islands with no names.

I closed my eyes, felt the tree move in the small breeze up here, smelled the marsh, heard a squirrel bark from somewhere behind us.

"Huger Dillard," I whispered. Two words, brand-new.

Unc held my hand tighter, my eyes still closed, and I watched this all, watched colors rise, the marsh now a green I couldn't name, mixed in and down inside it browns and reds and a color like bone. Miles of color.

I watched it all, there with my father.

This book is for
Jeff Adkins, John Astles, John Astles, senior,
Jeff Deal, and, especially, Joel Curé.

And this is for Melanie and Marian,
with thanks for your faith.

ABOUT THE AUTHOR

BRET LOTT is the author of the novels *Jewel, Reed's Beach, A Stranger's House,* and *The Man Who Owned Vermont;* the story collections *How to Get Home* and *A Dream of Old Leaves;* and the memoir *Fathers, Sons, and Brothers.* His stories and essays have appeared in numerous literary journals and magazines, among them *The Southern Review, The Yale Review, The Iowa Review,* the *Chicago Tribune,* and *Story,* and have been widely anthologized. He lives with his wife, Melanie, and their two sons, Zebulun and Jacob, in Mount Pleasant, South Carolina, and teaches at the College of Charleston and Vermont College.